Slept Away

★

ALSO BY JULIE KRAUT

Hot Mess: Summer in the City

with Shallon Lester

JULIE KRAUT

Slept Away

Delacorte Press

Copyright © 2009 by Julie Kraut

All rights reserved. Published in the United States by Delacorte Press, an imprint of Random House Children's Books, a division of Random House, Inc., New York.

Delacorte Press is a registered trademark and the colophon is a trademark of Random House, Inc.

Visit us on the Web! www.randomhouse.com/teens

Educators and librarians, for a variety of teaching tools, visit us at www.randomhouse.com/teachers

Library of Congress Cataloging-in-Publication Data
Kraut, Julie.
Slept away / Julie Kraut.— 1st ed.
p. cm.
Summary: Fifteen-year-old Manhattanite Laney Parker, a city girl all her life, is horrified when her mother insists that she spend the summer at sleep-away camp in the Pennsylvania countryside.
ISBN 978-0-385-73737-1 (trade)—ISBN 978-0-375-89270-7 (e-book)
[1. Camping—Fiction. 2. Interpersonal relations—Fiction. 3. Self-perception—Fiction. 4. Friendship—Fiction.] I. Title.
PZ7.K8753SI 2009
[Fic]—dc22   2008044567

The text of this book is set in 11-point Goudy.

Book design by Angela Carlino

Printed in the United States of America

10 9 8 7 6 5 4 3 2

First Edition

For Mom and Dad.

You guys make being a daughter too easy.

TXT from Kennedy to Laney:
How many times are you checking over your work? Just call me if you want to come to the pool . . . that is if you're done before 2015.

Chapter 1

"OK, look at that girl over there," Kennedy directed. She pulled her Diors down her nose a bit so I could see her eyes gesturing over to a girl in a tankini lying out across the pool. "Total brownout."

I took a peek over at the napping tankini-ed stranger. "Brownout" is a term we coined for a girl who was totally hot because she was blond, but if you put brown hair on her, she'd just be normal to fugly. And the truth is that you can't tell someone's brownout status from far away. You need to get a good look at her face. But Kennedy had just recently decided to go dark and was trying to convince herself that she and Cameron Diaz were the only two women on planet Earth who look hotter as brunettes. So I nodded, agreeing to the brownout situation across the pool, not sure if by bashing every woman who dared to look good blond in Manhattan I was enabling the rapid growth of a cancerous mega-ego or just easing a friend through a bad hair period.

"Yeah, highlights are definitely God's gift to *some* women," she said with disdain. As if three weeks ago she hadn't been one of those plebes who enjoyed the exponential hottening factor of professionally applied peroxide.

I sighed, running my hand through my head of what I was trying to sun-bleach into auburn waves, but was really just plain brown and in a sweaty tangle. My mom thought fifteen was too young for highlights and had denied me the parental credit card for a salon trip more times than Nicole Richie has denied anorexia allegations. And after one attempted at-home highlights session left me looking streakier than the love child of Kelly Clarkson and bargain-brand glass cleaner, I realized that I was just going to have to wait for college to fully research the age-old question of whether blondes really do have more fun.

Was I seriously thinking about this? Not even a full two hours ago I was double-checking the sines and cosines on my trig final—which I dominated, thank you very much—and now I'm considering how hair color affects your general sense of amusement? It's like after a hard-core round of studying and testing, my brain just isn't capable of real thinking and I sink to the level of a VH1 reality show contestant for a few hours. Whatever. I definitely deserved some chill time after trig. Taking advantage of Ken's mom's

Soho House membership for the afternoon was the perfect way to do it.

I flipped over to my stomach, smushed my cheek into my towel in a way that I knew was going to give me an acne-looking imprint when I got up, and closed my eyes for an afternoon nap. But just as I was starting to doze, I heard Kennedy yell, "Hey, bitch!" She was completely unaware of how loud she was being, thanks to whatever guyliner band she was iPoding into her ears.

"Your mom's here?" I swear I didn't mean for that to come out. It's just that I was in that halfway-to-sleep level of consciousness where I have absolutely no filter. And as much as I loved Kennedy—we've been friends since Baby Gym, where my mom took me and her babysitter took her— her family still scared me after all these years. It's like the *Nanny Diaries* family except for there's no one playing the Laura Linney desperate housewife role. Kennedy's parents were divorced, and both were these crazy career-driven, emotionless, would-probably-sell-their-daughters-for-their-organs-if-they-could-make-a-nice-profit human ice sculptures with dyed jet-black hair in one of those super-blunt bobs with straight-across bangs. OK, that last part was just her mom. But still, her mom hadn't warmed to me at all in the past fourteen and a half years. And I was seriously cute in grammar school. It was pretty impossible not to fall in love with my fatty cheeks, but Mrs. McEllen managed not to.

"No, my mom's at work, duh," Kennedy replied to my half-conscious, all subconscious comment. "Why'd you ask?" For the record, I believe that we all have different gifts. And I also believe that my best friend's most bountiful gift wasn't wit. But she was really good at burping the ABCs, so it all evened out. "I'm thinking that I should try and convince Conrad to have a little summer kickoff soiree. What do you think?" she asked. She dove into her bag to pull out her phone before I'd even answered.

Conrad was Kennedy's loving boyfriend slash total dick ex, depending on the day, or on some days, depending on the hour. This had been going on since the very first weeks of freshman year, and after two years, I was pretty fed up with the Kennedy/Conrad time bomb. But she's my best friend, so fed up or not, I had to be there with her every time she set the bomb, every time she watched that bomb tick down to zero, and every time it exploded. It's probably what it would be like to be Britney's personal assistant. Except I don't get paid. Or a tell-all book deal.

"Wouldn't a Conrad bash be awesome this weekend?" she prodded before hitting dial.

"Totally," I said. And it would. No matter how much I hated the romantic hostage situation he was holding Kennedy in, it's a fact that Conrad has the best parties in Manhattan. Well, the best parties for the sixteen-and-under crowd in Manhattan.

Kennedy suddenly stopped her chatter with Conrad and turned to me. "He's totally down to play host this weekend, just needs to know which day. What do you think, Laney P., would more peeps show up tomorrow or Sunday night?"

Even the thought of a party on Sunday night was enough to induce a panic attack for me. Hello! Was I the only person left in the Manhattan private school system who had a mom who wouldn't let her out on school nights? My mom would flip before I could even start the curfew negotiation. And she totally wouldn't care that we were done with finals and that all we'd be doing on Monday was watching *Stand and Deliver* while the teachers graded, which pretty much took the attention span of a drunk monkey. I could already hear her start in on the "fifteen-year-olds and gallivanting on Sunday nights don't mix" tirade. To be honest, I wasn't one hundred percent sure what gallivanting was, and to be even more honest, even though I'm technically fifteen, I'm pretty much already sixteen. Everyone else in my class is, and my birthday's in November, which is practically right around the corner. I definitely act just as mature as my friends. But somehow, bringing up the "sixteen at heart" argument never seemed like a good idea when my mom was in Mominator mode.

I tried to sound nonchalant and not like a baby who had to ask her mommy permission to do anything after dark when I said, "Probably Sat. Things always come up on Sunday for people, you know?" What was I even talking about? What comes up on Sundays for people? *Law & Order* marathons?

"Laney thinks Saturday would be better," she said into her phone. "Yeah, cool. Should I bring anything?" And then she started giggling like crazy, so I'm sure he responded with something shady like "Nothing but your sweet ass." He's such a creep machine.

Probably resisting her desire to have a full-on phone flirt session with Conrad, Kennedy snapped her phone shut. "All set! We're going to party like we don't have to use our brains for three whole months! Do you know how much time that is to grow back brain cells?"

"Um, three months?"

"Exactly!" She giggled at her own ridiculousness and I couldn't help myself and started too.

Through the laughter, I managed to get out, "And what do you mean grow back brain cells? Are you planning on huffing Wite-Out or something? Don't forget that we technically still have school on Monday, lady." Sheesh, I sounded so much like my mom.

She shrugged. "We're just going to watch that stupid movie about gang members learning math for like the millionth time. I get that they need to show us an inspirational movie, but hello, there have been like a hundred better movies that have come out since the math one. I wonder if I can put in a request for *Stomp the Yard*."

She had a point on the movies, but this was her attitude on school in general and I always felt like I had to bug her about it or she'd fail out. "Oh, come on, Ken. How are you in senior slump like two full years premature?" Her face contorted in a way that if I didn't know how much she hated bio this year, I'd have thought she was just really constipated. "What about our college roommate plan?" Since middle school Kennedy and I had been planning on heading to college together and being roommates. The thought of going off somewhere and knowing no one was nausea-inducing for me. And Kennedy, while probably not the most responsible of roommates, would make that transition so much easier. She might have been going through senior slump early, but I've been having separation anxiety since I hit puberty. I pretty much freaked when she threatened to switch down to nonhonors English last year. I talked her out of it, but I've spent more than a couple lunch periods recapping Shakespeare and reenacting scenes from *A Raisin in the Sun* because she couldn't keep up with the reading. "And sister, I

8

love you, but not enough to turn down an Ivy to go to community college in the Dominican Republic or wherever F students go."

"Fine," she said through a pout. Acting like I'd just grounded her, she put her earbuds back in and dialed up the volume. Her music was so loud, I could hear every single word of "Thnks fr th Mmrs" from a foot away, which gave me an idea I so should have thought of months before.

"Maybe you would have been into bio this year if you'd studied Pete Wentz. Seriously, how is he able to look more feminine than me without any surgery? Someone has to do a bio study on his hormones or something," I said to no one, as Kennedy was currently rendered deaf by emo's poster she-male.

"I heard that." Or maybe just partially deaf. "I'm choosing to ignore the nastiness you're directing at the man I'm going to be a lovely second wife to. I hope you think of something nice to say for your maid of honor toast." She kind of moaned to herself at the thought of becoming Mrs. Wentz and then quickly changed the subject to another douchetastic male. "I'm so pumped Conrad wants to have a party. It's like totally the p dubs to start the sum." I shot her a what-the-eff look. "Oh, come on. That one was legit. Perfect way to start the summer!" she explained.

Kennedy had recently taken up the annoying habit of shortening every word with more than two syllables. In her opinion, this made her sound "important, like I don't have time to waste on unnecessary syllables and stuff." But the truth was that after each sentence she said, she spent so much time translating from Text Message–ese to English, the time-saving factor was pretty much nonexistent.

I rolled my eyes and grabbed the coconut oil, reslathering

myself carefully. The chemically fruity scent of summer drifted up around me. I couldn't wait for summer to officially start. "Walking out of school on Monday is going to be so freaking liberating."

"Yeah, like taking off a strapless bra after a night out. It's just like, *free-dom!*" She pumped her fists in triumph as she bellowed the last word.

I laughed but seriously had no idea. The only time I haven't been in a training bra was when Kennedy convinced me to wear her sister's Cleavage Cupcakes to one of her dad's benefits. I thought they made me look even more like a cross-dressing twelve-year-old boy than I normally do, but she said I looked hot.

Then suddenly this shot of dread ran through me as I remembered again that I didn't have a real reason to be so excited for summer. I mean, aside from not having to wear a gray skirt and navy cardigan every freaking weekday. I had nothing planned for the next three months, and the last day of school was only a weekend and a day away. I'd been dodging Mom's questions about my summer plans for months now. In my opinion, I worked my hiney to the bone during the school year with a GPA that sparkled, multiple columns in the school paper, and a position as student government secretary; summer should be my downtime. But in my mom's not so humble opinion, chillaxing was not an appropriate summer activity, so I was going to have to come up with something "character-developing and worthwhile" soon or my mom would do it for me. I turned to Kennedy. "Wait, what are you up to for the summer again?"

She sat up in her lounger. "You know," she said, whipping off her Diors and circling her finger around her nose and then pointing to the tiny bump on her bridge. There was an incident involving Kennedy, four inches of Louboutin, and a spiral staircase at Spring Formal this year. She bit it hard, tumbling down like five stairs and winding up with nosebleed stains down the front of her Cavalli. And of course it turned into a total YouTube nightmare, since some freshman douche had managed to whip out his iPhone in time to capture the humiliation in medias res. Kennedy handled it well for the most part. But she was still focused on the mini-bump that remained from the broken nose. She was getting it "fixed" this summer. But seriously, with the major double-D mountains she had, I'm sure no one was paying attention to the minuscule lump on her nose. What, me? Jealous? Never!

"Post-NJ, I'm so going to be Ashlee minus the trashy Skechers campaign and sluttier older sister."

"Yeah, because you're way sluttier than your sis," I joked. But seriously, she was.

She pulled her shades back down to soak up the last rays of sun. I sank back into my chair, wondering what the eff I was going to do all summer while my ticket to the Soho House pool was Frankenstein-ing her face and on bed rest.

A few silent minutes of sun-steeping went by. The three months of total nothingness in front of me was suddenly not liberating but completely nerve-wracking. If I didn't come up with something quick, my mom might spring another relaxation retreat on me. This past winter break, she and her then boyfriend, now "live-in partner," had taken me with them on this week of spiritual cleansing. It was an entire week of tofu and yoga and stating what we were grateful for on an hourly basis. The trend in the group—or, as they preferred to be called, "the community"—was to be grateful for boundless joy and laughter and that you are fifty-something years young. I abstained from participating in the grateful group for most of the week. But after four days of bullying from my spiritual superiors—and yes, bullying, they were only love, peace, and smiley-faced emoticons when you were on their side—I finally caved. But my announcement that I was grateful for calorie-free sweetener and the fact that the cleanse only lasted three more days went over about as well as a dead baby joke at a funeral.

I definitely needed to think of summer plans quick because I just couldn't live for an entire three months on vegan desserts. Desserts need butter. It's a scientific fact.

After several minutes of thinking, I was finally struck with some summer inspiration. "Hey," I yelled over the screamo boy crap being earphoned into Kennedy's brain. She pulled a bud out and looked over. "Why don't I intern at some fabulous up-and-coming fashion house and get tons of free clothes seasons before they hit the racks?" I couldn't have come up with a more perfect solution. Despite the sweaty, gnarly mess that sat in my lounge chair now, I really was a fashionista. Well, as much of a fashionista as you can be when wearing a uniform five days a week. And even Monday through Friday people were always complimenting me on my style, like my shoes and whatever vintage pin or necklace I had on.

She contemplated that for a second and then blurted, "No, wait. Better-idea alert!" She let my anticipation build with a dramatic pause. And then, "You should go on a TT!"

I took a second to try and decipher what the shit she was talking about.

A televised trial?

A ten-speed tricycle?

A Tibetan time-share?

"Hello! I'm talking about a teen tour! My cousin went on one in Europe last summer and said it was awesome. I'd one hundred percent go on one this summer if it weren't for the incident that shall not be named." Again she gestured to the microscopic imperfection on her nose. "She stayed in super-swank hotels every night and only had to see boring history stuff like a few hours a day. Most of the time she was on the bus and she said that you're so unsupervised when you're on the road and the boys are super-hot. Make-out central!"

Backseat make-out sessions? Not quite what I envisioned writing my "What I Did This Summer" essay on when I got back to school in September.

Laneybelle,

We're out until late tonight. Fix yourself a healthy dinner. There are some protein slices in the fridge.

Love ya,
Mom

Chapter 2

Kennedy and I packed up our bottles of oil and back issues of *US Weekly* and headed uptown, home-sweet-homeward bound. Our cab stopped at Park and Eightieth, right outside my building. I fished a crumpled and coconut-oil-covered ten out of my bag, but she shooed my cash away.

"I've got this one."

Having a friend whose parents buy her love does have its benefits.

"Thanks, friend," I said as I started my less-than-elegant scootch out of the cab. "Want to come over tomorrow?"

She flashed me a smile. "Def! We need to pick out our ensembles for Conrad's par-tay." She reached into her bag and pulled out her phone to slate me in.

"You got it, sister," I confirmed before slamming the car door. I stood for a second, watching her cab zoom up Park, then realized I was wasting precious time. I zipped upstairs to my apartment, blowing by the doorman with a quick "Hi." My mom and her vomitous selection of male companionship would be freak-festing themselves about town until late, and I savored every second in the apartment by myself.

My mom and I have obviously lived together since I was born. But Dr. Douche was a rather recent addition. Before him, we were on our own for fourteen years—Real Dad and Mom divorced nanoseconds after I was born. They were both fresh out of law school and new superstars who were moving and shaking their way up the corporate ladder at the same firm. Then the story takes a turn for the ugly. While my mom was preggers, my dad was apparently moving and shaking with his secretary. Mom found out, as did everyone else in the firm, and the rest is history. He moved to California and I only hear from him on my birthday and on Christmas via Hallmark cards with twenties slipped in.

The disappearing-daddy act actually didn't bother me at all. I barely even thought about the missing parental unit because my mom and I were so happy and good together. The only time I remember us really getting into a fight was when she tried to give me an at-home haircut in first grade. I get that asymmetrical bangs are in right now and they look good on certain people, like designers on *Project Runway*, but on a chubby-cheeked six-year-old? I think not. So when I looked in the mirror, I flipped out in a big way. There was screaming, yelling, full-throttle tantruming, and at one point I remember staring my mother in the eyes and saying, "I know where you sleep, Mom. And one night I'm going to come in and cut you some horrible bangs and see how you like it." If we'd only had pea soup in the house, it seriously could have been a scene from *The Exorcist*. I was that crazy mad. Anyway, after a trip to a salon and a perma-ban on DIY haircuts, Mom and I have been a modern day Brady Bunch—well, as Brady as a single mom and an only child living on Park Ave can be. We're definitely not creepy fake best friends like Dina and Lindsay. She's totally annoying about mom stuff like getting enough calcium, taking school seriously, and not going to rehab before I can legally drink. But that's part of her job, and I've always respected it without too much eye rolling.

That was all before Dr. Mark entered the pic, though. And it's really not some bizarre jealousy thing where I don't like to share my mom or something. It's that Mark sucks harder than Mischa Barton's acting. Mom's had other boyfriends I've been cool with. Like the one who gave me his company's box at Madison Square Garden when the Spice Girls reunited and I don't even really like Victoria Beckham. And I was cool with this other guy who restocked my mother's Absolut without even saying anything to me when he realized that Kennedy and I had drunk it all and replaced it with water. See? It takes very little for a mom suitor to endear himself to me, and Mark is still miles away from even qualifying as human.

Mark is technically a doctor. But after a divorce, a midlife crisis, an ear piercing, and a fifties singles trip to Nepal, he decided to abandon Western medicine and become Internet certified in holistic healing. From what I can tell, holistic healing involves burning a lot of incense, men wearing drapery as maxi-skirts, and not showering with anything close to frequency. He goes around and offers private consultations where he chants and shakes some blessed spices and probably shimmies around to tribal music. He charges only for the hour that he's there, but it's a real bargain because I'm sure his stench lingers for days after. At least, it does in this apartment.

How he bagged my powerhouse lawyer mom, I don't know. What I do know is that my mother is a smitten newly vegan kitten who now, as soon as she walks in from a day at the office, kicks off her pumps and trades her pants suits for bizarre kente-cloth dashikis and headdresses. They are both really involved in this New Agey crap and spend a lot of time at meetings and healing stuff with their minds and talking in Yoga-ese or something. I'm now part of a family that I didn't think existed outside of *Wife Swap*. It's pretty much every self-conscious embarrassing-mom fear realized.

I think I'm handling it well, but the madre and I just don't get along as beautifully as we used to. Ever since she's become more and more Earth Mother and less and less my mother, it's like everything she says or does or thinks irks me. Like, when I asked her to sign a permission slip for the school trip down to the Hearst offices for a special career talk, she asked me to return the favor by taking some time to contemplate my being. Come on, all I have time to contemplate is how I'm going to afford all the therapy I'll need in my midtwenties to fix the emotional damage she's doing now.

Anyway, it's times like this, when the dippy doctor and

the shell of the woman formerly known as Mom are out, that I like being home most. I can watch "spiritually depleting programming" on television, eat food primarily made out of preservatives and gelatin, and listen to music that doesn't involve a rain stick. And that is what forces me to think that maybe this summer I should try and blow this Upper East Side abode and see what living sans adult supervision for a few months would be like. It would be good practice for college, which is only two short nonleap years away, and it would certainly be beneficial for my sanity. And if the fashion internship idea worked out, it would totally be downtown. Perhaps Mom would even spring for subletting a one-bedroom near the design studio for the summer, or at least put me up in one of the NYU dorms.

I decided to spend an hour hunting for a summer gig. Googling "Awesome Summer Fashion Internship NYC" didn't exactly pull up LaneyParkersDreamJob.com. Even for intern positions, a lot of these places wanted to see resumes, portfolios, and recommendations. Realizing that drumming up a portfolio in the hour I gave myself to job hunt would be impossible, I started looking for less demanding listings. I found a couple of openings for unpaid internships in fashion PR, which I knew from *The Fashionista Diaries* meant even more swag-bagging opportunities than working for a designer. I printed out the two that were the farthest downtown, figuring even a few blocks deeper into TriBeCa would add to my case for a summer prison break—I mean, departure from my loving vegan home. The Summershank Redemption planning took way longer than the hour I allotted, as did the Chinese takeout ordering and binging, walking Perez, my pooch, and the few—fine, four—episodes of *Made*

I watched. By the time I wrapped up, I heard the front door open and the Parenthood of the Embarrassing Yoga Mats come home. I quickly turned off my light, jumped under my covers, and squeezed my eyes shut, hoping that they would be humane enough not to wake me to tell me "namaste" or whatever. At some point, my mock sleep turned into the real deal, and I barely remember hearing their footsteps when they walked past my door to their room.

The next morning I woke up to breakfasty smells and Perez's barking. I wrapped myself in my binky—come on, I'm sure a lot of successful, sophisticated women are still attached to their baby blankets—and shuffled my way slowly to the kitchen, squinting at the light coming in through the windows and grunting a greeting to my mother.

My mom has always been an "up and at 'em before the sun rises" kind of person. And now that her chi was centered or whatever, it seemed to be even worse.

Flush-cheeked from couples yoga, she chirped, "Good morning, Laneybelle." She waited for a response. After fifteen years, you'd think the woman would get that "morning person" isn't a hereditary trait. But every morning I see her, I get the same greeting. "Aren't we a grump bunny on this blessed morning." Well, the "blessed" part was obviously new, probably part of the Hinduism or Buddhism or Branch Davidian or whatever it was that she was going to temple for now. "How about a non-melet, hon?"

For those who don't speak veganese, a "non-melet" is like an omelet but made with vegan egg substitute. It tastes like wet newspaper.

"I'll pass." I dragged myself over to the cupboard, pulled

out a box of Lucky Charms, and brought it to the table, where a bowl and the soy milk were already sitting. I poured out what probably counted as three recommended serving sizes and commenced shoveling the high-fructose corn syrup and food coloring down my gullet, loving every bite.

I was so immersed in finding the last three clovers in the Leprechaun Village—that's the way it always is, the first seventeen are gimmes but those last three, they're like the Holy Grail of whole-grain cereals—that my mom's voice kind of startled me.

"Hon, are you going to be around tonight?"

I nodded and through a mouthful of soggy marshmallows said, "Fol dinnah. Den I ma goin to Conlad's pahty." I swallowed and wiped the sugary milk-substitute dribbles off my chin.

"Oh great!" my mom responded, as if she could understand any of my cavewoman speak. "I've got news that I think you're going to love!"

"Oh good. I wanted to talk to you too." Dinner would be the perfect time to discuss my dearth of summer plans, the great opportunities downtown, and the fact that I wanted to be a long-distance daughter for the season.

"Perfect. Then I'll be back here around six. I'll cook, OK?"

"OK. Six at this table? I'll be here. And if you're cooking, I'll be sure to eat a snack before." My mom shot me a look. "I'm so kidding about the snack." I was so not kidding about the snack.

Kennedy came over after breakfast for some hanging. "An apartment downtown? Like a rental? That's so alterna!"

she cooed, looking up from the craigslist postings she was scrolling through for me. "Are you going to cut blunt bangs and get a sleeve of tattoos and sport Converse when you get back?"

"First of all, blunt bangs are not alterna." I looked up from the *People* I was barely skimming. "Tyra had them and I wouldn't exactly call her a hipster. And second of all, why are you worried about me coming back from this summer different? You're the one that's going to have a different freaking face."

She shifted her body and repositioned my MacBook on her lap. "So not a dif face! I'm just getting my old preformal nose back, OK?"

She actually looked a little hurt about the rhinoplasty ribbing. Which was bizarre because Kennedy has a self-esteem shell around her that's made of Teflon and Pope-mobile Plexiglas. She could normally take crap on pretty much anything. Had I really just offended her?

"I mean, preformal, my face looked like Angelina's, right? Because I totally asked for her nose!"

I rolled my eyes, relieved that I wasn't looking at a best-friend divorce. "Yeah, it's like whenever I look at you, I'm always about to call you Angelina until you turn around and I realize you don't have Sanskrit prayers etched on your back."

"You're not the first person to say that to me," she said, and then tried to do a super-glamorous hair flip over her shoulder but in her overdramatization almost flipped herself off my bed. After she caught her balance and I was sure I wasn't going to have to deal with broken nose numero dos this year, I couldn't stop laughing.

"OK," I managed to get out, about to start in on the

outfit picking when I immediately shut up because just then, I got a whiff of Dr. Mark coming down the hall. We had to shut our mouths to keep from gagging when he and my mom stopped in my doorway. They were wearing matching outfits, both in hot-pink fabric bedazzled with rhinestones. Hers was a sari, and his piece of fabric was fashioned into some sort of tunic. It was like looking at one of those matchy family portraits . . . only on acid.

"Namaste, ladies. Studying hard or hardly studying?" Captain Crunch said, and then yukked it up at his own joke. My mom chuckled along with him and they continued their trek down the hallway.

A second later, she hollered back, "We're off to worship, but I'm still planning on dinner tonight." And then the front door clicked closed.

We were silent for a second, me from embarrassment, Kennedy probably more from shock. She's met Mark like a hundred times, but you just never get used to his weird factor. She finally unmuted herself. "Dude, your stepdad and mom are bah-zar."

"OK, for the last time, he's not my stepdad." He was way too antiestablishment to believe in the sanctity of a piece of government-issued paper. He connected with my mother on a higher spiritual plane or whatever. And judging from the fact that most of his clothes were made from hemp, I'm pretty sure that spiritual planes weren't the only thing that guy was high on. "And I know. They're so totally weird. I'm like the only person in this apartment who wears pants on a regular basis." There really wasn't anything to say to that. She just sighed and I shook my head at my familial freak show.

• • •

That evening, after we'd both tried on every single piece of clothing in my closet and watched a mind-numbing number of episodes of *The Hills*, Kennedy headed back to her place and I sat down to a veggie-surprise stew at my kitchen table. I waited to bring up my summer plans until I'd pushed my goulash around my bowl enough to look like I'd eaten a few bites. "So, you know how for this summer I have nada in the works?" I asked.

"Actually, honey, that's what I wanted to talk to you about. We've, I mean I've," she corrected herself—she knew how much I hated when Dr. Fakedad got involved in my life—"been doing some thinking about your summer." She rearranged her kente-cloth headdress. "Hon, don't you feel like you're missing out on so much of your childhood by being raised in the city?"

Missing out? Not at all. I was stunned. It's like the total opposite. I'm getting a head start on just about everything by living here. I mean, how many books, TV shows, and movies are there about a girl's big dream to go to NYU after high school? Well, I'm in high school now and pretty much living the dream. But apparently, my mom couldn't have cared less about how I felt. Before I could even begin to respond, she exploded with her announcement.

"So that's why this summer, you're going to Timber Trails!" She grinned at me in a manic way.

Timber Trails? For a second I thought Justin Timberlake had finally broken the third wall of his hustler-wannabe persona and created some sort of basketball shoe, but then I saw the brochure that my mother was unfolding on the kitchen table.

I glanced down at it. "What is this?" I demanded, completely confused. "Some sort of orthodonture convention?" I looked up at my mother for an answer.

"What? No!" My mother took a closer look at the brochure. "Well, I guess a lot of these kids do have braces. But no. This is a sleepover camp in Pennsylvania!"

Summer camp? What the shit was she thinking? What had the evil doctor convinced her to smoke? I mean, an unair-conditioned summer of Popsicle-stick crafts in the boonies of Pennsylvania? Suddenly, I was jealous of Kennedy's summer of facial surgery. A little swelling and bed rest sounded like a five-star vacation compared to what I was seeing in the brochure. "Um, thanks, but no way," I answered. I got up from the kitchen table and bolted to my room, wanting to end this conversation and never revisit it.

"This isn't really a discussion, honey. You're going," she hollered after me.

Dr. Mark, in a predictably irksome way, added, "So you better get packing!"

Get packing? Yeah, like I'd have time to pack when I was going to be so busy with all the FAH-REAKING OUT I needed to do.

TXT from Laney to Kennedy:
My life is over. I need hard alcohol and
distractions. Be sure Conrad has stocked
up on both. Thanks in advance.

Chapter 3

I slammed my door behind me with a strength I didn't know human biceps were capable of—or at least my jelly-bean biceps. I flopped onto my bed and started mentally cursing out my mother. The crap I was thinking would make Alec Baldwin look like the dad on *Seventh Heaven*.

How could she just sign me up for something as life-ruining as this without consulting me? What happened to when we were a team? I swear my mother used to ask my opinion about everything. She'd ask me about outfits for work, what to make for dinner, where we should go on vacation.

And ever since Lord VoldeMark entered the picture, it's like she doesn't need my opinion on anything at all . . . even stuff that really matters to me, like my entire summer, for example.

I wondered if he brainwashed her with voodoo or yoga or something. If that theory didn't mean that I'd have to believe that Mark's spiritual crap actually had some effect, I would totally go with it.

For a second I considered calling the family lawyer to ask about the possibility of investigating this brainwashing theory. But then I realized that my mom was our family lawyer and she'd probably catch on to my "Let's just say I have a family member named Shmom who's being brainwashed by a guy with a gross old-man ponytail named Shmark." Really, my only option at this point was to just thrash around on my bed, crying and whimpering about my life being over.

There was absolutely zero question in my mind—I'd completely hate camp. Scenes from *Wet Hot American Summer* flashed through my head with weird red backlighting, like a horror movie. Sitting in dirt. Swimming in fish-poop water. Molly Shannon in shorts. It was horrifying.

I was imagining myself in the middle of the woods, cutting down trees to burn for warmth, eating roasted-chipmunk sandwiches for dinner, and getting terrorized by a nature-dwelling chain-saw predator, when I heard my mom's knock on my bedroom door.

"Babe, you want to talk?" she asked, as if this were something I'd want to chitchat about, like, well, I don't know. I couldn't think of anything that I'd wanted to talk to my mom about recently.

"Did you say something, Mom?" I yelled at my closed

door. "It's hard for me to hear you over all the frantic Googling I'm doing. Apparently, there's this process called emancipation that pretty much means kids can divorce their parents—did you know that?"

"Laney, come on. Quit it." Her voice was getting stern. "This behavior isn't like you."

"What?" I asked incredulously, and then stomped over to the door and opened it. I was so pissed that my face was suddenly hot. "Me? This behavior isn't like me? Look who's talking. When did you start acting like the kind of crazy mom who makes decisions without asking the person whose life you're ruining first? When did you start letting your boyfriend make your decisions for you?" I was focusing all my energy on not crying. "Because that behavior isn't like you. Well, it isn't like the Mom I remember, anyway."

"Laney, Mark has absolutely nothing to do with this," she explained very calmly. At least, very calmly compared to me, who was pretty much foaming at the mouth. "I've always had misgivings about raising you in the city. I feel like you haven't experienced so much of what's wonderful about childhood just so that I don't have to commute more than ten minutes to work. That's something I've always felt guilty about. And I thought this was my chance to make it up to you. It's such an opportunity for you, Laneybelle. And at fifteen, this is the last summer you're able to enroll as a camper at Timber Trails. I can't let you walk away from this." She was talking in one of those soft fairy godmother voices by the end of her diatribe. And if she hadn't just confirmed that she was in fact completely destroying my summer, I would have been soothed by her tone.

"Yeah, well"—I stumbled for words—"well, I still know

where you sleep, Mom. And maybe tonight I'm going to come in and cut you some horrible bangs and see how you like it." I don't know. It made sense when I said it a jillion years ago, and that's the only other time I remember being this mad at my mother.

In what I guess was a testament to my mother's maturity, but was still completely annoying, my mom just walked away, not validating my crazy-lady threat.

I slammed my bedroom door, threw myself back on the bed, and stopped trying to hold back my tears. They came fast and hot. I wasn't sure why exactly I was crying. The loser summer that stretched out before me? The shock of the total disconnect with my mother? Leaving my friends and nothing being the same when I got back? Missing an entire season of *The Real Housewives*? It was probably a little bit of it all.

I wiped my snotty tearstained face on my binky and resolved to not let this bomb ruin my entire night. I was still set on going to Conrad's party. Staying around the apartment wasn't going to make me feel any less shitty. Maybe the party would.

Conrad's was already in full swing by the time I arrived, which was no surprise. *Gossip Girl* makes growing up in Manhattan seem like one long rave, filled with drugs and sex and hair extensions and frequent cab rides to Brooklyn, which it's totally not. But Conrad's parties are like the one place where I feel pseudo–*Gossip Girl*–y. I don't know how his parents let him get away with this shit, but they do.

Conrad's place was packed with kids, most of whom didn't look familiar even though I'd known Conrad since grammar school and I should know everyone in his social circle. Fergie was spelling out words too loudly for me to even think, and everyone already looked thoroughly housed. It was perfect. Totally the place to be to forget about my mom's horror story newsbreak.

I started to bob and weave my way over to the bar, or what I liked to refer to as the "stress-relief buffet." I was trying to squeeze past a super-weird-looking group of guys with bangs who were wearing what looked like juniors section girls' jeans when I heard Kennedy's trademark drunken screech: "LANEY'S HERE!"

I turned and saw her parting the sea of private-school prepsters and indie-rock wannabes. And it wasn't a Moses-parting-the-sea kind of entrance, it was more of an I-wanted-to-crowd-surf-but-nobody-caught-me kind of entrance. She tripped toward me and gave me a hug slash body slam that nearly knocked the wind out of me.

"Lanes." Her breath smelled like she'd just chugged a gallon of nail polish remover. "Where have you been? I've been waiting for you since, like, forever. And why is your life over?"

I took a step back from the leaning tower of BFF, hoping that she could support herself. "Sisterfriend, you don't even want to know why I'm late, but I'm going to tell you anyway. Let me just grab a beverage."

"Totally," she said, and then took hold of my hand and turned toward the bar. "Coming through," she yelled at the top of her lungs, and she shoved herself into the dense crowd, pulling me behind. "Come on, people. Out of our way. We got a thirsty girl here. One Converse in front of the other, that's how you do it." I swear, Kennedy is sometimes like the pushy alcoholic mother I've never wished for. Although, any mother sounded like better parent material than mine at that moment.

At the bar, she mixed herself a drink that smelled like it could disinfect a wound. I popped a can of beer and we moved ourselves over to a corner of the party that seemed to be a little less packed and a little more quiet.

I gulped a few huge gulps and then started in on my nightmare evening.

Kennedy's mouth went slack with shock when I told her about the brochure. "No. She. Did. Not."

"Yeah, one hundred percent she did. And she means it. I really don't think I have a say in it at all."

"This is a legitimate catastrophe. What happened to the teen tour? Or your fashion idea? Even being a tester for a new herpes vaccine would be better." She took a long sip from her chalice of future vomiting.

"I totally didn't even get a chance to bring it up." My hands were starting to shake with anger as I retold the story. A little beer spilled down my wrist. "And now that I refuse to talk to her, I'm definitely not going to be able to ask her."

"So how far away are you going to be?"

"Judging from the brochure, it's a land that's far, far away where everyone is forced to do their hair in ponytails and wear athletic shorts at all times. It sounds horrible, right?"

I could see in her face that my best friend was deciding what a real friend would do—lie to me and tell me I'd be all right or give it to me straight and tell me to fake my own death and escape.

Saving her from the awkward decision, Conrad swooped into our conversation. "How are the two most beautiful ladies at the party doing this evening?" You know how some of your friends' dads are just really creepy in a way that makes you never want to sleep over there? That's totally what Conrad's going to grow up to be. He always hugs just a little too long, "accidentally" misses my cheek during a greeting kiss and ends up half frenching me, and seems to frequently confuse my chest with my eyes. But this was Kennedy's man du jour, or at least he was four jours out of the week, so I had to be nice.

My drunky friend gave Conrad a long and overly spitty kiss. I tried to avert my eyes. After wiping her mouth with the back of her hand, Kennedy remembered that I was standing a foot away from the two of them. "Oh, Lanes, tell Conrad your awful news." And then she turned to Conrad. "You're never going to believe this."

I dropped the camp bomb on him and waited for a reaction.

"Wait, so that means that you're not going to have your own room for the entire summer?" He said it like it was a human rights violation, and it kind of felt like it was, at least to this human. "Inmates on death row have better accommodations than that."

Conrad might have been a creep who applied cologne to his crotch when he thought he was going to get lucky, but he had a point.

"Well, why don't you make the most of your freedom while you can? You ladies should stay late night. The hot tub's all ready for action." He winked. So freaking gross. Though even with his off-the-charts yuck factor, I was still a little jealous that Kennedy had someone to lust after. I hadn't had a crush in about forever, and I was definitely missing the excitement and the obsession and the anticipa-tion. All the guys we typically hung out with were so, well, typical. Plus, I'd known them all since age five, and they were starting to feel more like brothers than real boys. But I was certain I wouldn't find any candidates to fill my boy-crushability-candidate slot hanging out with Conrad and his buddies.

I groaned when Kennedy enthusiastically RSVP'd for both of us. And even though brushing my teeth with sand-paper seemed like more fun than skinny-dipping with Shady McCreeps and company, I kept my mouth shut. If I knew my best friend—and I do—she'd never make it to the after party. In about forty-five minutes we were going to be in a cab back home, her a drunken sobbing mess and me unable to think about anything but pepperoni pizza.

Luckily, Conrad decided to make his exit and I was able to get back to stressing about camp with Ken.

"Am I overreacting?" I asked. "I mean, could it really be that bad?"

"Laney, no. You're being totally reasonable. Your mom made a huge decision without consulting you and now you're going to be in a situation where you're uncomfortable for the entire summer." She was surprisingly lucid and wise for being so wasted. "Plus, I mean, you're totally going to have to wear water sandals. Suicide wouldn't even be an overreaction. Because if you're going to wear shoes that heinous, you'd already be dead to me." There we go, that's the drunk Kennedy I know!

I could feel my face contort with fear and disgust.

"I'm kidding. You're going to be fine," she reassured me. "I mean, sure, you're not going to be able to straighten your hair all summer, but there are worse things than that." Her eyes got cloudy for a minute. "Well, I can't think of anything worse right now, but there definitely are worse things. We'll just alert Frederic Fekkai to up production on his frizz control. You're going to need a few gallons."

This was doing very little in the way of making me feel better. Mercifully, she changed the subject to something other than my sabotaged summer.

"Ugh, I can't believe Conrad invited his cousin." She rolled her eyes as she pulled a pack of cigarettes from her purse. Much like her text-message speak, this new habit of smoking seemed to just be putting a whole lot of effort into looking lame. "His mom must have made him."

I looked over at Ryan Bellsinger, Conrad's way less popular cousin, who was hovering over the bean dip and baby carrot display Conrad's mom had put out for us. Yes, his mom. How she didn't notice the beer tower and Everclear martini bar whilst arranging the decorative baby carrot arch, I don't know.

Ryan snagged a handful of carrots and retreated to the chaise in the corner of the room to munch in miserable solitude, not even looking up at any of us. Conrad's mom might have forced him to invite Ryan, but I'm pretty sure Ryan's mom forced him to come too.

I wasn't sure why Kennedy and, well, everybody had such a problem with Ryan. Actually, that's kind of a lie, I did know. In third grade, Ryan got a little experimental with his dad's electric razor and wound up shaving off both his eyebrows. Instead of just letting him take it like a man, or hell, even like a nine-year-old, Ryan's mom forced him to draw on eyebrows in this horrible reddish eyeliner pencil until they grew back. Of course this led to the kind of merciless taunting that only elementary schoolers can execute. Ryan's name was pretty much officially changed to "Fag Face" and he obviously fell to the bottom of the social totem pole. No one's really ever let him climb back up.

"Ken, come on. That eyebrows thing was nearly three-quarters of a decade ago." God, I couldn't believe I'd been alive long enough to say that. "Can't we get over it yet?"

She ashed onto what I'm sure was a priceless Oriental rug. "That's not as long ago as you think. You know what else was nearly three-quarters of a decade ago? *Newlyweds: Nick and Jessica.* And Jessica Simpson still hasn't gone away."

She had a point. Or did she? I couldn't tell, the beer was definitely starting to kick in.

TXT from Kennedy to Laney:
I woke up this morning still in last
night's dress with my mouth tasting like
parm cheese. Did I have fun last night?

TXT from Laney to Kennedy:
That depends. Does your definition of
fun include puking?

Chapter 4

Per expected, Kennedy and I did not partake in any after partying, hot tubbing, or even post-11:30ing. Instead, I was home early and fast asleep well before the stroke of twelve. At some point in the middle of the night, I heard my mom crack my door enough to see that I was home. I'm sure she didn't really think that I was planning on running away and joining some sort of lost girls' orphanage, but I still felt a twisted sense of power at her having to check. This made the score for the game Sanity: 0, Crazy Laney: 1. At least technically I was winning.

My hangover was pretty major. And I didn't think it was from the Jell-O shots. It felt more like an emotional hangover—dehydrated from crying, tired of hating someone I really loved, and queasy from the thought of a summer away from everything I'd ever known.

I sat up in bed and contemplated my Sunday game plan. The agenda included two things. First, silent-treatmenting my mom. Second, scouring the Internet for other last-minute summer options. Neither involved anything that normally made me happy, which would be ice cream, reality television, and puns. So the day was looking pretty bleak.

Finally, I willed myself to get out of bed, head to the kitchen, and eat some Lucky Charms. As I was lapping the pastel soy milk from the bowl, the president of Douchebags Anonymous waltzed himself and his half-attempt at a goatee through the front door.

"Morning, Lanezilla," he said as he headed past the kitchen and back toward my mother's room. And isn't that every teen girl's dream, to be referred to as a monster reptile first thing in the morning? It's amazing I don't have self-esteem issues after living with this guy.

"Morning, Dr. Evil," I replied through a milk-mustached grimace.

And then my mom appeared in the doorway. They must have been coming back from an early yoga class.

She stopped in the kitchen to say good morning, but per my silent strategy, I pretended to be far too busy digging through the cereal box for my temporary tattoo prize to notice her.

She sighed deeply at my very apparent silent treatment and started pulling out soy yogurt and homemade granola for her breakfast. I moved over to the coffee machine and started it up. Today was going to be a long day of bonding with Google and I needed all the energy I could get.

As the coffee machine dripped my brain fuel into the pot, I made my way around the kitchen to collect a mug, milk, and Splenda. But when I went to our normal Splenda stash, I couldn't find any. I opened almost every cabinet in the kitchen hunting for the fake sugar but found none. Normally, this would be the time when I'd ask my mother where she put the Splenda, but since I was silent-treatmenting her, I couldn't. So I just poured myself a cup and sulked off to my room to slurp down the bitterness. Symbolism much?

As I walked into my room, my phone was vibrating. It was obviously Kennedy. It was too early for phone calls, but clearly she was stalking her phone for signs that I was awake, and my prebreakfast text back was an invitation. I picked up without even checking the caller ID.

"What, Ken?"

"Good morning, Sunshine!" she chirped.

"Why are you so peppy? Shouldn't you be wallowing in hungover anguish, asking to be put out of your misery like that mom in *One True Thing*?" I asked.

"No, my dear. That's the beauty of puking! You wake up refreshed and ready to carpe diem." She sounded like an infomercial for purging. "So, what are we doing today? Brunch and then shop?"

"Sorry, I'm being a major dork today and staying home." I started pawing through my drawers for some comfy clothes to research in.

"Cool, I'll come over," she offered.

"No way. I really want to get stuff done and find something for this summer to counter my mom's offer. And your

40

version of getting stuff done—eating snacks and rating Conrad's frenching technique—is in no way going to help my situation." I love how Kennedy and I are so close that this brand of brutal honesty is totally acceptable.

"Fair enough, but you know what's going to happen. You're going to try and do stuff for like fifteen minutes and then take a five-minute break and you'll wind up g-chatting with me for like six hours about Conrad's frenching, not getting anything done, and not even eating any snacks."

I groaned into my phone. She was totally right. "Fine." I sighed at my total lack of self-control and she squealed with success. "Bring Combos," I added before hanging up.

I changed out of my pj's and into velours. Not really much of a step up, but staying in my pajamas all day long reminded me too much of a Cymbalta commercial. I propped my pillows up on my bed, leaned back, and waited for Kennedy to ring the doorbell.

About four and a half minutes later, she was knocking on my bedroom door.

"Ready or not, here I come," she said as she burst into my room.

"How'd you get in?" I asked.

"How do you think? Your mom let me in." She plopped down next to me on my bed and opened the bag of Combos she'd brought.

"Wait, did you talk to her?" Somewhere in the back of my head, I knew I was being a wee bit nutso, but I just couldn't help it. "We're not talking to her," I instructed.

Ken rolled her eyes. "Listen, your mom has been my best friend's mom since forever. I can't not talk to her in her own home."

"Fine," I snapped. "So are you now down with this whole summer camp thing too?"

She started patting my back up and down like she was looking for something. "Is your psycho switch back here?" she asked, still continuing her searching pantomime. " 'Cause it somehow got turned on and I want to turn it back off."

"What?" I asked, pushing her hands off my back.

"You're being ca-ca-cah-razy! Of course I'm not down with this whole summer camp thing. I just said hello to your mom and told her that today's tunic selection was lovely." I continued to hairy-eyeball her for a second. "And that's not code for 'Let's cart Laney off to the boonies so she'll freeze to death and be forced to eat human flesh to stay alive.' "

I was seriously confused now.

She clarified, "I'm kind of picturing camp as that movie where that plane full of rugby players crashed in the mountains and they ate each other until help came." She pulled the blanket from the foot of my bed over her legs. "Anyway, what I'm saying is that talking to your mom for a hot second doesn't mean that I'm not on your side here. I've actually come up with a plan to help get you out of this."

"A plan?" Scenes from *It Takes Two* flashed through my head. "You found my long-lost twin sister and we're going to send her to camp instead of me?"

"I wish it were that simple," she said. As she reached down to pull her bag up to the bed, I grabbed a fistful of Combos and shoved them in my mouth.

"I'm going to spend this next week trying really hard to get addicted to drugs and alcohol so I have to go to rehab this summer instead of camp?" I guessed again, pretzel crumbs flying from my mouth.

42

She shook her head and took out a small book from her bag, laying it flat on the bed to show me.

"*The Secret?*" I wasn't sure what to make of this.

"Yeah, I saw it on *Oprah* a while ago. Basically, it's about the Law of Attraction. If you think hard enough about something, it'll happen."

"Really?" I picked up the book and flipped through the pages. "That's what it says?"

"Well, I don't know. I didn't actually read it. But that was the gist on *Oprah*." She straightened her back and sat up. "So let's try it."

We both sat on my bed, facing each other with perfect posture and closed eyes. It felt a lot like when we were super little and would play with the Ouija board. After five totally silent minutes, I cracked an eyelid. Kennedy was still fully focused, but I decided to interrupt anyway.

"OK, let's see if it worked." I jumped off my bed and over to my laptop. I opened CNN.com. "Well, no reports on Pennsylvania and all of its unair-conditioned nature breaking off from the continental U.S. and floating into the Atlantic. So I guess it didn't work."

She giggled. "Well, it was worth a shot, right?"

I shrugged. "I guess." My eyes were starting to tear up at the thought of camp. This was such a nightmare, but I was awake.

Kennedy was obviously daydreaming too, not about my veritable prison stint, but about something almost as disturbing for me.

"So, like, do you think Conrad's going to do anything super sweet for me when I'm on post-NJ bed rest this summer?"

I reached for the bag of Combos, hoping that having a

mouth full of food would be a good enough excuse to get out of this convo and continue with my mental pity party.

As I pushed the metal door open and walked out of school for the last time as a sophomore, I totally didn't feel the pang of energy I thought officially becoming an upper-classman would give me. Instead, I was in a daze. And while some of that could be credited to spending three hours in a dark classroom watching a boring movie that was made before I was born, it was kind of like I was in a fog of my own stress-out.

But with school finally over, I had nothing more to distract me from my imminent starring role in *Into the Wild 2: Same Nature, Different Dead Body*. I kind of wanted to stand up to my mom and tell her that this summer conversation ain't over until the fat lady sings. And since she'd gone vegan, I weighed more than her. But also, the thought of disobeying my mom made me nauseous. It was so stereotypically sitcomy and just not me. I could only fight this so much.

After an afternoon at Kennedy's, I went home for dinner and plopped down in front of a steaming plate of vegan lasagna with my mom and Mark. How was I even considering throwing down with my mom when I couldn't even bring myself to be five minutes late for a super-gross supper?

I leaned to the side and offered Perez a bite off my plate. She sniffed it a few times and then turned her nose away. I laughed and scratched her chin. "Good girl, Perez. Such a good girl."

I decided I was ready to end the silent treatment with

my mom. "In the likely event that I don't make it back from this summer alive, I want Perez to have my room. You two can't change it into a yoga studio or soy-plant greenhouse, OK?" I said.

"Oh, for crying out loud," my mom whinnied. "You're going to camp, not off to war. There's no chance you're going to die. Turn down the dramatics, please."

"Yeah? Well, it feels like you're killing my soul," I said, trying my hardest to make my mother feel at least a little remorse.

"You know, in Inuit culture, a man's soul is considered an actual part of his body. Just as real as a hand or neck," Mark said, and then smiled proudly, as if this comment were at all interesting or on topic.

"Good point, Mark." I smirked overly sweetly at him and then continued, "If my soul is a physical part of me, then this qualifies as physical abuse. I'm calling Child Protective Services."

I huffed off to my room, obviously not to call CPS to report my mom and nondad for sending me off to an expensive sleepaway camp, but to do something far more drastic—e-mail my father.

Dad,

I know that this isn't one of our Hallmark-sanctioned communication periods, but I hope that you'll still be down for some father/daughter interaction because I have a serious issue I want to talk to you about. Mom has gone crazy and is sending me to summer camp for the entire summer. And I know that it probably doesn't sound that bad, but it really is. So I'm begging you, you've got to help me out. Tell her what a horrible idea it is and ask for custody for the summer. It can be like that movie with the Rock when his daughter comes to live with him. We'll both learn a little something from each other about the meaning of family and love. Sounds nice, huh? Seriously, hurry up and save me.

Just to reiterate, I'm totally not overreacting.
Laney

Chapter 5

"Wake up, Laney Parker! Today's the day!" my mother shrieked enthusiastically as she yanked my curtains open.

Squinting, I turned my head away from the glaring sunlight and caught a glimpse of my alarm clock. "Mom," I mumbled, "it's six freaking a.m. What time zone do you think we're in?" Using my drool puddle as a guide, I repositioned my head back exactly to its sleeping position.

"Honey, it's your first day of camp. You need to catch the camp bus that takes you down at noon." And with that, she pulled my blanket off me and waited with her arms crossed for me to hop out of bed.

"Noon! I have forever till then. Let me sleep for a few more hours." I made a move to grab my comforter back, but thanks to hours of downward dog, my mom had Madonna arms and almost pulled me straight out of bed.

"The bus doesn't exactly come to our front door, Laney. The stop is at Rockville Centre."

"Wait, this camp doesn't even provide transportation from Manhattan? I have to go out to Long freaking Island?"

My mom didn't answer, but she did take my comforter as she left my room, yelling down the hall, "Hurry up, Laney!"

I lay in my bed and tried to pull my T-shirt down as a makeshift blanket to cover my legs, but all I wound up doing was stretching out the letters on my MAKE OUT NOT WAR shirt.

Completely uncomfortable without a blanket and unable to fall back asleep, I caved. I rolled out of bed and trudged down to the kitchen, shaking my head at the fact that not everyone thinks of Manhattan as the center of the universe. It's like the sun, but with a more intense mix of famous and homeless people.

I slumped down in a chair and avoided eye contact with Mark as my mom got the fixings together for breakfast.

At the sound of my butt hitting the chair cushion, my mom turned around, spatula in hand. "Oh good, you're here. I was just about to head back into your room to really wake you up. Right now I'm working on a protein-rich, ginkgo-infused breakfast. Should give you the energy and brainpower to meet a bunch of new friends today." For some reason, the way she was holding the spatula struck me as menacing.

"Mom, if you did any more of a thorough job waking me up, you'd have given me shaken baby syndrome," I grumbled.

I grabbed the comics from Mark's piles of papers and started reading, trying my hardest to pretend none of this was happening.

My mom plopped a plate of tofu scramble and a giant glass of some sort of green goopy smoothie in front of me. It smelled like fresh tar. I looked over at Perez's bowl of Purina and contemplated switching with her.

"And here's some breakfast reading so you can get excited." She slid the Timber Trails information packet in front of me.

I groaned and put down the Sunday comics, switching my attention to the packet. D-day had officially arrived, and there was no longer any point in imagining myself fighting the parental power. This summer was going to suck and denial wasn't going to change that. Might as well find out the details.

I shoveled a spoonful of the vitamin-rich goop into my mouth and flipped through the pages, nearly choking when I got to the pricing page. And not because I got a piece of undissolved polenta lodged in my throat. Well, not just because I got a piece of undissolved polenta.

"Wow, Mom." I pointed to the expense grid. "A summer at Timber Trails is really expensive. Don't you think we could find a better use for the money? Like a new purse or a charity or something?" I took a second to think, but all I could come up with was "Like, what if I joined Big Brothers Big Sisters and got a little sister from the Bronx or the East Village? I could mentor her and stuff." Even through my desperation-induced haze, I knew this was a bad idea. I mean, what would I mentor her in—how to keep a tube top up even when you don't have boobs? I had a feeling that wouldn't fly on the Big Brothers Big Sisters application, let alone with my mother, who was actively ignoring me at the moment.

I continued flipping through the camp booklet. I still wasn't over the massive plague of braces that had apparently struck Timber Trails. Every single picture was of a camper in a T-shirt and drawstring shorts, smiling widely to display a mouthful of metal. The packet went on and on about keeping your kids well supervised and safe from harm. Really, what was there to be worried about safetywise in the boonies? You probably didn't even have to look both ways before you crossed the street there because you can hear a horse-drawn carriage coming from a mile away. It seemed to me that the only thing these parents should worry about was protecting their kids from a strong magnet in the deep part of a lake.

Finally, I landed on the packing list page and my breath caught. The high-gloss paper reflected the light and gleamed. I might actually have a glimmer of hope. "Look at this. I really can't go, Mom. I mean, I haven't even packed yet and there's no way I'm going to have time to get all my travel-size shampoos together and stuff." I gave a huff that tried to sound defeated, but this was as close to a real escape as I'd come since Mom brought up the whole camp idea. "Maybe I should just stay here for the summer and go to camp next year."

My mom may be many things. Weird? Yes. New Agey? Uh-huh. Painfully poorly dressed? For sure. Have bad taste in men? Duh. But easily shitted? Certainly not. "Oh," she said in what she tried to make her sweetest voice, but I could hear her angry don't-you-mess-with-Mama tone, "I took care of the packing, sweetie."

I nearly choked on my lentil smoothie. "What? How could you have done that? I mean"—I looked down at the list—"ten pairs of athletic shorts? Where did I get ten pairs of athletic shorts?" I don't think anything in my closet could be considered "athletic." Short, I had plenty of, but I knew that my mother hated all my going-out gear and would never pack that.

"I told you, I took care of everything. I bought you some athletic shorts. Well, I guess they're more like skorts. Very cute!" She looked genuinely excited. But me in a pair of skorts? For serious? I could hear an icy sheet forming in hell and Britney accepting a Parent of the Year award.

I opened my mouth to alert my mother to the fact that I would wear skorts the day after never, but my mom cut in before I could say anything. "Laney, you can sit here and try and fight me for an hour before I send you off to camp or you can spend the next hour getting ready. Either way"—she whipped an index finger through the air in a sassy S shape she'd learned from watching one episode of *Everybody Hates Chris*—"You've got one hour before you need to take that frown down to the garage for us to drive you out to the bus stop."

"An hour? That's nowhere near enough time to get ready." And it's not like I'm some super-high-maintenance glamour girl who needs to go tanning and get extensions and a face peel before heading out. But six weeks away from home? Come on, even Gandhi would have needed more time to prep for that. And he'd only have to pick out which cloth diaper things to pack. I had makeup, hair products, Fiber One bars, moisturizer, and so much more stuff that I couldn't even think of.

I slammed my still-soy-filled dishes into the sink and

whisked by my mother, who was practicing attitudey pursed lips in her reflection on the spatula.

By the time I got to my room, I was already hyperventilating. Six weeks away? Speed-showering? Praying there was enough undereye concealer in the one tube I had to last all summer? Saying goodbye to all my friends? Researching Wicca and figuring out how to put a hex on Mark and my mother for doing this to me? One hour just wasn't enough time for all of it. And yes, I know that technically, I'd had since school ended to get ready for this, but "technically" doesn't mean anything when you're "actually" in the middle of a full-blown panic attack.

I pulled open my makeup drawer and stared at my nail polish section. Which ones to bring? I was going to be in nature and stuff—should I just go with the pale pinks and beiges for my natural look? Or, since I was probably going to be sick of nature and generally miserable, should I go with the blacks and dark blues?

I decided on the most logical course of action: a little bit of everything in the drawer, including the free sample of age-defying wrinkle creme I'd never used. My mind spun—what next? I was paralyzed and reality was crashing down around me. I was going to camp for real. I dug back into my makeup drawer and pulled out two more handfuls of whatever I could grab. Just as I was dumping the load into my makeup bag, I heard my text alert.

I glanced at my phone to see "u up???" from Kennedy. I immediately speed-dialed her.

"Hello?" a groggy Kennedy said from her end.

"What are you doing up?" I asked, surprised and happy to hear her tired voice. Kennedy getting up on her own, sans hangover, before noon is absolutely unheard of. For school, she puts her alarm clock on a high shelf across her room and even has this crazy obstacle course of baby safety gates set up near the shelf so that she doesn't sleepwalk herself into snoozing through first period every day. She'd already dismantled the Fisher-Price prison to facilitate her summer sleeping in.

"I don't know. It was weird. I just suddenly woke up and was all, 'I need to call Laney and make sure she's OK.'" We were so like twins who were separated at birth but can still feel each other's pain when one is in labor or something. "So, you're OK, right?"

"Not even close to OK. Light-years away from OK." I blubbered out as much of my morning as I could without sobbing.

"Skorts? She seriously said the word *skorts*?" She was laughing as she said this, but I think it was that nervous kind of laugh that you do when something's so uncomfortably awful, your body just makes you giggle.

"For serious, she said that. Actually, I think the term was *athletic skorts*, whatever that means. And can we talk about how I have less than an hour to get ready?" I was stalking around my room, trying to use up some of my crazy nervous energy.

"An hour? Is that even enough time for you to get the malaria pills and shots you're going to need?" she asked, genuinely concerned.

I stopped in the middle of my room. "Wait, what?"

"Yeah, like whenever my parents go on long trips to weird naturey places, they always have to get shots and go on meds for malaria."

"Yeah, but they go on safaris in Africa and stuff. This is just Pennsylvania. I think the only thing I have to worry about catching there is homesickness."

"OK, when you get some weird strain of Pennsylvanian brain-dissolving virus, I'm not going to tell you I told you so, because I'm not the type to say stuff like that. Plus, with a brain of mush, you wouldn't understand me anyways. But know that I'll totally be thinking it."

I rolled my eyes at her nonsense. It was like she was already practicing being a naggy mother. "Really, so comforting, Ken. Just the kind of support I need right now."

"Come on, I'm kidding. Well, like thirty-two percent kidding."

"I'm going to miss you so much while I'm away contracting brain diseases," I said, and totally did get a little teary.

"No you're not, because it's going to be like we're still together I'm going to call and text you so much, OK? Don't even worry about that." I sniffled a little at her sweetness. "Seriously, you're going to come back and be sick of me. That's how much we're going to keep in touch."

"Yeah, yeah, you're right." I wasn't sure if I believed her or was just trying to convince myself that missing her wouldn't be so bad.

After a few deep breaths, I was finally starting to calm down from my near-tear encounter when my mom walked up to my closed door and yelled, "Thirty-minute countdown, Lane. And I haven't heard the shower at all."

"Ugh," I said into my phone, feeling the anger pulse through my body and turn my ears red. There was no escaping the Mominator. "I'll call you when I get to camp. Right now I have to take the world's fastest shower and pack anything aside from skorts I'm going to need for the next six weeks."

"Wait, what happened when you e-mailed your dad about swooping in to save you?" she asked.

"That would be a big fat nothing." I exhaled a sound of disappointment into my phone. "I got an out-of-office bounce-back saying he'd be away until the middle of July. By then I'll probably be so bug-bitten and, if you're right, diseased, that I'll need to be quarantined, so even if he was going to save me, he wouldn't be able to."

"That kind of sucks," she said bluntly.

"Yep, it does." It actually didn't *kind of* suck. It *really* sucked. "All right, I need to go." I felt my anger giving way to pure panic. I only had thirty minutes of freedom left and I had no idea what to do first.

"OK, be brave, babe. I'll talk to you soon."

I hung up and galloped to the bathroom, tripping on the carpet because my body was moving so quickly. Some hotels barely had water pressure, and I doubted that this camp was on par with your average Hilton. I decided to start my half hour of liberty by taking advantage of the massage setting on my showerhead and doing some serious loofahing while I still could.

I sat on my bed, petting Perez with one hand as I changed my Facebook status to "Downward spiraling into the worst summer known to humankind. Send help. Cash counts, so do baked goods."

"What are you going to do without me, girlie?" I cooed at my puppy. She rolled over so I could scratch her belly.

I heard my mom stomp up to my door. "LANEY! WE NEEDED TO BE IN THE CAR FIVE MINUTES AGO!"

"Yep, almost ready," I yelled back, and stuck my tongue out at the closed door.

Again, my mom is not easily, or come to think of it, *ever*, duped. She opened my door to see me wet-headed, back in my pj's, and playing with Perez.

"Oh, no, no," she said, taking in my disobedience. She marched toward my closet, yanked out a skirt and a tank, and threw them at me. "You put these on *now* and then we're off."

She stood hands on hips waiting for me to get dressed. Her face was red and she was clearly ticked in a major way. I wanted to say something super snotty about how not Zen she was being about this, which I knew would get her even more peeved, but I went another direction instead.

"I can't believe you're watching me get dressed. I'm not a baby."

"Fine, you keep getting ready. I'm going to get the bag I packed for you." She left the room for a second as I quickly shimmied into the outfit she'd picked out for me and started applying makeup.

She came back in with an army green duffel bag.

"Mom, what homeless person did you rob to get that bag?" I rolled my eyes. "This is turning way too *Into the Wild*." I was kind of joking when I made references to that before, but now I was seriously getting scared. "And that guy ate the wrong berries and died in the freezing Alaska tundra. His body wasn't found for like a really long time either. Is that what you want for me, Mom? A daughter-sicle?"

"OK, stop with the nonsense and head downstairs. Our car should be waiting," she commanded.

Reluctantly, I kissed Perez goodbye and did a sad shuffle out of the apartment. The clicking of the bolt behind me reminded me of a prison lockdown. I swear the elevator has never moved that quickly, and before I knew it, I was on the curb watching Mark get out of the car he'd just pulled up from the garage. Then he heaved the hideous olive sack of my summer garb into the trunk. I didn't even want to think about the horror of acrylics and breathable athletic mesh that lay within it. That would just make me a jillion times more upset, and I was already trying my hardest not to cry. My mom got into the driver's seat and adjusted the mirrors. I slumped myself into the passenger's. Through her window, I made eye contact with Dr. Demon and gave him a terse wave, which is about as intimate as the two of us get. Thank God he wasn't coming with us on the road trip to the great suburban yonder. I guess that was the silver lining to this huge, dark, horrible cloud.

I leaned back in my seat and closed my eyes. I felt like I was stepping into one of those haunted house rides where you know you're about to see something lame like a Frankenstein on wheels but you're going to be scared anyway. That's exactly what I was expecting from camp: a frightening level of lameness.

TXT from Laney to Kennedy:
Just arrived at what looks like an extras
casting call for When Kim Kardashian's
Closet Attacks. HELP!

Chapter 6

My mom and I drove in quiet hostility the whole long ride out there. When we pulled into the parking lot to meet the bus, she broke the silence.

"Well, Laney, this is where I leave you. I know you're a little upset now, but I bet when I pick you up here in a few weeks, you're going to be singing another tune."

She came in for a hug and pulled me close to her. The gearshift was poking my ribs. "I bet not," I whispered with my head smooshed into her hair.

"What's that?"

"Nothing. I'll miss you," I said in a meaningless mono-tone, and hopped out of the car.

I'd barely gotten the duffel out of the trunk when my mom blew me a final kiss and zoomed our sedan out of there. It was like she couldn't get away fast enough, though given how nasty I'd been the past few days, I seriously couldn't blame her. I held myself back from chasing after the car like an abandoned puppy. But that's exactly what I felt like. I took a deep breath and started the long duffel-bag lug toward the crowd of people in the far corner of the parking lot. As I got closer, I was accosted by suburbia in the most brutal way possible: a parking lot of middle-aged women in pastel sweatsuits yelling at children of assorted ages. Across this ocean of terry cloth and brewing mommy issues, I saw a bus with a banner reading TIMBER TRAILS BOUND hanging on its side and made my way toward it, trying not to disturb the locals.

"Um, excuse me," I said to a woman who was scolding her kids and blocking my path.

"You two," she yelled with a smoker's rasp, "you better wear sunscreen every day. Are you listening? Every day."

It seemed like she couldn't hear me over her own voice, so I begged her pardon again. "Excuse me, ma'am."

She continued, still unaware of my presence. "And Brandt, I better not get any calls this year about you putting toothpaste on your peepee again. OK? Say it. Brandt, I want to hear you say, 'I will not put toothpaste on my peepee.'"

Stunned and beyond horrified, I decided not to interrupt family hygiene hour and backed away slowly. I walked the twenty extra feet around them, passing a few more normal parental conversations—"Miss you." "Write soon." "Always

60

carry your inhaler."—before I found myself right in front of the bus.

I walked up to a guy who had a broken leg. He was wearing a Timber Trails shirt with the font in curly script so it looked like a Coca-Cola product. He seemed to be the most official person in the parking lot, and, at around seventeen-ish, probably the oldest nonparent. Every other camper looked so young, I was feeling like Grandma Laney. Well, maybe that's an exaggeration. More like Weird Older Cousin Laney who still had to sit with the kids on Thanksgiving even though she's so tall now, she can't fit her legs under the mini-table.

"Hi," I said as I dropped my duffel onto the blacktop. "I'm getting sent to sleepaway camp." My tone was way more attitudey than I wanted it to sound, but way less than I actually felt.

"Well, you're in the right place," he said, all smiles and rainbows. "Let me just check you off my list." He bent down to pick up a clipboard from the bus's staircase. He was moving rather deftly for a guy with a broken leg, so as covertly as possible, I looked down for a closer inspection of his injury. It turned out that what I thought was a cast was actually about twenty friendship bracelets, or I guess friendship anklets. He had so many that they formed a thick cuff from his midshin down to the Velcro strap of his athletic sandal. He picked up the board and flipped a page. "OK, so what's your name?"

"Laney Parker," I answered, feeling totally weird. It was like the exact opposite of getting checked into a club's VIP section by a bouncer—the last thing in the world I wanted was my name to be on the list. It struck me that if for whatever computer glitch reason my name wasn't on that list, I could pick up my bag, get on some smelly commuter train, and be in the city within the hour. And at this point in the summer, it was far too late to apply for any summer programs or internships. So I'd just have to spend my summer watching *Millionaire Matchmaker* marathons and taste-testing every single flavor of Ben & Jerry's Lighten Up line.

"Parker, Laney. Gotcha." Friendship Leg's voice broke through my daydreams of becoming obese and couch-bound over the summer and I sighed to myself. "So just go ahead and throw your suitcase under the bus and hop aboard. We'll be leaving in about five minutes." He then turned away from me and yelled out to the masses in the parking lot, "All right, parents. Time to say goodbye to your Timber Trailers. This bus will be heading out in five short minutes. See ya in six amazing weeks!" He did a little salute on "See ya." This guy was so cheesy. If I were lactose intolerant, I'd totally be stomach-cramping.

By the time I had hauled my sack of gear into the storage compartment of the bus, everyone else's requisite precamp mommy scoldings had been completed and there was a line forming to get on the bus. It was official: I'd lost the Just Say No war on camp. I moaned out loud and found a place at the back of the line. I looked at the column of campers in front of me and again realized just how young everyone seemed. At five three, I towered over like ninety percent of the kids. How could everyone be this little?

I dragged my heels as the line crept forward and eventually climbed on the bus to find that my seat options were limited. The choices being the open seat next to the counselor in the front row or a seat next to a kid so young he could seriously be in kindergarten. As exemplified by his woven shackle, the counselor was a friendly guy. And with six long weeks stretching ahead of me and not knowing a soul in the entire state of Pennsylvania, I could certainly use a friend. But befriending the cheeseball counselors was probably like being one of the suck-up girls at school who bring in holiday gifts for the teachers and compliment the substitutes on their weird polyester skirts, and I didn't need that rep. So I headed back to sit with the baby. I hoped he wasn't wearing a diaper . . . or maybe I should hope he was?

Wordlessly, I fell into my seat, fished my iPhone out, put in my earbuds, and leaned back to catch up on the sleep I was so robbed of this morning. Only about five seconds into "Put Your Records On," I felt a sticky finger tap my shoulder. I turned and looked down at my SpongeBob SquarePants–geared neighbor. Once I got a closer look at him, I realized that I recognized him from the parking lot.

"Hello. I'm Brandt," he said, waving up at me. Oh, Brandt, I know what you did last summer and I'm never going to be able to brush my teeth without thinking about it again. "I'm seven years old and my birthday is in March. You want to know something really cool?" he asked.

"Sure." I nodded, hoping he wasn't going to pull mouthwash from his underwear.

"One time I had a boogie that smelled like an elephant and I saved it in my nose." He sat up a little straighter, beaming with an absurd amount of pride.

I flashed a wide-eyed fake smile. "Cool," I said slowly.

It took all my inner strength not to speed-dial my apartment and inform my mother of the correct definition of "missing." Because if circus-scented boogers were what my mother thought I'd been missing by living in the city, then it was clear that she needed a vocab refresher. *Missing* wasn't the right word. *Avoiding* was more appropriate.

Instead, I cranked Corinne Bailey Rae back up and closed my eyes, hoping to sleep through the rest of the bus ride. But just as my lids closed, the crackling static of a microphone getting turned on erupted from speakers at the front of the bus.

"Sorry to disturb you guys."

I opened my eyes and of course it was Captain Friendship Anklets on the mike. The microphone dropped with a huge thud that was projected throughout the entire bus. He bent down to pick it up.

"Wow, this thing sure is slippery. Anyway, guys, I wanted to give you an unofficial welcome to Timber Trails! You'll get the official welcome once we make it through the Timber gates, but for now it's only me. So you know, folks, this trip is going to be a little less than three hours, barring any traffic and not including potty breaks."

This seemed to remind Brandt about his bladder situation. As soon as the counselor finished his sentence, Brandt belted out at the decibel level of the Big Bang, "I have to go to the potty!"

The bus had just pulled onto the highway and we'd been driving for all of twelve minutes. And that included the six minutes it took the driver to unparallel park the bus without hitting any of the waving mothers or their SUVs.

"Can you hold it until we're a little farther along, buddy?" the counselor asked into the microphone. Was he for real, talking about urination into a microphone? Maybe if I'd been in a better mood I could have seen the hilarity in this conversation, but I wasn't and I couldn't. Disgusting.

"Nope. Five minutes more is probably all I can hold it for," my seat buddy replied.

"Well, we're not really scheduled for a break," the counselor said while flipping through the sheets on his clipboard for something I assumed was labeled "wee-wee schedule."

"Just let the child go." This was from the bus driver, who up until this point had been completely silent. Thank God the driver said something, because I was about to. I didn't want to start off my camp experience by making a scene, but I really didn't want to take a three-hour ride next to a little boy with pissed pants. "I don't need my bus smelling like a port-a-john."

And so, without even waiting for a nod from the counselor, the driver shifted the bus over to the exit lane and within a few minutes we were parked in a rest-stop lot. Brandt shimmied off, doing the pee-pee crotch hold all the way to the bathroom, and the rest of the bus population scattered. Most of the kids bolted from the bus straight into the McDonald's ball pit. As I was stepping down the stairs to exit, I heard some of the girls who looked closer to my age— well, who at least looked like they were somewhere in the double digits—talking about going to the gas-station gift store and perusing the personalized license plate key chains. Since I didn't have much interest in a new key chain and was way over the size limit for the ball pit, and because no one invited me to partake in either, I just stood around the bus pretending to check my texts. I noticed the time on my cell clock: 12:37. I should have just been getting up, and then I'd be meeting Kennedy for eggs Benedict in about an hour if I hadn't been deported.

Before my mouth watering at the would-be hollandaise sauce turned into full-on drooling, Brandt came running back to the bus, followed by the rest of the gang. The counselor brought up the rear of the herd, counting the bopping heads in front of him to make sure there weren't any ball-pit casualties.

I climbed aboard and Brandt settled back in next to me. The bus took off and then Brandt seemed to focus all his energy on creeping me out.

"Hey, do you know why boogies are salty when you eat them?" he asked me, his pointer finger poised in front of his lips.

"Um, no. I don't," I admitted. "But I don't want to know," I added quickly, hoping that would keep him from elaborating.

"You don't?" His naïve shock might have been endearing if he weren't talking about snot. "Well, I do," he continued. "That's why I'm planning on doing a scientific experiment this summer. I'm not going to eat anything salty for the entire six weeks, like only eat dessert and Froot Loops, and then see if that changes the taste of my boogies." He took a break to deposit whatever was on his finger into his mouth. I tried not to look too closely at the green goo, convincing myself it was just a new kind of candy he'd picked up at the rest stop. "I'm going to keep a daily flavor log."

"Sounds very official, Brandt." And by that I meant officially the grossest thing I've ever heard, but I wasn't about to offend him. After all, at this point, he was the only nonstaff person from the entire Timber Trails population who had actually talked to me.

Though perhaps I spoke too soon, because just as I was trying to persuade myself that a summer with a friend who ate mucus wasn't that different from one with a best friend who drank till she puked regularly, a girl with a mask of too-thick drugstore foundation covering a mountain range of acne on her cheeks and an orange ponytail came up to Brandt's and my two-seater.

She leaned over me, grabbing my seat back for support and practically smothering me in her armpit in the process. "Brandty Boy, are you doing OK?" she asked in a baby-talk voice.

I moved my face out from her pit and smiled up at her, waiting for her to acknowledge me.

"Yeah, I'm fine," he replied in a monotone, clearly not appreciating her checking up on him.

"So you found a new little friend, Brandt? That's so nice." Even when talking about me, she didn't seem to recognize my presence, or if she did, then maybe she just assumed I dug whiffs of body odor.

"Yeah, she's cool, I guess," Brandt responded, and then turned to the window and commenced a deep finger dive into a nostril.

Finally acknowledging my existence, she turned to me, her greasy ponytail whipping around as she cocked her head. "He's my brother and this is only his second year, so I thought he might be nervous still, being so new."

For a second I was going to ask why then she wasn't sitting next to him, but with all the boogie and potty talk, I was pretty sure I knew. Blood wasn't thicker than snot.

"Well, I can relate. It's actually my first time at camp," I said way too cheerfully, hating myself for sounding like the lame-o counselor.

The girl stood up straight, no longer leaning on the seat,

and because I was sitting, she suddenly seemed gigantic. "Oh, I know that," she said, looking down on me and flashing a snide smile. "That's why it's great that you two are becoming such good friends." Perfect. Not even a full hour into camp and I'm already associated with the Boogie King.

I managed to grin back at her sweetly, despite feeling completely awkward. "Yeah, he's cute. But, actually, well . . ." I hadn't made a new friend since the fourth grade when Maggie Sommers transferred into our class in the middle of the year, and I was definitely rusty. "I'm Laney and I'm from the city. Where are you from?" Was that a good starter question? Should I have asked her about something cooler like music or snowboarding or intravenous drugs or something?

"Listen." She flared her nostrils like a rhino about to attack. "I know you're trying to be friendly, but you can just stop. I've been going to Timber since forever and I already have a ton of friends. I don't really need more." She pursed her lips and waited for her bitchiness to sink in.

I was completely dumbfounded and just stared at her. This fugs with a makeup line more defined than Chase Crawford's abs was putting me down?

"Maybe you should focus on befriending some of the other new campers," she continued. "Like our cousin from Philadelphia. He's coming to camp for his first time. He's six."

I could feel my face go slack with shock. Seriously? It was like I'd warped into some horrible mash-up of *Teenage Mutant Ninja Turtles* and *Mean Girls*—a movie where the popular bitch was a mutant created from a L'Oréal cover-up animal-test lab that escaped and turned into this weird cake-faced pseudohuman with an attitude.

Of course, my mind was so busy concocting the back-story of *Teenage Mutant Mean Girls* and where exactly the little brother with the toothpaste on his peepee incident fit into her mutation that I couldn't even think of an appropriate next conversation line. I just sat there helpless as she turned on her Croc-knockoff-clad heels and strutted down the aisle back to the posse of girls who I assumed were only a small fraction of her aforementioned "ton" of friends. I could almost see the needle on my self-esteem gauge drop to empty. And even though it was never even close to full when it came to meeting new people, empty was a completely rotten feeling.

Brandt jolted me out of my self-pity party. "I need to go potty," he yelled.

"Didn't you just go?" I asked. It hadn't even been twenty minutes since the last toilet break. This was astounding, even for me, who pretty much used my gym membership exclusively as a citywide Porta Potti service.

Brandt yelled his potty request again, even louder, and the driver didn't wait for the counselor to fumble his way onto the mike and start an amplified tinkle negotiation. At the very next exit, we were off the highway and back into a gas-station-and-golden-arches haven.

For the second time, everyone disembarked from the bus, and again, I was the only loser on my own. I stood there checking my texts while everyone else cliqued their way into the rest stop. As the redheaded Queen Bitch and her gang of shiny-faced followers marched past me, I heard her say, "I seriously hope she doesn't try to come with us to the gift shop and stuff. She's pretty much obsessed with being my friend. You should have heard her begging. And I'm all, why don't

69

you stick with talking to the little kids, 'cause you seem to be getting along so well with my brother. It was pathetic."

"Totes pathetic," a girl said through her veil of mid-afternoon sweat sheen and acne.

I literally winced at what they were saying. I couldn't believe it, but it really hurt my feelings so much. I never let stuff like this get to me. Actually, if I'm being honest, I've never had to deal with stuff like this before. How could I have sunk this low on the camp cool scale in under an hour? And even though I knew I shouldn't even give this chick any more thought because with her multicolored frizz clips and body odor issues she was clearly lame and gross, I still wanted to run up and inform her that telling someone your name does not qualify as obsessive or begging or pathetic. And didn't the fact that she was still talking about our minute-long interaction technically make *her* the one who was obsessing over *me*?

I leaned back on the side of the filthy bus and huffed to myself as I reread my old texts from my real friends, who would totally want me to accompany them into a grimy gas-station gift shop.

I took a deep breath, threw my phone back into my bag, and looked up at the bus driver, who was standing a few feet away from me enjoying a cigarette and I'm sure a few minutes of quiet nonkidness.

"Um, excuse me," I called to him. "Where exactly is this bus going?"

The driver pulled his cigarette away from his mouth, exhaled a thick gray cloud of smoke, and gave me a weird look. "To Timber Trails summer camp in the Pocono Mountains. Where do you think we're going?"

I exhaled too, only my breath wasn't a huge puff of cancer. "Well, that's where I thought we were going when I got on a few minutes ago. I'm just wondering if we took a wrong turn somewhere." I traced the outline of my cell through the leather of my bag and let out another deep breath. Completely depressed, I muttered what I was really thinking: "Because I feel like I'm on a bus bound for CrazyTown right now."

TXT from Kennedy to Laney:
What does that even mean? PS-I'm
thinking of getting my boobs done with
my nose. Thoughts?

TXT from Laney to Kennedy:
It means that everyone is wearing
velours that are two sizes too small for
their butts. You don't sound nearly
concerned enough. Send help (with some
chocolate). And getting your boobs
done is ridiculous. They'd be so big,
they'd offset the gravitational pull of
the sun and send Earth out of its orbit.
Stop thinking about your boobs and
start thinking about your best friend,
who's a friend in need, indeed.

Chapter 7

It took four hours, an anthology's worth of Brandt's boogie stories, and about twenty bathroom stops until the bus finally pulled off the highway. Suddenly, we were in nature. And not Central Park nature. Real-deal, not-a-skyscraper-or-marathon-trainer-in-sight nature.

We pulled up a long, dusty path and approached a set of incredibly unimpressive wooden gates. Even through the snot smears that Brandt had decorated our window with, I could see the long strips of paint peeling off the wood planks that formed the rickety entrance. TIMBER TRAILS CAMP was etched on the highest part of the entryway in the kind of choppy handwriting you see when angsty teenagers cut words into their thighs on made-for-TV movies. Below that, the camp slogan was written in the same cut-myself-to-feel font.

I read it out loud as we drove through the gates: "All for fun and fun for all."

"That's the camp slogan," Brandt explained. "I chant it whenever we're doing something where we need to get excited, like playing kickball or getting really high up in a Popsicle-stick building or something."

I didn't ask for more details on Popsicle-stick building competitions, knowing that it would probably freak me out about this place even more than the dilapidated welcome gates.

The bus pulled to a stop on the other side of the gates of fun and we all slowly filed out. The counselor stood by the door counting us as we descended the stairs, making sure we were all still there. As he patted my head and dubbed me "Thirty-four," I couldn't help but think that if he came up a few short at this point, there wasn't much he could do. I mean, was he going to go back to every rest stop between here and Long Island checking the bathrooms for renegade camp commuters? I displayed un-Laney-like self-control and kept this logic to myself.

Immediately upon my stepping into the naturey outdoors, my eyes started to water. Then came the sniffles and the itch deep in my throat. The sprawling greenness looked like a battlefield to me, where it was me versus the pollen and ragweed. And they had a very unfair home-court advantage. I sneezed and wiped my nose on the shoulder strap of my tank. Gross, I know, but it felt like the campy thing to do, especially after the past four hours with Brandt.

I was wondering if my mother had been mad enough when she hate-packed me to leave out my antihistamines when I heard a voice from behind me. "Laney Parker, I presume."

"Um." I turned around to see who was making nineteenth-century-lit references when school was out. "You're presuming correctly," I said to what would be best described as a pink troll incarnated into human form.

"Awesome!" The she-troll jumped up and down and clapped. The seams of her fuchsia shorts were working overtime to stay together. She came in close and grabbed me for a hug. Fake intimacy on first encounters is one of my biggest pet peeves. File it in between preachy vegans and that spitty sound Dr. Mark makes every time he swallows. I tried not to visibly recoil at her touch. She pulled back and yanked at something in her pocket. "I made you this name necklace since you're new!" A chain of braided hot-pink gimp attached to a hand-drawn rainbow made only of shades of pink with my name written on it dangled from her claw. It looked like a valentine had puked jewelry. She lunged at me and I flinched, throwing my hands up in self-defense. "Don't be scared. I'm just putting it on you. Kind of like knighting you, right?" She hung the piece of homemade horror around my neck.

My hands dropped from fighting stance and I fingered the plastic chain. "Oh, you shouldn't have." My skin had turned green from that fake gold bling ring I'd bought as part of my *I Love New York* Halloween costume last year. And that thing was actually kind of cute. I wondered how my body would react to this piece of heinosity.

"No biggy. Bubble cursive is, like, my thing. I can teach you if you want," she offered.

My response was to remain silent.

She continued, undaunted by my very apparent lack of enthusiasm. "So you're one of my girls." She bounced up and down some more as she spoke. I was getting motion sickness just maintaining eye contact. "We're in Bunk Redwood. All of the bunks at Timber are named for trees, and since we're the oldest bunk, we get to be the tallest trees. And I'm Mandi, with an *i*, of course. And I'm your counselor. Psyched for a dynamite summer?" Everything she said sounded like she was leading a group cheer, but super rushed. It was like watching *Bring It On* in fast-forward.

"Psyched isn't even close to describing how excited I am," I said through a forced smile. Technically, I was not lying.

She put both her hands on my shoulders and looked me in the eyes. "Then let's get this party started right! You probably can't wait to get to the bunk. I'm going to take you right now." She was beaming with uncut enthusiasm and she showed no evidence of noticing my foul mood. "So let's just get your bag and head up."

"Let's" actually meant "you," because it was just me who was lugging my body bag of summer outfits across the entire camp as we made our way to Bunk Redwood. I huffed and puffed while Mandi strolled next to me. The more we moseyed into the camp, the more green and lush and postcardy it looked. The trees were like national park tall and there were birds and little bugs flying around. It all would have been totally cute and picturesque if it were, well, a picture in *National Geographic*. But because it was where I was going to have to live, it was just overwhelmingly naturey.

"So, there's the mess hall," Mandi said. The building that she pointed to was gray and looked like a sad inner-city public school, except for without the graffiti and metal detectors. This building validated my prisoner-like feelings. "We eat our meals there. And the canteen is connected to the back of the mess hall. That's where you can get treats like chips or chocolate twice a week."

I slowed my already sluggish pace down to a halt. "Wait, did you just say we get chocolate twice a week?" I'm a chocolate-twice-a-day kind of girl, and that's not including if I eat Cocoa Puffs for breakfast—they're vitamin and mineral fortified, so they count more as vegetables than as chocolate. Even though I guess I was expecting some sort of cuisine limits, I thought there would be s'mores after every meal, not weekly rations of dessert. Summer survival didn't seem possible with these kinds of restrictions.

"Yep." She skipped ahead of me. "Now hurry up, slow-poke!"

I dragged myself and my bag onward and Mandi continued with her tour-guiding. She pointed out the boating area and the pool and the row of bunks for the younger girls. As we walked past, I could see through the bunk window a mom making up her daughter's bed and the father placing all her clothing on shelves. And even though I was mega-pissed at my mom, seeing this perfect little family made me wish that she had driven me down instead of shipped me on a bus like a FedEx package. It would have at least pushed the reality of camp back a few hours.

Finally, Mandi stopped and motioned to a set of log stairs that were set into a steep hill. "We older girls live up here." I craned my neck to try and see the bunk at the top of the stairs, but the hill was at a nearly vertical incline. All I could see was sky.

I turned back from the stairway to hell and looked at Mandi with a crinkled forehead. "I'm sort of done with physical feats of strength today." I shook out my tired arms. "Could we just take the elevator?" Looking at the dirt and log staircase, I knew this was wishful thinking, but I had to ask.

Mandi immediately started laughing. "Oh, you're funny, Laney! You're going to fit in great with us!"

She took off, bounding up the stairs, and left me to drag my millions of pounds of clothes myself. What were skorts made out of, lead? I was practically hyperventilating by the time I reached the top.

You would think that in this state of dehydration and exhaustion, my mind would be kind enough to reward me with some sort of mirage—like a spa or the open arms of Kevin Jonas or even just a building that looked like it had functioning plumbing. But no, not lucky enough to get a temporary hallucination. Instead, I just saw a row of brown shanties that didn't look zoned for human habitation.

Before I could even catch my breath, Mandi ran up to the door of one and stood in front of it like Vanna White. "This is our summer home!" she screeched. Then she did a reverse wave and motioned me in. She was so visibly pumped about beckoning me in, you'd think she was bringing me into the best surprise party in the world. "Come on!"

Easier said than done, Mandi. I was beyond exhausted and could feel my arm muscles spasming beneath my skin. It was the hardest workout my arms have had since we had to do that fitness test in gym and I was forced to hold a chin hang for a minute because I couldn't do a pull-up.

Mustering every ounce of strength left in me, I lifted my sack-of-skorts one last time and made my way into the bunk. The floor creaked under the incredible weight of my skort sack, and immediately my nose began to tingle and the throat itch came back. The dust in the bunk was so thick, I could see little particles dancing in the sun near the windows. There were about four girls hustling around and unpacking, but I couldn't focus on any of them. Instead, I was zoning in on the rust-covered bed frames. They didn't look remotely safe or from this century. The brown splintering walls matched the equally doody brown floor, and there was no ceiling, just a few supportive crisscrossing beams and then straight up to the roof. It was pretty much an outhouse with a few cots and a bunk bed. My eyes ran around the perimeter of the room and then over the window frames. I didn't see anything that looked like central air or even a box unit. The sweat from my neck dripped down my back. With no AC to cool me down, I could already feel the sweat hives surfacing.

Now, at this point, I can't technically say that I was shocked. After the stair-climbing torture, I should have expected something equally painful for living quarters. But still, my jaw dropped as I took in what was going to be home decrepit home for the next six weeks. What had I done in a past life to deserve this? Put gum in a handicapped person's hair and then pushed her and her wheelchair into oncoming traffic while I stole her boyfriend and called her mother a slut? It had to be that level of atrocious for me to be here now.

"You're here!" Mandi interrupted my thoughts—as if I needed reminding of where I was. I turned to her. She was prancing toward the set of bunk beds and pointing. "I've got top bunk!" That was a relief, at least. With the rusty frames on these beds, sleeping on the top was a death wish. Although I guess that meant that Mandi would be falling to her sleepy death on me.

I was stupefied by how shockingly bad this place was. I wondered if there was a site where I could rate these accommodations, like Hotels.com but for camps. Because I definitely had some fighting words that I needed to get out. And I was just about to let them out. I wanted to start screaming and yelling and freaking so hard that they'd be forced to send me home. But that's so not me, and I just don't have that kind of bad-girl follow-through in me. I mean, I'm a good student, a hard worker, and I never break curfew. Hell, I don't even jaywalk. Actually, I've never ever broken any rules, unless you count the legal drinking age, which I don't think anyone but my health teacher does. And while a little bit of me knew that being a total nightmare would get me kicked out, a bigger chunk of me knew that the real nightmare would be facing my mother afterward.

Deflated and annoyed with my good-girl complex, I dragged my bag near the bed. As gross and peed-on as the plastic mattress looked, I really wanted to lie down on it for a quick nap. But before I could make a move, Mandi plopped down in the center of the bunk floor and called out, "Laney, why don't you sit here next to me."

I walked over to the area of floor she was patting and squatted.

"Okay, now that Laney's arrived, we're at full capacity," she belted out to the other girls in the bunk. Then her voice suddenly changed to a robotic monotone. "Warning. Warning. One more camper and this bunk will explode." Back in her chipmunky normal tone, she turned to me and explained with gusto, "I'm really into fun impressions and jokes."

"Oh, we remember that you're funny, Mands," a girl on the far side of the bunk who was unpacking her bag said. "You've been our counselor for like, eons." She turned to put a pile of T-shirts onto a shelf and I saw that the back of her shorts declared her butt CUTE.

"Yeah, but I'm just trying to get Laney familiar with our little gang," Mandi explained. I knew she was trying to include me, but highlighting that she needed to put effort into including me just made me feel like more of an outsider.

Mandi cleared her throat and in an official-sounding booming voice called out, "OK, Bunk Redwood ladies, let's all get into a circle and go around, introduce ourselves, and say what we're hoping for most to get out of our Timber Trails summer."

Seriously? This sounded like the beginning to a bad family therapy session.

Immediately, the other girls in the bunk stopped making their beds and putting away their clothing and formed a circle in the center of the bunk. I noticed that at least two other girls were also wearing trashed-out booty gym shorts with writing on the butt. One's said SEXY and the other's said what I assumed was ANGEL, but currently, she had a wedgie and her butt read ANEL. I almost convulsed with repressed giggles . . . or maybe it was still muscle spasms.

When Sexy turned around from putting her last pile away, I locked eyes with her. The shorts were definitely false advertising, because she was certainly not sexy. It was my foundation-faced enemy from the bus ride down here. And I was certain that she interpreted my random assignment to her bunk as yet another indication of my obsession with her. I kept my fingers crossed she wouldn't say that what she was hoping for most out of her summer was to learn more about taking out restraining orders and embarrass me in front of everyone before I even had a chance to do it myself with a midnight bout of IBS or something.

Mandi nodded approvingly at the circle of cross-legged girls that had formed. "I'll go first. I'm Mandi with an *i* and I'm hoping that this summer I can help you girls have the best summer ever. OK," she said, turning to the girl to her right.

I wanted to shout out "You're going to fail!" at Mandi. There was absolutely no way this summer would ever go down as my best summer ever, or even in my top fourteen.

"I'm Aiden," Cute said as she fingered her dyed blond hair. There was already at least an inch of roots. Six weeks here without a colorist and that chick was going to have a reverse skunk's butt for her head. "This is my seventh summer at Timber Trails and I'm just hoping that this year lives up to how phenomenal my past six have been."

She nodded at Anel/Angel—depending on if you're going with pre– or post–butt pick—to start her intro. "I'm Aidan too," she started.

Mandi quickly rotated toward me and piped up, "But she's with an *a* at the end and she's"—Mandi pointed to Cute—"with an *e* at the end." Was this camp sponsored by Sylvan Learning Center or something?

Aidan with an *a* nodded to confirm the spelling of her name and continued, "And this is only my fifth summer at

Timber, but I'm hoping for it to be as slamming as the past four."

The next girl in the circle was the bus brat. I didn't even look at her, hoping that she'd notice how nonobsessed with her I was. She started her intro. "I'm Hayden, like Hayden Panettiere." It took all my self-control not to laugh at that one. Aside from the name, this Hayden had nothing in common with *Heroes* Hayden. The Hayden sitting in front of me had greasy red hair with freckles that were peeping through her gallons of too-dark foundation, an acne situation across her forehead and cheeks, and bug bites that wouldn't fill a training bra. She was nowhere near as sexy as her butt said she was. Hayden "Not at All Panettiere" continued, "And I've been going to camp for seven years, and I also want this summer to be my favorite, just like the past six."

Who sang that song about city girls finding stuff out early? Elvis? Well, he was wrong. Because apparently, suburban girls are the ones who find out how to live on their own early. It sounded like as soon as these girls were potty trained and eating solid food, they were packed up and shipped off.

I noticed then that each of the butt-shorts trio had a matching friendship bracelet around her wrist. Hayden was absentmindedly playing with hers as the introduction circle moved on.

Mandi nodded at the next girl to start. I looked over to see who was up and almost did a double take. I didn't know people this awkward-looking existed outside of *Degrassi High*. She had a unibrow, a triangle of frizzy hair, and a mouth so full of orthodonture that she probably shouldn't be allowed on airplanes because that much metal could certainly be used as a weapon.

She popped her rainbow retainer out of her mouth and set it on her thigh. If her name was Jayden, I might have to yell out "Connect Four" or something.

"This is also my seventh year," she said. "And I'm hoping that this year I can finally break into the archery bull's-eye club. Oh yeah, and I forgot, my name is Sylvie." This girl must have been even worse than I was in a past life to end up with that combo of bad teeth and hair.

With Sylvie done, all eyes were on me for my intro. My heart practically thumped against my rib cage and my throat dried up so I felt like I was gagging on chalk. How could five sets of eyes staring at me make me feel like this? Anytime I walked out of my apartment there were probably ten times as many people who checked me out and whenever I was with Kennedy, we were pretty much always the center of attention of our group. Why was I reacting like this?

I took a deep breath and tried not to sound as nervous as I was. "Hi, everybody. I'm Laney and this is my first year here." I heard Hayden stage-whisper, "Obviously." Aside from the smallest eye roll, I ignored it. "Um, and I guess that I want to love this summer as much as you all have loved your summers here." I hoped I sounded genuine, though there wasn't an ounce of sincerity in anything I'd said. I was just trying to fit in with the intro format the butt-shorts girls had laid out. I didn't want to be friends with horrible Hayden in any way, but fitting in seemed to be good self-defense against whatever evilness she was planning on spewing my way. You can't make fun of someone if she's just like you, right?

Wrong. I didn't even get a chance to add a pitiful smile to my sad intro and Hayden was already cutting me down.

She jumped in with, "And since this is all to introduce you"—she eyed me up and down, seemingly berating me for not wearing butt shorts—"to the bunk, you should probably know that I'm best friends with Aidan, she's best friends with Aiden, and Aiden's besties with me. And then we're second BFFs with whoever in the Timber Trio we're not first best friends with."

I sat totally still, feeling like I should respond but not knowing how to interpret the verbal Venn diagram of best friend-dom that had just been outlined for me. Mandi jumped in before I could react. "Well, there's always an opportunity to make new friends, right, girls?" Her voice shifted up to a wobbly soprano. "One is silver and the other gold."

"Theoretically, yeah. But"—Hayden eyed me up and down once more—"probably not." OK, now her meaning was perfectly clear—and it was "Suck on that, new girl!"

Bitch-festing was definitely not listed in the activities section of the camp brochure I'd read that morning. I was going to have to talk to someone about the concept of accuracy in advertising.

The Bitches of the Round Table dispersed, each girl going to her own slice of the bunk and continuing to unpack and set up. Mandi walked me to our shared bunk and we sat on the bottom bed. She turned to me, and while I tried to shift myself to mirror her angle, I couldn't. As soon as I sat down, the plastic shellac of the mattress had stuck to the back of my thighs and I knew that any movement would mean the room-shaking fart sound that skin, sweat, and synthetics create. I was already enough of a pariah in this bunk for absolutely no reason. I certainly didn't need to give them actual incentive to mock me.

I gingerly turned my head so I was looking at Mandi with the rest of my body facing front. I felt like one of those mannequins in the window of Forever 21.

"We are all so excited that you're here, Laney!" she enthused, nodding with every syllable. "I'm so excited! I'm so excited! I'm so scared!" she yelled in my face, and I jumped. I was scared too at that moment.

The rest of my bunkmates exploded with laughter. I quickly forced my expression from a panicked grimace to a smile, trying not to look as uncomfortable and confused as I was.

"You don't know that line?" Mandi asked, genuine surprise registering on her face. Clearly, I was doing a very poor job at looking unconfused. "It's a really famous line from *Saved by the Bell*," she offered.

"Do you watch the show?" Aidan asked, once her giggles were under control.

That show Mario López was on before *America's Best Dance Crew*? They couldn't be serious. "No. Never."

"Well, we're all totally obsessed with it," Aiden jumped in. "And we TiVo the reruns on TBS all year and then g-chat about it like every day."

I stayed quiet, trying not to react. I wasn't sure if they were being serious or pranking me.

"Yeah, so, I guess that's just another thing you don't have in common with us," Hayden said smugly. She pursed her lips and locked eyes with me.

Another thing? What was the first? That I didn't wear adjectives on my tush?

"Well . . ." I could tell from her tone that Mandi was about to say something that would turn these lemons into

Crystal Light. "That just means *another thing* you guys can teach Laney about, right?"

My "teachers" each stood next to their beds, glancing from Mandi to me and then back, not saying anything.

"One of you can invite her into our Addicted to *Saved by the Bell* Facebook group at the end of the summer."

I could feel my eyebrows raise in reaction to what Mandi had just said. My shock wasn't over her affinity for a prepuberty Neil Patrick Harris—wait, this was the show with him, right? All the big hair and scrunch socks kind of melt together in my mind—I was surprised that Mandi would want them to wait so long to invite me.

"Why at the end of the summer?" I asked.

"Well, because that's when you'll be back online and whatnot."

"Wait, what? *Back* online. I'm not sure I get it." She couldn't possibly mean what I thought she was saying. A whole summer without the Internet? That made *me* want to shout "I'm so scared."

Mandi opened her eyes wide to explain, like I was special needs for thinking that wireless Internet existed in the woods. "Well, like you don't want to be sitting in front of a computer all day while you're at camp." Excuse me. Who told her that? I had no problem sitting in front of a computer all day. My body started to get prickly with panic at the thought of leaving my Facebook profile dormant for six whole weeks. People would probably think I was dead if I didn't update my status at all. "But if you want to e-mail with your parents, we have this system set up where you can write a letter and then we'll scan it in and e-mail it to your folks," Mandi explained, smiling the whole time, unaware that she was pretty much giving me the worst news of my entire life and I was verging on a digital breakdown.

"But that's it?" I gulped. "Like no other access to the free world, I mean, to the Internet for the entire summer?"

She started to twirl her ponytail as she spoke. "Right, but don't worry. We'll totally remember to invite you into the group. Don't sweat it," she reassured me. I sank deeper into my quagmire of hate for my life as I remembered that I hadn't packed my iPhone charger.

Mandi continued babbling on about the group. But over her yammering about the weird nineties-show quotes and the quizzes I could check out, I heard Hayden say to the other two, "So don't invite her into the group, OK? We don't friend losers."

Ignoring this nastiness for the whole summer was going to be impossible. Tears were trying to push their way out of my eyes already and I hadn't even been on Timber Trails property for more than an hour. I wished Kennedy were here. She would totally know what to say. She always did. Like there was this one time in third grade when my mom packed a smelly pickle in my lunch and it made the entire cubby wall reek all morning. At lunch, when everyone found out that it was my lunch that contained the pickle stink bomb, Kat Richards yelled out to our entire lunch table, "Laney P.'s got a disgusting lunch."

I wanted to slide off my stool and under the table and never come out. But Kennedy grabbed my arm, refusing to let me die of embarrassment in peace. She stood, still holding on to me, and yelled back, "Could you please keep your meanie thoughts to yourself? We think your face is disgusting, but we're polite and never say anything about it." And that was when I decided to give Kennedy the other half of the best friends necklace I'd been saving for the right moment. It was also when I decided to start buying my lunch from the cafeteria instead of bringing it from home, but that's beside the point.

Sitting on my bed in the bunk, I tried my hardest to channel Kennedy, but the only comeback I could think of that didn't use the word *meanie* was "Yeah, 'cause they don't let you friend *yourself* on Facebook." And that was so lame, it made *meanie* sound badass. So again I let Hayden go unchecked. I made a mental note to think of a list of generic comebacks I could use for her next assault. "Your face is disgusting" actually might still be a winner after all these years.

Tuning back in to Mandi's chattering, I heard, "And then my best homefriend took the quiz too and I was all, 'We can't both be Jessie Spanos!' But that's what that quiz said, so whatever." I didn't have the slightest idea what she was talking about, so I just smiled and nodded and sniffled, trying not to let my rejection tears seep out of my eyes. "But I'm sure you'll be hearing a lot about the awesomeness that is *Saved by the Bell* over the summer, so I won't bore you with those deets now. What I should be doing is running to the infirmary to get everyone's health forms."

With a toothy smile, Mandi launched herself from my bed and bounced her way to the opening in the wall that served as a doorway but didn't actually have a door on it. I felt a weird pang of separation anxiety as I realized she was making an exit.

"You're leaving?" My desperation was audible. I was seriously worried Mandi was that one crucial Jenga block that was holding the whole tower up. If she left, my bunkmates' carefully created building of viciousness could topple and totally crush me.

Captain Cheerful was of course oblivious to my faceful of fright. With a great big grin she looked back and chirped, "Yep, just jetting to get your lice-check sheets and whatnot. I'll be back before you can say 'At Timber Trails, my summer rocks!' "

Considering I'd probably never utter those words, I had little hope that I'd ever see Mandi again.

I hunched over as I sat on my bed, trying to make myself small and unnoticeable. I was alone. Well, not technically alone, as I was in a tiny wooden shack with four other girls, but still, alone in the sense that I've never felt lonelier . . . and I was an only child who'd refused to speak to her parental unit and faux parental unit for the past few weeks, so that said a lot.

"Look what I brought again, girlies," a member of the trio across the bunk yelled out. I'm not sure why I felt the need to look. She was clearly directing her shout to the girlies on her side of our shack, not even acknowledging Sylvie and me on our reject side. As I turned, my stomach dropped with panic. I had forgotten about the plastic peepee protection on the mattress and braced myself for a mortifying pootie sound. But as my thighs slid across the plastic coating, there wasn't a sound at all. I breathed a sigh of relief. I looked down at my skirt and saw that I'd completely sweated through it, leaving my legs well past the point of being sticky and now just plain soaked. I never thought I'd be so happy about my overactive sweat glands.

Relieved after not farting, I looked back over to the girlies. Against the backdrop of a bright purple and green tie-dyed wall tapestry that she'd just hung, Aiden was holding up a plain white T-shirt.

"What WHAT!" Aidan hollered back, and then crumpled onto her bed in a fit of giggles.

Hayden started laughing too, but she got her chuckles under control enough to turn to me and say, "We have a lot of inside jokes from being friends for so long. There's no way that even with the whole summer in front of us we're going to have time to explain them all. So, like, don't ask, OK?"

"Your face is disgusting like a pickle lunch," I hissed to myself, and then looked around the bunk to see if anyone had heard my butchered slam. Hayden and her ladies-in-waiting were still too busy cracking up over whatever inside joke they weren't able to explain to hear my crapback. Thank God. I turned to my right to check if Sylvie had heard. She was deeply engrossed in the dual activities of Sudoku puzzling and biting her nails and seemed oblivious to the outside world. I smiled, glad that my dig had gone unnoticed. And then my smile quickly melted off my face as I assessed the true horror of what was my current reality: my home was pretty much a shack, my bed was a rusted-out cot, I was talking to myself, all of my possessions were contained in a tatty sack, and I smelled like a boys' locker room from how much I was sweating. I was a cardboard sign and a round of "Amazing Grace" away from being homeless.

With a deep sigh I grabbed my duffel to unpack my summer duds. I opened the bag and cringed at what I pulled out. Or maybe it was more of a squint than a cringe, because my pupils needed to readjust to the practically glowing contents of the sack. The shirt I was holding in my hands was the shade of orange reserved for traffic cones and bikinis in early-nineties rap videos. I wanted to shriek at the grossness of it, but definitely didn't want to bring any attention to this from the trio of torture across the bunk. Even I wanted to make fun of this shirt, so those girls would probably rip me to shreds because of it. I frantically pawed through the other clothes in the suitcase, hoping that the rest of the outfits were in some way more wearable. But the deeper into the duffel I got, the more horrible it got. Neon blues, fluorescent yellows, and Day-Glo pinks were the only shades I saw. Where had my mom found this much horrifyingly bright clothing? At the Crossing Guard Vest Warehouse? I couldn't decide if my mom packed like this to punish me or if she really thought this raver look was cute. My packing nausea increased as my hands reached the bottom of the bag and I realized that they'd never felt any makeup. The bag that I'd dumped my entire makeup drawer into was still sitting on my bed. I'd totally forgotten it during my forced march out of the apartment. The thought of a makeup-free summer made me want to cry, but I held back my tears. My current eyeliner had to last as long as possible since it was the last drop of makeup my face was going to feel until fall.

I choked back my disgust as I continued removing the hideous clothing from the bag stack by stack. I started to shove the piles into the set of shelves that sat by the head of my bed, purposely trying not to take a closer look at any more of the terrible T-shirts. But when I got to the items in my bag that qualified as shorts, I just couldn't help myself from unfolding a few and checking out if my mom had really managed to find skorts or had only been bluffing over breakfast—I couldn't believe that skorts threat had just been that morning. It felt like eons away.

I peeled a pair off the top of the pile and my mouth fell open in horror at what I saw. First, they were a barfy neon green. But their style was far more gross than the color. They looked like they hit at just about the knee and were balloony, like pirate pants. My breaths were getting shallow and quick at the sight of them, and the room started spinning as I fully understood the nightmare of what these were. My mom was wrong about these being skorts. They were decidedly more heinous than a pair of skorts. Technically, these were culottes, if I was recalling VH1's *I Love the 80s* correctly. I looked down at the pile and saw that there were culottes in every color of the fluorescent rainbow.

Touché, Mom, touché.

I considered destroying them all. I could run to the bathroom and flush them down the toilet one by one or throw them into a bonfire or the lake. But then what? I'd be pantsless the entire summer. And as horrifying as this place was, at least it was a summer camp, not a nudist colony.

Just as I finished cramming the culottes into my shelves, Mandi galloped back into the bunk.

"Girlie girls, I've got our lice-check forms!" she announced, and then waited for our reaction. I looked up at her and for the zillionth time that day felt like an abused, helpless, lost puppy. First the crossbunk meanness, then the wardrobe catastrophe, and now I was being checked for bugs like Perez at the vet? This felt incredibly inhumane. Mandi's face fell as she noticed that no one in the bunk was thrilled. "Come on, you guys, this is like the official start to the summer."

I always thought that was Memorial Day. But I'm really glad that now I know the summer actually doesn't start until you have your head fondled by a veritable stranger looking for insects.

"Laney, why don't I do you first?" she said, coming over to my bed and combing through my hair before I could object. Did I really look like the type to have lice?

"You know, I'm pretty sure I don't have lice," I said, wincing as she yanked her tiny comb through my hair without mercy. "The last time I was in a place where I could have possibly contracted lice was"—I tried to think of a recent time when I was somewhere naturey or even Central Park and came up totally blank—"well, a long time ago. I mean, I don't even go into the dressing rooms at H&M 'cause they're too gross for me. Maybe you could just stop." This was mortifying. Someone was digging through my scalp because she wasn't sure I was good enough at showering to avoid harboring an infestation in my bangs.

"Sorry," Mandi said happily from behind me. "Camp policy."

Wait, I thought the camp policy was All for Fun and Fun for All. I didn't remember anything about humiliation for the new girl.

I was declared insect-free, thank God. I honestly would have shaved my head if she found anything buggy in there, and if there was anything that could make me look more heinous than this summer wardrobe could, it was for sure a bald head. I finished unpacking the rest of Mom's bag of tricks and made my bed up. Fortunately, my mom wasn't cruel enough to forget my binky. I folded my blanket, slipped it under my pillow for safekeeping, and perched back on my bed. Now I truly had nothing more to do to distract me from a hard-core case of homesickness. I let my mind wander, thinking about how I should be roof-deck tanning with Kennedy right now. Or sitting on my gorgeous canopied double bed, not this peepee-guarded bunch of squeaky wires and yellowed-laminated fabric. I swallowed hard, trying to push the lump in my throat back to where it came from.

All of the bunk ended up being bug-free. And while a tiny piece of me—OK, maybe a medium piece of me—did want Hayden to be a lice carrier, I really was relieved. I mean, being in the vicinity of actual lice? This was pretty much my first time being in direct non-skyscraper-blocked sunlight for an extended period of time. I think that would have been too much nature at once.

Mandi bounced up from Sylvie's bed after her head check and announced, "Yay! All clean, and now it's din-din time. Who's hungry?"

I was surprised that the visual of my head being used as a rec center for a colony of bugs had done nothing to my appetite. I was actually pretty hungry. Still, I didn't join the chorus of "I am's" that came from the other side of the bunk. For now, my strategy of dealing with those three was to keep a low profile. At least until I thought of a better dig than the pickle line, anyway.

The bunk got prepped for mealtime, everyone moving in a frenzy. Mandi slithered out of her pink shorts and into a pair of even more saturatedly pink sweatpants about four feet from my face. It was no surprise that her underwear was pink too. I felt weird knowing the panty color of someone I'd just met that day, but she was pretty predictable. I probably could have guessed pink, so actually knowing wasn't that much different. The three besties passed a lip gloss around their triad a few times. Aiden turned around at one point and her lips were so overglossed they looked like an oil spill. So trashy. Sylvie changed into a pair of overalls and thankfully did it discreetly enough that I didn't know what kind of Underoos she had on. Since I sure as shit wasn't going to change into the hot yellow tracksuit my mom had packed, I just sat on my bed. I tried to look like I was immersed in *The Glass Castle*—a summer-reading book my mom had packed probably with the intention of showing me that she wasn't the worst mom in the world. I'd give her that. But she was definitely still in contention for second worst.

I zoned out from my reading and started to get pumped for dinner. Food was going to be the best part of the whole camp thing. Campfire-cooked hot dogs and hamburgers every night? As my kitchen at home had become the *How It All Vegan!* cookbook sample station, having meat on a daily basis would be a totally welcome change of pace. And unless you're counting the Ben & Jerry's flavor, I'd never had a s'more, but I already knew I was going to get along with those. I loved anything with melty chocolate. I'd probably eat a newborn if it were covered in enough melty chocolate.

I had a little pep in my step—at least until I got halfway down the horrible stairs. Then it was less pep, more strained quad in my step—on the way to dinner. But we weren't heading to some open fire pit with nonvegan product and warm chocolate bars. Instead, the girls in front of me were barreling toward that sad, institutional building Mandi had pointed out on the way to our even sadder-looking bunk this afternoon. The mess hall.

I deflated as I realized that my daydreams of charred meat were not likely to come true, and any pep left in my step quickly drained out as I walked through the dingy screen doors of the mess hall. The intense smell of Clorox immediately assaulted my nostrils and burned off my nose hairs. I stopped and looked around. The inside of the building was surprisingly no less tragic-looking than the outside. It was more like a hospital waiting room than the rustic log cabin with picnic tables and a brick fireplace that I had in mind. The room was overstuffed with tables of varying sizes surrounded by mismatched plastic chairs already packed with campers ranging in age from my bunk down to what looked like girls who were too young to know how to wipe themselves. We were clearly the oldest ones in the room.

Mandi was waving me over to a table where she and the four other campers in my bunk were already sitting. When I'd stopped to take in the prisonlike interior, the rest of the girls had paraded forward and left me behind. I pushed my way through the forest of plastic chairs and yelping girls until I reached our table.

By the time I arrived, Mandi had disappeared, so I sat in an empty seat and looked around the room some more. I noticed that the entire room was filled with only girls. I thought I remembered brace-faced boys in the "Deport Your Kids for the Summer" Timber Trails brochure, but maybe they were just really athletic girls.

Out of the corner of my eye, I saw Mandi's pinkness by the far wall, picking up several bowls and platters of food and then making her way back to our table.

"Here," she said as she passed one tray my way and the bowl to Sylvie, who was sitting on her left. My platter held several slabs of something brown covered by a layer of murky gel. My stomach churned a little at the repulsive onion-and-burnt-rubber smell coming from the dish. I looked at the meat chunks and couldn't believe that I had psyched myself up for something this horrendous.

"You take one and pass it," Mandi instructed me, as if my hesitation with the food was because I didn't know how family-style worked.

"What is this?" I asked Mandi quickly, trying not to inhale through my nose.

"Meat," she replied, as if that were a sufficient answer.

And then I heard myself say a sentence that only yesterday I would have guaranteed I'd never say in my life: "Um, is there a vegan option?"

TXT from Laney to Kennedy:
One good thing guaranteed to come from this summer: I'm going to be turn-to-the-side-and-disappear skinny when I get back. Get ready to be jealous. Very jealous. (Insert evil laughter here.)

Chapter 8

Apparently, another part of camp life was reenacting Cinderella—the slave work with the horrid stepsisters part, not the slipper, pumpkin, falling-in-love part. We had to bus our own table, which meant scraping the leftover food on our plates all onto one plate and then carrying that to a counter that contained about seventy similar plates piled with a conglomerate of scraps. As I'd found the full platters of food revolting, seeing a table's worth of the partially chewed meat and veggie mush was a complete gagfest. Totally the reason I knew I'd never try bulimia, even though every college docudrama makes it look like it's a mandatory part of your freshman year.

Post–scrap piling, the table needed to be wiped down. Mandi held a damp cloth in her hand and pushed the crumbs and sauce dribbles around. "I'm doing this tonight, but starting tomorrow, this is going to be a different girl's responsibility every day. I thought it would be nice and helpful for me to show Laney how it's done before she has to do it." She accidentally shoved a pile of moist bread pieces off the table and onto my skirt. I thought I was going to retch but instead I managed to nod and keep my eyes on her wiping technique.

"Now that our tummies are full," Mandi said. And even though I was still grossed out to the point of mouth vomit at the entire meal experience, I laughed at Mandi's joke.

The table of girls all turned my way with quizzical looks.

"What? No one else thought that joke was funny?" I said.

"What joke?" Mandi asked.

"The one about us being full from this meal," I responded, realizing only after the words had tumbled out of my mouth that Mandi hadn't been joking. "Or, I mean, it actually wasn't funny. Because it wasn't a joke. Not because you're not funny, Mandi. You are. Just your nonjoke wasn't." I took a deep breath. "Wow, this mountain elevation must be getting to me." I made the crazy finger gesture by my head, wanting to crawl under my chair and hide for the next six weeks.

An ample pause passed wherein all pairs of Bunk Redwood eyes were on me. I pretended to suddenly become incredibly engrossed in the crumb mush on my skirt to avoid their stares.

Mercifully, Mandi ended my moment in the spotlight and continued with her nonjoke. "As I was saying, now that our tummies are full, let's head over to the amphitheater, because we counselors have been cooking up a surprise for you guys!" One more cooking surprise tonight and I was going to hurl. But the other girls seemed exponentially more enthused than I was. They pushed their chairs out and bolted en masse to the amphitheater. I slowly followed them.

As I stepped out of the mess hall, I got a sudden chill. The temperature had dropped about twenty degrees since dinner began. The other girls in my bunk all seemed to be slipping into sweatshirts that magically materialized as we made our way across the fields. I shivered along after them, eager to get to the amphitheater and warm up and kind of pissed that Mandi was too busy showcasing her panties to suggest that I bring a sweater. Wasn't her job to be my stand-in mom this summer?

We arrived at what looked like a giant Lincoln Logs explosion. There were rows and rows of huge logs cut in half, stacked unevenly on stumps, the wood wet and rotting. Girls from my bunk filed in between the logs and sat. I followed their lead and tentatively sat, hoping the log could hold all of us without collapsing. A broken tailbone was the last thing I needed this summer. Though at least now I had a culottes collection that was baggy enough to fit over my butt cast. It's all about the silver lining, right? Actually, I'd have liked any kind of lining then. The moisture from the rotting log was soaking through my skirt. It had only just dried from it's earlier sweat-soaking, and I shivered at the wet coldness and rubbed my bare arms.

The amphitheater benches quickly filled. It was too dark for me to make out anyone's face, but I could still see that on the other side of the aisle, there were definitely guys. So at least I knew that the pics I saw in the camp brochure were of actual dudes and not just androgynous girls. That made me feel a little bit better. I mean, that many boyish girls in one place that wasn't a drag show dressing room would probably have meant that something was wrong with the water.

The counselors organized us so we were segregated by age as well as by gender. Girls to the left, boys to the right, youngest in the front, oldest in the back. The way the rows crescendoed in height from front to back was like a life-sized display of Russian dolls. Though I'd probably have been warmer in Russia than I was in the amphitheater.

I uncrossed my arms and tried to rub my goosebumped legs for warmth as all the counselors paraded into the clearing in front of the rows of benches.

"Good evening, campers!" a counselor standing at the front of the bunch yelled. "We've put together a little welcome routine for you, so let's hit it!" She bopped her knee a few times and then belted, "A-five, a-six, a-five, six, seven, eight."

On her count the rest of the counselor bunch started gyrating and then singing a capella. I recognized the song but couldn't quite place it. It wasn't until they were a full minute in, when they finally all got their voices synced up, that I realized it was Britney's "Piece of Me" with campified lyrics. It went:

I'm Mrs. "That you came so glad you made us,"
   You wanna camp with me

I'm Mrs. *"You're all so special in no way nameless,"*
 You wanna camp with me
I'm Mrs. *"This summer at camp we all will win,"*
 You wanna camp with me
I'm Mrs. *"Next summer we'll be back at Timber again,"*
 You wanna camp with me

After the chorus, the singing deteriorated into garble again, but the freestyle dancing continued full throttle until the very end of the song. The words *uncoordinated, painful, running man,* and *who told you that was OK to do in public* came to mind as I watched the spectacle. I sat shaking my head and quaking with shivers. I probably looked like I was having a seizure.

Finally, the singing stopped and I was overwhelmed with sweet, sweet relief as all but one counselor left the stage area. The remaining guy looked to be about twenty and must have been the guy who wrote the Brit parody, because he was about to explode with how proud he was over the routine.

"Thank you," he yelled out over the applause. "Thank you. Thank you." By the second thank-you, no one was still clapping. "Really, that's enough. Thank you so much! You were a great audience." A cricket chirped in the background, literally. "OK, OK, let's all simmer down." He waited a bit for the crowd to tame their silent sitting down. "And with that, you all are officially welcomed to a very Timber summer! Good night, and see you all tomorrow for your first full day of fun!"

A "full day of fun" sounded a lot like a threat to me. I'd barely survived this day, and it hadn't even gotten Timber-fied until noon.

I sat on my section of the wooden bench. The rest of the camp population took the announcement of tomorrow's full day of fun as a cue to stand and file out of the rows of benches. So I got up and trudged behind the girls from my bunk, assuming we were heading back to the cabin, but I was so turned around they could have been marching me to Mexico and I wouldn't have known. I only got my bearings when we reached the mountain of stairs. Those I definitely remembered.

By the time I made it up the massive hill and arrived in our doorway, all the girls had already changed into their pj's. I changed into mine as discreetly as I could still gasping for breath from my climb and in an open room with five other people, then I grabbed my toothbrush from my toiletries kit and headed toward the sound of running water.

My arm hair stood on end and my body went into fight-or-flight mode as I walked into my first group bathroom experience ever. It was like *Girls Gone Wild* but not like *sexy* wild, like *feral beast* wild. Everyone was shoving each other around, with foam coming from their mouths, and speaking unintelligible garble through their toothpaste. If I wanted to avoid reliving my seventh-grade bout of acne, I needed to get in there and wash my face. So I fought my way in between Sylvie and Hayden and started to brush and wash. About four seconds into my dental hygiene routine, Hayden elbowed me in the gut when she went to spit. I almost snarfed up my toothpaste lather.

"Sorry." She turned to me, the corners of her mouth white with foamy leftovers. "I didn't see you there." She pressed her lips together in a tight, bitchy smile.

"Yeah right," I responded. My brush was still in my mouth, so no one could hear my sass back. But I now completely understood how jailyard riots broke out. Being locked away from reality makes you do crazy things. I got pushed on the street all the time and never thought anything of it. Less than one day into lockdown and I was considering drop-kicking Hayden in her sleep as revenge.

I continued brushing my teeth, taking my rage out on my tartar instead of on Hayden. When I spit and rinsed, my teeth were fresh-out-of-the-dentist-office clean and I had simmered to the point where I didn't think I was in danger of starting a gang fight. I shuffled back toward the sleeping/living area.

Teeth brushed, face washed, and wearing the hideous grandma nightgown that my mom packed me, I tucked myself into my cot and closed my eyes, more than ready to say goodbye to the single longest day of my life.

Mandi came around to say good night to each of us individually. She started on the opposite side of the bunk, hugging each girl and then wishing her dreams of unicorns and glitter. I kept my eyes closed even when I could sense she was by my bed, hoping she wouldn't want to disrupt a sleeping camper. But my faux sleep didn't deter her in the slightest from bending down, giving me a nice long hug, and then kissing me on the forehead. My reflex was to yell, "Bad touch, bad touch!" But I refrained.

I thought it was weird that someone probably just four years older than us was giving us goodnight snuggle kisses, but I had expected her to mother me into appropriate attire earlier in the evening. And this was just as mothery as that, I guess.

"All right, my girls, I'm heading to the staff lounge. You be good and I'll see you in the morning for our first full day together!" With that, she clicked off the light and I could hear her bouncing footsteps head down the stairs.

I fell asleep immediately, dreaming of neither unicorns nor glitter. But my dreams were even more fantastic. I dreamt of concrete and skyscrapers and noise pollution. Home.

The next morning, I opened my eyes to the blinding light of seven a.m. sunshine unobstructed by buildings, smog, or curtains. It felt like the rays were actually burning my eyeballs, and I closed them immediately. It was clear that for safety purposes, I had to go back to sleep until conditions improved, which either meant sunset or the end of summer. I wasn't sure which.

Not so shockingly, Mandi was a morning person. The solar-powered Energizer Bunny bopped her way over to my cot. Her thumping woke me up, but I still wouldn't open my eyes.

"I spy a sleepyhead camper," she said in an eager voice, like a detective character on some PBS children's program. "It's a beautiful day here at Timber, and I wouldn't want Laney to miss it."

I groaned softly and then pulled my binky over my head as a useless form of self-defense. The blanket only seemed to provoke the bubbly beast.

She began belting out some song about little birds spreading their wings and saying good morning to each other. By the second verse, which was about a baby bird telling the mommy bird good morning, I couldn't take it anymore.

"Fine. I'm awake," I croaked. I sat up and threw my feet out of the bed.

"That's not how you say good morning here at Timber," Mandi scolded.

"Well, it's all you're going to get. Deal." Mornings have never been my shiningest time of the day. And even though the day before I'd been trying to hold back my inner bitch, I had zero control over my mouth first thing in the morning. I managed to find my flip-flops under my bed with my feet and stand up. I felt light-headed and wanted to lie back down as soon as I stood, but I could sense Mandi watching me, making sure I was up for good. I waited until my head cleared to the point where I could walk, and dragged my grumpy self to the bathroom.

Again the herd of girls by the sink looked like animals poised to pounce. But I was far too tired to be scared or to feel any emotion aside from crankiness. I muscled my way through the horde to a sink without making eye contact with anyone. I splashed some water on my face and nearly screamed at how frigid it was. Apparently, Arctic temperature was the way faulty plumbing said good morning at Timber. Even though my lips might have gone numb for a second, the ice-cold blast did help me feel slightly more awake.

I shuffled back to my bed, careful not to sit on it for fear that the Mandi morning alarm would go off again, and slipped on what would basically be my uniform for the rest of the summer—a pair of elastic-waist culottes and a matching T-shirt. Today's ensemble was a shocking shade of orange. I looked like a tangerine on steroids. The synthetic fabric immediately began to irritate my skin, and I scratched the whole way down to the mess hall. I was waiting for some sort of slam from Hayden and Co. about having my hands down my pants, but it never came. They must not have been morning people either.

"It's our first morning together!" Mandi announced as she ushered us through the mess hall to our assigned table. I sat slumped in a plastic chair at our sticky table. Mandi skipped off to get us our meal, which I prayed was not another mystery-meat-and-powdered-vegetables concoction. Then again, if it was, maybe I could get down to a Mary Kate weight. I'd probably look good with sunken cheeks. I've just always loved spoonfuls of chocolate frosting too much to pull it off. I need brain food when I'm studying and stuff. And sometimes I need entire canisters of brain food.

Hayden slammed both her hands down on the table, creating a sonic boom. My whole body tensed at the sound. Sudden movements like that should be forbidden before anyone's had caffeine.

"You guys," she announced, and eyed each of her two besties intensely. I could see them go rigid with fear at whatever she was about to say. "We seriously need to get started on our bracelets earlier this year. I don't want to end up wearing something that looks like this shit again." She lifted and slammed her arm down again on the table to display the thin red braided cord that wrapped around her wrist. "Everyone at school was all, 'Are you into kabbalah?' And, like, that's so not the point."

I had no idea where she was going with this but was afraid nonetheless. If she was taking this tone with Aiden/an, she'd probably breathe fire at me.

Aidan nervously twisted some flyaway frizz at her temple and whispered, "I worked really hard on that last summer."

But Hayden either didn't hear her friend or was actively trying to win the title for biggest bitchface in the universe and continued, "The point of a friendship bracelet is to show everyone at school that I'm really popular at camp over the summer. Not that I pray to Madonna or whatever." Everything immediately clicked. Of course. Hayden was one of *those* girls—those girls who didn't have a social life at school but insisted that they were the shit at camp or Jewish youth group or horseback-riding class or on Mars. I'd always suspected it was a super-lame excuse for not having any friends, and now that I'd seen the flip side of it, I *knew* it was a super-lame excuse.

Mandi arrived at the table with an armful of mini cereal boxes before Hayden could further bully her friends. She unloaded her variety-pack loot into the center of the table and headed back to the kitchen to get some more grub. I glanced down at the selection, and the thoughts of sunken cheeks and two-digit weights evacuated my brain. Before my eyes I saw three of my favorite things: sugar, food coloring, and cartoon mascots. I quickly grabbed two boxes of Lucky Charms and one of Froot Loops. Everyone else grabbed boxes of their own. I noticed that I was the only one who took three, but didn't really care that I looked like a heifer. I'd practically gone without dinner last night and I didn't have high hopes for lunch. Hayden reached for the skim and poured and passed and we all dug into our multicolored bowls, slurping and chomping without speaking.

Out of the corner of my eye, I saw Mandi shimmying her pinkness back to the table once more. It was hard to miss.

She weaved a path among the mismatched patio furniture and fellow counselors dashing back and forth for parts of their bunk's balanced breakfast, and I prayed that she had something else fabulous, like a chocolate croissant. Even if it was just a plain butter one, I'd totally take back every horrible thought I'd ever had about Timber. Mandi returned baked-good-free, but what she had in her hands was even better. Mandi was carrying a steaming mug of coffee. Could this be more perfect? I could almost hear the chorus of angels singing in the background as the delicious caffeininess wafted in my direction.

"Great!" I said, my mouth full of sugary spittle. "Where can I get some of that?" I pointed to her mug.

Mandi turned to me, the steam from her cup between our faces. I was salivating like a German shepherd at the smell. "Oh no. Campers aren't allowed to have coffee."

That shook me out of my dry-roasted daze. I slurped back my drool, my food coloring/sugar high immediately plummeting. I could already feel the light beat of a caffeine-withdrawal headache coming on. Another half an hour and it would turn into a heavy pounding. I needed something. "Um, then is there Diet Coke?" I asked, trying my hardest not to tear up at the situation. Mandi shook her head. This was too terrible to really be happening.

"Fine, then regular Coke?" Desperate times call for desperate measures.

"Honey, campers aren't allowed to have caffeine here. Camp policy!"

I dropped my spoon into my bowl. I was shocked. What was the process for presenting amendments to camp policy? Because this policy seriously needed some revision. My sanity depended on it. I stayed silent. My caffeine-deprived brain was at least functioning enough to tell me that a hissy fit was not going to help this situation. I just hoped my mother had packed enough ibuprofen to last through an entire six weeks of daily caffeine headaches.

I ate my three bowls of cereal quietly, then followed my bunkmates as they pushed back from the table and started a silent march toward the bunk. My head was pah-pah-pounding from withdrawal, so the silence was more welcome than a second season of *Living Lohan*, and my fingers were perma-crossed that it would come back on air. The only way that show could be more entertaining was if they had to tap-dance through the whole thing. I loved it.

Of course we came to the 179-degree-incline stairs that led up to our cabin. I tried not to even look up and rested after every stair or two so I wouldn't turn all hot pink and sweaty and BO-y. Washing my face in freezing-cold water was one thing, but taking a shower with that plumbing would be torture, so I wanted to put it off for as long as possible. Mandi made a point of slowing down to clomp up the stairs with me. I opened my mouth to huff out that I was fine on my lonesome but Mandi cut in before I could speak.

"So, when we get back to the bunk, it's cleanup time!" she cheered.

I didn't return her full-face grin. I just plain couldn't make my facial muscles fake it.

She was undeterred. "Basically, this is a chance for us all to work as a team. The cleanliness of the bunk is an indication of how much we respect ourselves as a unit." She prattled on for the next thousand stairs or so, but I couldn't really hear her over my pounding headache and burning lungs. When we reached the top, I started to catch my breath and managed to hear bigger snips of her sentences between gulps of air. ". . . and the last responsibility is to scrub down the toilets on a daily basis. You'd be surprised at the kind of funk a group of girls can cook up." She giggled, then galloped ahead of me into the bunk. Panting and sweating by the time I reached the top, I made a mental note that the slow and steady technique hadn't done much in terms of cutting down the sweating or windedness.

I was too tired to react to what Mandi had said until I had a chance to sit on my bed for a few minutes and stopped breathing like a gorilla in heat. Gradually, I started laughing to myself. There had to be hidden cameras around here or something. There was no way this was for real. I glanced around the bunk, sure I would find evidence it had been wired from some budget *Punk'd* show, or maybe it was *True Life: My Mom's a Practical Jokester*.

"I was totally buying this all until the toilets thing. Everyone can come out now," I said to whatever tech and crew guys were probably hiding in the bunk rafters or wherever. How embarrassing that my first time on national television I would be makeup free and dressed like a bottle of SunnyD.

Mandi looked down at me from her bunk. Her face was upside down, but I could still see that it was crinkled with concern. "Laney, are you OK?"

I sat mute, still waiting for a clandestine cameraman to come forward. "Wait," I said, finally getting that this wasn't reality television, just plain reality, "you were serious about the toilets?"

She nodded. Her face was going a little purple from all

the blood rushing to it. "Of course. It's camp policy that we maintain our own bunks." The cereal in my stomach started to churn at the thought of what kind of diseases I could get from touching a toilet. I've thought it before and I'm sure I'll think it again: Eff camp policy. "I know that you're going to enjoy the sense of pride and ownership you have from a job well done," she continued.

Now, I don't care if this makes me a snob, but I will never be proud of myself for cleaning a toilet. I actually think that never having to clean a toilet is a better indication of what to be proud of.

"And you're going to be responsible for mopping the showers today as well." She pushed herself up and back onto her bed fully.

"Wow, that's a lot of opportunities to make myself proud. I hope it doesn't go to my head." I just couldn't hold back at this point. The combination of the headache and the humiliation and the elastic from my culottes digging into my waist made being on good behavior an impossibility.

But people who wear pink on a constant basis do not comprehend sarcasm. And that's a fact. "Glad you're on board, Laney!" She bent back down over her bed to flash me a bright smile. "Need me to show you how to do the toilets and showers?" she offered.

"I'll be able to figure it out," I assured her.

She nodded and hoisted her upper body back onto her top bunk. "OK, girlies. Cleanup time!" she hollered from above.

I couldn't wait to hear the temper tantrum the terrible trio was going to throw at the cleanup call. I was assuming that someone with PRINCESS scrawled across her hindcheeks wouldn't take kindly to a broom and dustpan. But you know what they say, assuming about butt shorts makes an ass out of you and the chick who's wearing the butt shorts. Well, she was an ass to begin with, but still.

Sylvie, Aiden, Aidan, and Hayden all jumped off their beds and ran to their respective cleaning stations. Sylvie started sweeping the floor, the crumbs and dirt heading into a dustpan Aiden was holding. Aidan disappeared into the bathroom with a cardboard can of Comet and attacked the sinks. Hayden went outside to pick up litter. This all happened without one complaint or groan. I couldn't even freaking introduce myself to these girls without some sort of group eye roll, yet they were willing to roll around in trash and dirt without giving Mandi any crap? I was officially living in a nonsensical nightmare.

I sighed and groaned enough to make up for the other four as I dug through my cubby of shelves to find my iPhone. Might as well get the most out of the short battery life I had left while I could. I cued up some KT Tunstall and went to work in the bathroom—which if I'm being honest wasn't as bad as I thought it would be. It took all of four seconds to clean the toilets, as I just went into each stall and flushed twice. The shower floors were a bit more time-consuming because I had to at least get the entire area wet to pass off as an attempt at cleaning.

I was listlessly pushing the mop around the floor when Hayden waltzed into the bathroom.

"Oh my God!" she shrieked so loudly I could hear her over my blaring music. "Is that an iPhone?" She was practically drooling over it.

Like a million years ago they were hot enough to induce

a freak-out, but a reaction like that now was pretty surprising to me. Maybe Apple hadn't spread their product out to the suburbs yet. Kind of like how the message that David Hasselhoff is a giant drunk douche hasn't spread to Germany yet.

"Yeah, it is," I answered. I felt a sudden rush of compassion swell within me. Maybe it wasn't her fault she was such a jerktits. It seemed like she hadn't heard of the Internet before, and I'd be in a perma-bad mood too if I didn't know about FunnyorDie.com. In an act of charity, I popped out my earbuds and offered the phone to her. "Want to check it out?"

But before I could even finish my sentence, Hayden had turned around and was yelling, "MANDI! MANDI!"

I heard Mandi throw herself off her top bunk and run over to the two of us.

Despite Mandi's proximity to us now, Hayden continued yelling. "MANDI, LANEY HAS A CELL PHONE!"

I spun around to show the phone to Mandi for her to ooh and ahh over.

Mandi looked from my hands up to my face. "We're not allowed to have cell phones here. So I'm going to have to confiscate it." Everything clicked. Hayden was still a megabitch. She had totally seen an iPhone before and just wanted to get me in trouble. I hated myself for misjudging the situation so drastically. Without a word, I wrapped the earphones around the phone and handed the bundle to Mandi. "I'm sorry, Laney. It's just that it's—"

"Camp policy?" I finished.

"Exactly."

"I figured," I said.

Screw camp policy.

Mom,

    Hi. It's your daughter. Nope, I'm not writing from 1991, it's actually just me handwriting a snail-mail letter from camp. Apparently, there's a no-Internet policy here. EVEN PRISONERS IN JAIL GET THE INTERNET. Interesting point of comparison, no?

                             Rather be in Rikers,
                             Laney

Chapter 9

I wish I could say that being stripped of my only form of communication and entertainment plus the child labor were the lows of my day or even that the awfulness plateaued there, but I can't because it's just not true. The day got even worse.

It started with the fact that after cleanup, we all had to put on bathing suits and athletic gear and set out for our day's activities. Thanks to Mom—and if I'm being totally honest with myself, my own fruitless silent precamp protest—my swimsuit selection was rather limited. In searching through fighting this futile, but my swimming skills were probably on par with the toddlers in my group. "Fine, whatever. I'll stay in one."

Mandi went back to talking to my belly button. "OK, chickadees, let's all practice getting in the water. Is this anyone's first time?"

None of the four boys raised their hands.

"Great! Then you fellows"—she paused to look up at me—"and Laney will be pros at this. OK, everyone in." The brat pack threw off their T-shirts and ran into the pool. I peeled off my pantaloons, tried to arrange the butt of my suit so it wouldn't expose anything X-rated, and climbed in as well.

"All right, guys and Laney, let's practice bobbing," came Mandi's baby voice from above us on the pool ledge. "Just jump up and down in the water." She demonstrated by bending and straightening her legs. All the boys started bopping up and down, closing their eyes as they went under. Of course, when you're over five feet, bobbing in the shallow end is a totally different experience. I bent my knees, water coming up to my waist, and then straightened out, the water settling down at my hips. This was humiliating. I just hoped that Hayden was too busy triple-lutzing off the high dive to notice me plummeting to rock bottom.

I moved over to the far side of the group of boys, hoping that putting them between the high dive and me might create a little camouflage. The little guy nearest to me turned around. His eyes were already pink from chlorine burn. "Hey, are you Laney, my bus friend?"

I looked down at the slick-haired boy and registered him as boogie Brandt from the ride down, little brother to Satan's spawn herself, Hayden.

my cubbie shelves, where I'd crammed the contents of my duffel, I found three suits. All one-pieces. All Speedos. All hues in the neon spectrum.

I slipped on the electric-green one and immediately realized that it was too small. Had my mom not noticed that I'd gone through my growth spurt at some point during the past five years? I squatted and pulled at the spandex, trying to stretch the suit out, but finally resigning myself to the fact that I'd have a daylong wedgie to deal with. I slipped my orange "shorts" over the suit and for once was grateful to have such small boobs. If my chest stuck out any more, I'd probably be able to see the neon of the suit in my peripheral vision. And the less I saw of my heinous outfit, the better.

First stop on my schedule of torture: instructional swim. Again I was at the tail end of the Bunk Redwood parade as we walked through the gate of the chain-link fence that surrounded the pool area.

"Level nine!" Hayden said to a counselor with a clipboard who was standing at the gate. The counselor directed Hayden to the far corner of the pool, where a group of girls was waiting.

"Level eight," Aiden announced, and followed the counselor's finger to another group. Aidan and Sylvie both announced their numbers, eight and nine respectively, as they entered the pool area as well. And then it was my turn.

"I'm not sure what number I am," I confessed to the clipboard holder. "I'm new to instructional swim and actually to camp altogether. Probably an eight or a nine with the rest of my bunk? Maybe eight and a half?" I'm not sure why I found any comfort in sticking with this group of girls who had been nothing but nasty to me. I was identifying with my captors. Total summer Stockholm syndrome.

The pool counselor looked down at me blankly. "Can't just put you in a level. You need to be officially assigned." She said this with the seriousness I would expect to come with a positive blood test for mono. "Just go and stand with all the other new kids." She motioned to a grouping of campers only a few feet away.

I looked over to where she was pointing across the pool and started my waddle over to the group. It wasn't until I reached the new-kids-at-the-pool bunch that I realized that everyone was at least seven years younger than me. I guess I thought that from a distance, everything looks smaller. But no. I towered over every other new camper by at least a foot. And they were all boys. I felt like everyone should call me Laney her Largeness. And of course the too-small Speedo riding its way up my butt wasn't helping my height dysmorphia. I stood with the elementary schoolers in silent humiliation until the clipboard counselor came over.

"All right, campers. Any of you taken a Red Cross swimming program before?" Hands shot up all around me, and one of the little kids started crying for no apparent reason. But the clipboard lady didn't care about the sniffle session going on next to me and continued. "All right, then form a line and let me know what level you were in. I'll get you into the right Timber group." The crier stopped crying and said he was a level four, and a good chunk of the rest of the little campers reported their levels and then were sent to the corresponding groups around the pool. Most of the little guys wound up in swim level three, four, or five.

As the group dwindled to five, I was pumped to see Mandi walking up to us. "Well, looks like you guys are in my group." I breathed a sigh of relief. Again, I'm not sure why being with Mandi would make me feel any better. Being with her for every other element of camp hadn't seemed to help much. She crouched down to be at eye level with the other four members of my swim group. Of course, she was more at belly-button level with me. "So, group one–ers, I know that none of you have taken Red Cross swimming lessons before, but no one needs to be scared. Group one is about fun in the pool!"

For a hot sec I was still too excited to be in Mandi's group to register what she'd said. But then, with a slow and horrible realization, I got it. Group one? Even without Hayden anywhere nearby to mock me, I knew this was bad in the worst of camp social hierarchy ways.

"Um, Mandi. I'm not sure if I should be in group one. Don't you think I should be in nine or something with the rest of our bunk?" But as I said it, I looked over at the deep end of the pool and saw Hayden on the diving board. She took three quick steps, jumped hard on the board once, piked her body to touch her toes with her fingertips, and then stretched out vertically before she dove into the water for a splashless finish. I felt like I was watching the Olympics. "OK, well, maybe not nine. But at least four or five. There are a few girls my age in those levels." Of course this was the moment when all of level four decided to demonstrate their flawless butterfly strokes, moving as a cohesive unit down the length of the pool. Did no one here know that pools weren't made for swimming in? They were exclusively for lounging around. I'd be in level twenty-seven of lounging if they had that. I grunted and accepted that not only was

"Yeah, I am. I remember you too." We jumped up and down next to each other in the cold water for a few beats in silence. I crinkled my nose and remembered that this wasn't Brandt's first year at camp. He shouldn't be in the newbie club with me. "Hey, why are you in group one? I thought this was your second year."

"Yeah. I should be in two. But they don't let pool pee-ers make it to the next level." He shook his head and gave a sigh, as if restricting his potty breaks to actual toilets were a human rights violation. Immediately, I was grateful for my extra foot on him and that my mouth was nowhere near the pool water.

"Well, maybe this is the year you'll move up to two," I offered. Some of Mandi's uber-optimism seemed to have rubbed off on me.

"Not unless they change the rules," he said, and shrugged.

My optimism quickly transitioned to disgust as I bobbed myself away from Brandt.

After I'd toweled off the peepee pool water, all the cabins headed in different directions to their second activity of the day. By my count, we had actually already done about ten activities, including waking up, eating breakfast, reenacting that *20/20* about child labor law violators, etc. But the official Timber count was only at one.

I trudged out of the muddy pool area and across the fields, following the gaggle of girls that was my bunk. The gang slowed down as they approached a lake, and I watched as they all stopped and sat cross-legged by the water. I scrambled to catch up. The closer I got to the lake, the stronger the smell of stagnant water and fishiness got. It smelled worse than Chinatown on garbage collection day. Why was everyone rushing to get here? I normally run from this kind of stench.

I let out a groan as I popped a squat on the sandy bank with the rest of the girls. Something about the combination of boats, life jackets, and stanky water led me to believe this activity was going to be even worse than instructional swim.

A burly guy with a hairy chest he wasn't ashamed of stood in front of the group listing the rules and procedures for boating on the lake. He blabbed on for a long time, but basically, the only rule of the lake was "Don't drown." This was one camp policy I thought was fair enough.

"All right," the hairy man said, clapping his hands in front of him, "partner up and let's get out on the lake." My stomach sank. Why hadn't I even tried to convince Kennedy to come to camp with me? I could hear my speech now. "Who needs a new nose when you can have an entire six weeks' worth of new experiences?" But I hadn't, and here I was. All alone and obviously about to be last pick for boat partnering.

Hayden immediately grabbed Aiden's arm. "Besties who boat together stick together," she said, ignoring Aidan, who seemed completely bewildered. I'd like to think that she was more taken aback by Hayden's complete butchering of that expression than by the fact that she was excluded by her two best friends, but I'm not sure.

"Aidan, I'll be your boat partner if you want." I stepped toward her. My voice sounded sweet, but I wasn't trying to make her feel better. I just didn't want to be the odd one out who had to be in a boat by herself. Who knew what kind of pirates or tidal waves there were in this lake?

"Uh, gross?" She said it like it was a question, but she wasn't asking if I was gross, just telling me. "You still smell like piss from being in the baby side of the pool. I'd rather go with her." She pointed at Sylvie, who was lost in her copy of *The Luxe* and didn't look up. "Sylvie, you're with me in the boat, OK?" Why hadn't I thought of asking Sylvie? Now I was going to be alone and plundered for doubloons.

Sylvie marked her page in the book and shrugged as she walked over to the life vests and picked one out.

I just stood on the sand with my head down. I wish I could say that I wasn't hurt by Aidan's rejection. But I totally was. And I was definitely showing how wounded I was. Mandi rushed over to me with a concerned look on her face.

"Oh, Laney. I'll go in the boat with you." She rubbed my arm to console me, and I cocked my head up at her. "I totally don't mind the pee smell."

That didn't make me feel any better. But still, I nodded at Mandi, taking up her pity partnership offer.

Mandi handed me a life jacket and I slipped on the moist piece of orange foam. I thought that my mom had picked out the world's most unflattering pieces of neon gear, but this thing was far more unflattering than anything I had in my cubbie back at the bunk. It simultaneously smooshed my nonboobs and added four inches to the radius of my torso. It also reeked of lake water, which I'm sure meant that I'd smell like a Porta Potti for the rest of the day. Lovely. Mandi set two paddles aside for us and then gestured for me to help her hoist a canoe from the rack of boats.

"One, two, three," Mandi counted down to the boat heave. On three she pushed her end of the boat up to the sky, and with a huge groan and all the muscle I had, I got my half about a centimeter off the rack. We shimmied the boat down, sidestepping as we went. My upper arms were burning and I finally had to let the boat drop to the grass.

She was still holding her side. "Come on, silly. We can't canoe on land!" she said through a huge smile, as if I were actually joking and not standing there rubbing the hurt out of my biceps. Then she dragged the boat the entire twenty feet to the lake singlehandedly. If her cheeriness weren't the furthest thing from 'roid rage on the planet, I would have sworn she was on steroids.

She stabilized the boat in the water. "Come on, Captain Laney. Your ship's waiting." She chuckled as I gracelessly fell into the floating tin can, and then she hopped aboard the back end and pushed us off. As we glided on the water, she shouted up to me, "I can canoe. Can you canoe?" Her giggle fit lasted a few seconds before she yelled up to me again, "It's a boating play on words!" I nodded but didn't turn around. I was pretty sure I couldn't even fake a smile at that joke.

We paddled around the puddle of a lake for a while. To be honest, Mandi must have been doing most of the paddling, because I kind of just smacked my paddle against the side of the boat like a deaf kid with a drum set.

After an attempt at rowing, I gave up and tried to think of the canoe as one of those Italian boats with the romantic bridges and the serenading striped-shirt guys. I was about to ask Mandi if she knew any Italian opera, but the instant I opened my mouth, my face was covered in a sticky gossamer. I immediately wished I had followed Kennedy's advice and filled a prescription for some antimalarials.

"Oh my God, oh my God. I think we just paddled through a spiderweb, Mandi!" I shrieked. "I'm covered in it.

What should we do?" I could feel the stirrings of a panic attack, my heart racing and all the blood rushing to my face.

"Excuse me, *we* paddled?" She chuckled to herself for a second. "I don't remember *us* paddling."

I knew she was just trying to be funny, and normally, I would attempt to fake laugh or at least be able to ignore a lame attempt at humor. I would certainly never cry in a normal situation. But, this wasn't a normal situation. This was camp and there was nothing normal about it. And I don't know if it was the bitching from the bunk or the humiliation of the swimming group or the malnutrition of having ingested nothing but simple carbs in the past twenty-four hours, but I lost it.

"I'm sorry about the paddling, Mandi," I screeched in a shaky voice. "I just didn't know what I was doing and so I stopped, and now I'm covered in tarantula poop or whatever and I'm totally grossed out." The bottom half of my vision was blurred by the tears collecting on my lower lids. I tried hard not to blink so I wouldn't actually be crying.

"OK, so here's my advice." Her voice was calm and I turned around, ready to do anything she said if it would help with this spiderweb facial. Mandi leaned forward and pointed a finger at me in a true advice-doling gesture. The pink ribbon in her pony flopped in the summer breeze. "It takes more muscles to frown than to smile, missy. So turn that frown upside down!"

My body suddenly flipped from panic-attack mode to the makings of a full-blown temper tantrum. I gritted my teeth and balled my fists so hard I could feel my fingernails carving crescents into my palms. I'm sure if she knew how many muscles it was taking me to refrain from punching her, Mandi would be a little more discriminating with sage advice.

"Get your paddle in the water, Lane-a-doo," she continued with a smile that was so bright and shiny it was probably causing more global warming than burning Styrofoam. "Let's steer this ship back to shore with those landlubbers." She rolled the final *r*. "I'm Captain Jack Sparrow," she carried on with her bizarre accent that made her sound more Canadian than pirate.

I dunked my paddle in the water and kept it there, not stroking or helping at all. If she wouldn't help me when I was practically being eaten by a daddy longlegs, I didn't see why I had to help her paddle.

But despite my paddling protest, we made it to shore. Mandi jumped out of the boat and I tried to follow, only instead of a graceful dismount, I caught the tip of my aqua sock on the ledge of the canoe and tripped my way out of the boat splay-legged. I face-planted into the sand—as if my pores needed any more reason to break out, with the spiderweb, tears, and sweat, now my T-zone was caked in sandy gravel. The fall knocked the wind out of my lungs. As much as I wished this weren't happening, I couldn't deny what a perfect next step this was in building my day's tower of suckiness.

As I sputtered on the ground, covered in sand, flailing, and hyperventilating, I could hear the two other boats pull up to the beach. Great, so Mandi wasn't the only witness to me eating sand. Just as I was spitting out a mouthful of grit, I heard the bitchtastic trio's shrill laughter. The sound of their cackling made me feel even worse about writhing around with my head in the sand like an ostrich. I closed my eyes, deciding that if I couldn't see them, they couldn't see me. They then stampeded past me to the life-vest shed. As they ran, their feet kicked up a mountain of sand around me, which made getting up even harder.

"Here." I heard a voice from above.

I opened my eyes and looked up, expecting to see a tunnel with a bright light at the end and God beckoning me to come closer. I had no doubt I was about to become the first person on record to actually die of embarrassment.

But the only bright light I saw when I looked up was the glare of the midafternoon sun reflected in the metal cross wire of a retainer. Sylvie was standing above me, smiling her tin grin and holding out her hand. It wasn't the pearly gates, but seriously, with the sun behind her, she kind of did look divine. Like the Angel of Orthodonture. "Here," she said again. "Take my hand."

I wanted to kiss her hand, I was so grateful. But I just reached out, held on, and let her hoist me up. Once I was upright, I spent several seconds brushing the sand off my face. Sweat's similarities to superglue is really quite amazing.

Sylvie had officially just become my everyday hero. Like a virtual Ty Pennington but without a Sears sponsorship or the leathery face. I started to thank her only to realize when I looked up that I was talking to myself. She was already migrating back to the bunk, trailing a little behind the rest of the girls. I unhooked my life vest, which had actually served its purpose today. Without it, I probably would have broken a rib during my crash to the ground. I hung the damp and sandy orange piece of foam up with the rest of the supply and slid my paddle back into place on the pegs on the side of the boating shed. Then I speed-walked, trying to catch up with the rest of my bunk. By the time I was at the bottom of the stairs to the cabin, the terrible triplets were already on the top step. I stopped, prepping myself for the upward hike, and noticed that their butts read like a cannibal's game of Mad Libs: PINK, JUICY, BABY. I would have laughed if I hadn't been on the verge of a deep, dark, camp-induced depression.

Ken,

OK, so I've been stripped of my phone and my dignity. Remember that time we took that awful field trip to Medieval Times? Camp is a lot like there. Weird clothes, gross mass-produced food, and no Internet. I wish there were jousting here, though.

Can't write much now, I'm being rushed off to some activity that will surely be equal parts humiliation and near-death experience.

Send word from the outside world soon, K?
XOXO,
L

Chapter 10

"Good morning, my campers. Good morning to you and you and you and you."

And so began another day with a Mandi melody original, composed exclusively of flat and sharp notes.

I grumbled to myself as I pulled my sheet over my head to put off the torture of being upright presunrise for a few more seconds. "Every freaking morning for the past . . ." And then my griping trailed off. How long had I been at camp? It felt like a lifetime and not like *my* lifetime, like the lifetime of someone who has lived to be ninety-nine years old. But really, how long had it been? Two days? Five? Forty-seven? I'd honestly lost count.

All I knew for sure was that camp had seriously kicked my butt in whatever amount of time I'd been there. My feet had blisters from walking around in my damp aqua socks. My culottes tan was so bad that I looked like I was another race from the knees down. My fingernails had shimmery crusts embedded in them from an unexpectedly oozy glitter pen in the arts and crafts shed. I was pretty sure I was developing scurvy, considering I'd only ingested food coloring and what seemed to be marinated cardboard in the past however-many days. And I'd been worn down to an emotional nub by the twisted triplets and their constant Laney bashing.

Their latest display of bitchery having been last night right before I was about to go to sleep.

"Hey, Laney," Hayden had whispered from across the room. I pretended to be asleep. "Hey, Laney," she said a bit louder, and then continued saying my name at increasingly higher decibels until she was full-out yelling.

"What?" I finally said back.

"Are you Amish?" she asked, and then giggled to her girls. "I just thought that maybe you were Amish because you dress weird and I know that Amish people dress weird." At this point the other two were in hysterics, whispering things like "I can't believe you asked that" and "So weird, I was wondering the same thing" when they caught their breath enough to speak.

"No, I'm not." I was kind of embarrassed that I was actually validating her question with a response, but if I didn't defend myself now, this would totally go on all summer. "Actually, the Amish dress very differently from how I dress."

"I know that," Hayden said. "Well, like I kind of knew that. But I just thought you were on that Amish vacation thing. You know how they get a month to do whatever the frick they want and they just go crazy and make out all the time and try acid and stuff?"

"Well, I am going crazy. So maybe you're on to something," I said, and rolled over, my need for sleep overpowering my desire to fight back.

It was really unbelievable that I hadn't melted into an emotional puddle of self-esteem issues and wrist banging from their abuse.

"What do you think they're serving for breakfast today?" Mandi said, snapping me back into my morning grump session.

For however many umpteen mornings I'd been at camp, breakfast had been cold cereal and orange-flavored Kool-Aid everyone referred to as "orange juice."

"Oh, I don't know, Mandi. Hard question," I deadpanned. "But if I had to bet, I'd say cereal and OJ." I knew she was just trying to be nice, but pre–morning cereal sugar rush, I have absolutely no tolerance for pep.

"I guess we're just going to have to find out when we get there. Race you to the mess hall." She took off, sprinting out of the bunk.

How was Mandi always so damn perky? I wouldn't even have summoned the energy to wipe away my morning eye goop by the time she'd finished her one-hundred-meter dash.

After breakfast, I found myself back in the bunk holding a broom, moving it listlessly around the bunk floor. I was doing more to stir up my allergies than to clean anything, but the sneezing was a burden I was willing to bear to continue my silent (and unnoticed) protest of chores. Since the shower floors and toilet scrubbing, I'd followed the chore rotation and also experienced the joys of sink drain cleaning and litter and garbage duties. And yes, litter duty was very different from garbage duty. Litter duty involved me walking on the grass around the perimeter of the bunk and picking up trash—a lot like when Naomi Campbell was sentenced to community service at the sanitation department. Garbage duty was when I had to take the bathroom trash cans full of used tampons and pads out to the Dumpsters—which was similar to no sentencing in history because it was so unsanitary that it would be considered cruel and unusual punishment. Every camper rotated through the chores, and why no one had revolted against the vile garbage duty was so far beyond me I'd need binoculars to see it.

"Hey, girlie girls!" Mandi stood in the middle of the bunk floor, clapping her hands to get our attention. "Keep on cleaning up, don't want to interrupt you guys at work." I decided then to sweep the middle of the bunk and went at her feet with my straw bristles. She jumped out of my way, trying to continue her speech, but had to scoot as I swept my broom across her toes again. I know that a Cinderella foot assault wasn't in any real way solving my summer issues, but making her move like a wet Pop Rock held some sort of sick entertainment value, and at that point in the summer, I'd take my kicks wherever I could get them. I finally got back to sweeping the floor and not her toes and let her speak. "I just want to go through today's schedule." She walked over to the wall and took down our activities clipboard. "We've got instructional swim"—I let out a groan—"ceramics, and a nature walk that will be led by yours truly! Fun, fun, fun. So, my girls, we're all going to need to wear swimsuits, shorts, and hiking boots with nice thick socks."

"Add a defined six-pack and we're going to look like an Abercrombie catalog gone wrong," I joked . . . to myself. Of course, no one in the room laughed. I tapped the tip of the broom handle. "Hey is this mike on?" Did no one have a sense of humor in this place? "Is it even working?" Again, no laughter.

I saw Hayden make eye contact with Aiden. She stage-whispered, "Definitely Amish!" Aiden then started laughing so hard I was afraid she was going to piss her butt shorts and I was going to have to clean it up. Inaccurate religious sterotypes . . . *that* was what counted as comedy here? I rolled my eyes to myself and got back to spreading dust around the bunk.

Once my chores were done, or at least fake done, I sat on my bed in my swimsuit putting on thick wool socks for my fashion don't ensemble. I was spending a lot of energy trying to look as un-Amish as possible and didn't even notice that Sylvie had come over to my bed until she spoke.

"Hello there," she said, tucking a lock of frizz behind her ear.

"Hi," I responded, smiling for the first time all day and quite possibly all week. Yes, this girl was odd-looking. Yes, she was wearing overall shorts with a very defined camel-toe situation. But since my iPhone had been confiscated, she was the only person not high on pink Pixie Stix who would talk to me without mentioning the Mennonites. I was going to make the most of this. "What's up?"

"So, I'm guessing you hate it here," she said.

"Well, *hate* is an intense word, you know? But honestly, in this situation, it's nowhere near intense enough." She laughed and nodded. She actually got my joke? I could almost feel tears of joy collecting in my eyes at the sound of her short chuckle.

She smiled at me. "OK, here's what I tell myself. It's only six weeks. And prisoners have been held in Guantánamo for years. We're just in the Poconos. We'll survive."

I giggled. "True, true." Wait, stop the friendship bracelet weaving, Sylvie was funny? "So you're totally miserable here too?"

"Um, my days are filled with crafting fluorescent plastic key chains and interacting with the Billboard Butts and a human incarnation of a pink Webkinz. Do you think that's my idea of fun?"

The Billboard Butts? Hilarious. Why hadn't I thought of that? Totally going in my next letter to Kennedy. "Um, haven't you been coming here since like the turn of the century? If it's so horrible, why do you keep coming back?" I scooched over and made some space for her on my bed.

"I don't know." She plunked herself down next to me. "My mom went here when she was a kid and loved it. And my sisters all went here and they loved it. And everyone's always talking about how great Timber is, and then I get the sign-up pamphlet every fall and see all the pictures of kids having fun and think it's going to be better next time and sign up again. Kind of like a bad boyfriend or J.Lo movies . . . you always go back, thinking it's going to be different this time, but then aren't that surprised when it's the same suckass situation. You know?" I nodded. I knew exactly what she meant. I'd seen *Maid in Manhattan*, *Shall We Dance*, and *Monster-in-Law*. "Well, I'm kind of just guessing on the boy-friend thing. I've never really had one. Not like I want one that's bad or watches J.Lo movies. But, you know."

"Totally." I continued nodding. I wanted to keep talking to her, but I wasn't sure what to ask. It was like I'd lost all my social skills. I sat there struggling to come up with a topic and let our convo lull into an awky silence. Everything I could think to say sounded like I was more of a super-lame creep at a club than a potential friend.

"The silver of your retainer wire really brings out the hazel flecks in your eyes."

"What's your sign?"

"Those overalls are becoming on you."

Fortunately, just as my conversation skills seemed to be putting my sexuality into question, Mandi interrupted.

"Are we all ready for our day?"

"Crap, I still need to get into my suit," Sylvie said, get-ting up from my bed and hustling over to her area to get her-self together for the day. I restrained myself from reaching out to grab her hand and pull her back, but just barely. I didn't want what could possibly be my single pleasant social interaction for the whole summer to be over so fast. Well, *pleasant* might be an overstatement, as it was probably the most awkward thirty-five seconds of my life. But still.

"Well, hurry, hurry," Mandi urged us all in a way that was half cheering, half chiding. "We don't want to be the last bunk to the pool."

Being the last bunk to the pool actually sounded like a good plan to me. The less time in the peepee water, the bet-ter. But by this point, I'd learned better than to express these sentiments. Instead, I grabbed my towel and waited cross-legged on my bed as the rest of the girls shimmied themselves into their gear.

Mandi stood in the middle of the bunk in her tankini, tapping a pink hiking boot. While Mandi's very apparent love of pink typically made her look like a walking Pepto-Bismol promotion, these shoes were freaking cute . . . especially compared to my heinous brown pair with diarrhea green detailing. Though, aside from the dozen plain white granny Jockeys my mother had packed, my hiking boots were the only item in my entire camp wardrobe that could be considered a neutral color. So I was actually kind of glad to have them.

"Ready!" Sylvie announced once she was properly outfitted in her mountain-climber-goes-to-the-beach costume. And with that, our day of activities began.

Instructional swim was doing more to teach me about the effects of repetitive and extended periods of degradation than anything close to swimming skills. For an hour, everyone else within six years of my age practiced swan dives, floating with synchronized leg extensions, and lifeguard rescue techniques. There were even some guys who were obviously way younger than I was butterflying and tuck diving with the higher groups. I stayed in the baby end, bobbing around, "learning" how to hold my breath, and then accidentally choking down chlorine by the gallon. I obviously knew how to hold my breath without Mandi doing exaggerated fishy faces from the pool ledge, but with all of Brandt's splashing, I was inhaling tons of water even with my head way above sea level.

Finally, I heard the glorious sound of the whistle that indicated the end of the water torture. I climbed the shallow stairs out of the pool and snaked my way among the towel-snapping boys to my bunkmates. They were drying off and slipping their clothes back on.

"Since we're all ready, let's go to ceramics," Hayden commanded. She sounded like a drill sergeant, and Aiden and Aidan totally responded like soldiers at attention. They grabbed their towels and started off toward the pool gate.

I was still soaking wet and hadn't even started to get dressed. I wondered if she thought *Amish* was a synonym for *invisible* and that was why she was pretending not to see me. "Um, I'm not ready at all," I said quietly to no one in particular, and then frantically reached for my tank and culottes. I didn't like the girl, but it still sucked to be left behind.

In my haste to get dressed, my toe got stuck in a fold of my shorts and I hopped around like a flamingo on speed for a full minute until I finally got my foot through the hole. By the time I was finished, the girls were out of the gate and out of sight.

Worse than being abandoned was the fact that I had no idea how to get to ceramics, so I just stood by the pool clutching my towel like a blanky and sniffling. I probably looked like I did when I was seven and slept over at Kennedy's for the first time and got so scared in the middle of the night I had to call my mom to pick me up. Except for this time, my mom definitely wasn't coming. And even if she would come and rescue me, I had no phone to call her with. I let out a huge sigh and started toward the gate.

"Wait, are you OK?" I heard from behind me. I turned

and saw Sylvie. She rushed to my side and rubbed my back. Further confirmation that I looked as pathetic as I felt.

I nodded, but I still felt like crying and/or punching someone in butt shorts. "I'm fine. I guess I'm just grossed out from swallowing the entire pool." And while the pee water wasn't the main reason I looked so bummed, it definitely didn't help the situation.

"You'll get used to it, I promise," she said as we started walking. "I remember my first summer here, I probably drank an entire pool in the first two weeks, but then all of a sudden I just got the hang of the underwater stuff, and holding my breath was totally a nonissue." She had stopped rubbing my back, but she was clearly still trying to soothe me.

"Yeah." I rolled my eyes with the pool gate slamming behind us. "But that's when you were like five or something. This is so embarrassing because I'm like a million years old compared to everyone in my group and someone my age should totally know how to swim. But believe it or not, they don't give Red Cross certification at the Soho House."

"OK, yeah," she conceded, "I was talking about when I was little. But that doesn't mean I was the Little Mermaid. I was still learning. And if a six-year-old can catch on in two weeks, you're going to get it sooner than that, OK?"

I took a deep breath and let it out in a whiney moan. She was right about me improving at swimming, but that didn't make me feel much better. It wasn't really the swimming that I cared about. It was embarrassing myself, and I had a feeling that situation wasn't going to improve much for the rest of the summer.

By then, we'd arrived at the ceramics shed. I had to duck when I walked through the tiny door and into the dusty room. Whoever was on sweep duty here during cleanup was even worse at their chores than I was.

Sylvie sat down at the long table across from the Billboard Butts. She turned around and looked at me, patting the space on the bench next to her for me to sit. As soon as I sat, Mandi popped herself between us to slam down two huge mounds of gray clay. I involuntarily jumped at the boom of the clay on the table.

"Here you go, girlies. *Let's get creative, let's get creative,*" she sang to the tune of "Let's Get Loud." Sylvie cocked her head toward me and mugged in a way that let me know that she was completely weirded out by Mandi too. Finally, a compatriot in my silent judging crusade! It felt so good.

Sylvie started kneading her clay, so I mimicked what she was doing and began kneading mine.

"Hey, you guys, we need to make matching pinch pot bowls like we did last year," Hayen demanded.

"Yeah," Aidan responded. "And then when they're done, we can all use them to hold stuff in. You know, like a bowl!"

"Are we at special needs camp?" I asked myself. And then I realized that I definitely said it loudly enough for Sylvie to hear, because she was giggling.

She leaned over and whispered to me, "Yeah, it's a special camp for those who suffer from the unfortunate birth defects of mean spirit and slow wit."

I laughed quietly and continued messing around with my clay, making nothing in particular but kind of enjoying myself. Though after instructional swim, picking my cuticles would have probably seemed enjoyable.

Following an ugly bawling out of Aiden for pinching

her pinch pot bowl so it was far thinner than Hayden's or Aidan's and therefore not part of the matching plan, Mandi led us out into the wild Timber yonder for a nature hike.

We walked from the camp's dirt paths into the woods in a triangle with Mandi as our pink point, followed by Sylvie and me and then a row of the butt-shorted brigade.

A few feet into the forest, Mandi started a prepared speech about enjoying the beauty of nature and respecting the outdoors by leaving only footprints as the evidence of our presence in the woods and taking away with us only memories. As she spoke, I couldn't help but notice her break a low-hanging branch of a tree to use as a walking stick. I'm obviously no nature expert, but killing the fauna seemed like she was leaving a wee bit more of an impression on the woods than her footsteps. I didn't say anything because I needed to focus on not tripping on any roots and was thinking hard about how I could go about striking up some sort of conversation with Sylvie.

"So, um," I fumbled for something to discuss, "um, back at the bunk you said that you'd never had a boyfriend," I started. Nice, Lanes. This girl is funny and sweet and—contrary to what her orthodonture paraphernalia may imply—pretty cool. And the only thing I can focus on is that no boys are interested in her. Great. Cancel the order I mentally made for two half-heart best friend charms. This friendship was over the day it started.

"Well, yeah," she answered back, slowly and without the pep in her voice she normally had—and yes, by "normally" I meant the three times she'd spoken to me prior to this conversation. I stared at the ground, not sure who I was more embarrassed for, me or her. "But I would be interested in getting one."

I looked up at her. "Really?" I could barely contain my excitement. I wanted to scream like a *TRL* audience member.

She nodded and smiled. Finally, something I could actually *do* here. I could feel a summer project coming on. And this one didn't involve gimp or a life jacket. "I think I can help in that department," I said, trying not to squeal.

Dear Mom,

I'm not sure who I hate more, Mother Nature or you. But as I'm not going to be in charge of selecting Mother Nature's nursing home, I think you should be more concerned than she is regardless.

Still questioning your sanity for sending me here,
Laney

Chapter 11

Camp was approximately a jillion times better with Sylvie as my friend. Please note that this does not mean that camp was anywhere close to a level that could be considered tolerable, let alone good, but it was better. Definitely better.

Instructional swim was still torture, though. And we had it every single morning. Rain or shine. Feigned case of meningitis or not.

"All right, little guys and Laney, let's practice head dunks. I want you all to be comfortable underwater," Mandi cheered from the rim of the shallow end of the pool. She was loud enough for her squeaky voice to be heard all the way at the deep end.

As I considered myself a master of head dunking, I took a break from the lesson and noticed that across the pool, Hayden had also given herself an instructional-swim recess. She was using her time to do an impersonation of Mandi. I could barely hear her over the pool's worth of shrieking children, but I made out, "All right, little Laney, let's practice wiping our butt. I want you to be comfortable doing this yourself."

Aiden and Aidan treaded water and cackled in unison.

"Yeah, cause Amish women don't poop," Aidan added.

"Good one!" The two slapped hands.

What had the Amish ever done to these girls?

Just as I was about to attempt suicide by chlorine-fume huffing, Sylvie caught my eye. She was down at the deep end with the Billboard Butts and the rest of the camp's nine-and-up female population. "They're idiots," she mouthed, shaking her head. I immediately felt better. And I'm not sure why. I mean, obviously I knew the trio weren't the brightest glow sticks at the rave, but it was just nice to have a witness to concur.

I made the nuts finger swirl by my ear and mouthed "Crazy too" back to Syvlie. That got a huge smile from her and a knowing nod. My shallow-end shame a little bit assuaged, I turned back to my swim level ready to head dunk till it hurt.

I was sitting on Sylvie's bed writing SOS letters to every single person on the island of Manhattan while she filled out a crossword puzzle in her book of mind-benders.

"Give me a six-letter word for 'postdinner drink.' "

"Um." I tapped my pen on my pad. "Fresca?"

She looked over the top of her oversized paperback to see if I was joking. I wasn't.

"Note to self "—she took her pen and pretended to write on her hand—"People not to call for trivia help if I'm ever on *Cash Cab*: One, Laney Parker."

"Note to Sylvie"—I pretended to write on my pad—"If you're ever on *Cash Cab* that means that you're in New York and if you don't call me—trivia-related or not—I will beat you."

She laughed and continued the pantomime writing. "Telegram to Laney: Is that threat supposed to entice me into calling you? Full stop."

I didn't even look up from my pad. "To whom it may concern: The beating beyond recognition is certainly not a threat. It's a promise. Sincerely, Laney Parker."

"Dear Captain of Badass Promises." She looked up at me, "OK, this has gotten too ridiculous. I give up."

"Too ridiculous? No such thing in my book."

We both cracked up with that kind of breath-catching laughter that only happens when you're really having fun. Her little cot was actually shaking from how hard the two of us were laughing.

When I was finally able to come up for air, I decided to dive into the conversation I'd been dying to have with Sylvie since her earlier confession. I took a deep breath, "Hey, speaking of unrecognizable, should we start step one of Project Sylvie Gets a Guy?"

Sylvie instantly perked up and dropped her game book. "Oh yeah. Let's do it." And then she recoiled slightly. "Wait, did you say unrecognizable? Should I be scared?"

I squinted and tried to looked menacing. "My answers are yes and yes, respectively." I gave a loud, evil, mwaha-haha-type laugh. What I had to do to get this booty train out of the station was clear, but it was going to be tough to convince her. I jumped off the bed and ran the foot and a half to my cubby area. I rummaged through my junk shelf until I found what I was looking for.

"Got it!" Swiss Army knife in hand, I jumped over my bed and back to Sylvie's.

"OK, Crazy. Now I really am scared. A knife?" Her eyes were actually going a little wide with fear. "Listen, I'm not down for *Extreme Makeover: DIY Edition*, OK? This isn't at-home plastic surgery, is it?"

"No, better." I clicked open my weapon of choice. "This is totally going to change the contour of your face and open your eyes wider." I brought the implement close to her head, she flinched a little. "Hold still."

I got to work, trying to be as gentle but as quick as possible. Who knew how long she'd last before the pain would get to her?

"Shit, Laney! That hurts." She pulled back, rubbing her face.

"Oh my God." I rolled my eyes. How could I explain to her that a little pain goes a long way in terms of looks? "It's just a little plucking, OK? And this is JV compared to waxing. Just be glad I didn't steal any of the candle-making crap from the arts and farts shed."

She took a deep breath and moved her head closer to me. "Fine, go for it. Wait, do you have a leather strap I can chew on or something?"

I sighed. "This is eyebrow shaping, not childbirth. Just grow a pair and deal with it." It was time for tough love.

"I thought this whole thing was about trimming down my pair . . . of eyebrows that is. *Ba-dum chi!*" She mimed a drum roll.

I had to drop the serious face. A good—or even just above-mediocre—pun is hard to come by. "Hilarious!" I giggled, and then continued with my de-unibrowing while she was distracted with her own humor. "This is going to make such a difference, I swear. Your face is going to be more open and feminine and less Chewbacca-y."

Crap attack. Did I say that out loud?

"Wait, are you saying I look like Chewbacca?" She was careful not to move her forehead at all when she spoke.

"Well, no," I backtracked. "Like not exactly Chewbacca. Maybe like his older, prettier sister," I offered, not doing much to take my foot out of my mouth. Note to self: Making friends would go a lot more smoothly if you didn't compare them to Wookiees.

"OK, now the talking is hurting more than the plucking. Let's just get back to tweezing in silence."

I silently agreed, but felt bad that my dig was more painful than the brow trimming. This was at the turning-Frida-Kahlo-back-into-Salma-Hayek level of hair removal. Even I—a hair-removal veteran at this point—was having sympathy pains. After a few long minutes, I was finished. I stood back to admire my work. "Looking hot!" And she really did. Sylvie had great skin, already tan from our hours outside; these amazing hazel circles around the outside of her irises; and cheekbones that would make even Kate Moss jealous. And now all these great features were able to shine, because no one would be distracted wondering if she was the long-lost sister of Bert and Ernie.

Sylvie seemed too busy rubbing the pain out of her reddened brows to care about how they actually looked.

"Come on, I want you to see how hot you look." I dragged her into the bathroom and up to the dingy mirror I hadn't cleaned even though my cleanup task this morning had been mirrors and windows.

She glanced at herself and then struck some *ANTM* poses. "Um, Miley Cyrus, what are you doing here? I was expecting to see Chewba—I mean, Sylvie in this mirror." She giggled and took a closer look. "But seriously, folks." She turned her head, getting looks from every angle and fully taking in her foxiness. "This is pretty remarkable work, Laney. Thank you!"

I took a look at her in the mirror too and realized that this was my first activity at camp where I actually did a good job. I smiled even wider.

"Sister, stick with me. By the end of the summer, you're going to be Kristen-Bell-minus-the-lazy-eye hot! And that's not a threat. That's a promise!"

The afternoon's activities were kicked off by an hour of volleyball. So a newly eyebrowed Sylvie and I, along with the rest of our bunk, stood on the volleyball court, which was really just the far end of the field where someone had drawn curvy white boundary lines in powder and strung up a net between two trees. From what I could tell, there was a volleyball counselor who was supposed to teach us how to volley and then set up some sort of game or an hour's worth of drills or something. At least, that was how it had worked with tennis the day before and soccer the day before that. However, there was one difference here. Our v-ball counselor was a guy. He was probably the first guy I'd seen over four feet tall since our hairy boating man.

And our volleyball specialist seemed to be more focused on flirting with Mandi than on schooling any of us in serving, setting, or spiking. And Mandi was equally focused on reciprocating his cheesy advances. It was totally weird that they were kicking game that hard with the entire bunk well within earshot. I was flashing back to my sixth-grade trip to the Central Park Zoo when two snow monkeys started going at it and I wanted to be like, "Hello, you're not alone here. Why don't you go take care of that business in the fake plastic cave they built you back there?" But this was even more absurd because it was humans.

"I really like what you did with your shirt. You know, cutting the sleeves off and stuff," Mandi cooed.

"Thanks. It wasn't that hard. I just did it at arts and crafts. I could show you how sometime." I think he was talking to Mandi when he said that, but he seemed to only be able to make eye contact with his own bicep.

"Yeah, I'd like that." Seriously? What girl would want to cut the sleeves off her shirt? Side-boob central. "And maybe I could make you a headband or something out of the sleeves." Her extra-sugary flirty voice was making me meganauseous.

"That would be crazy hot," he said, running his hands through his hair like he was in a dandruff-shampoo commercial.

All five of us campers were standing around watching this pathetic display of heterosexuality. It reminded me of when Suze Chang got really sick in fifth grade and didn't make it to the bathroom in time and everyone in the hallway saw her hurl. We all knew it wasn't her fault, but we still felt incredibly bad for her. Like I couldn't say that this was either of the two of their faults, but I was still just as painfully embarrassed for them.

But when life gives you incredibly awkward eighteen-year-olds flirting, you know what they say, make lemonade. So I seized this as a teaching opportunity.

I leaned over to Sylvie. "OK, first lesson on flirting with boys—what is going on here"—I casually pointed to the counselors—"is not good. And another general rule of boys: avoid any of them who cut off the sleeves of their shirts. Or actually who wear sleeveless shirts in general."

"Roger that," Sylvie affirmed.

I tuned back in to Awkwardpalooza: Counselor Edition, partly excited, but mostly scared to hear what came out of their mouths next.

"Yeah, I like hanging out. Do you?" Mr. No-Sleeves asked our counselor.

"I totally love hanging out too." And then she giggled for a while at nothing in particular. I contemplated feigning an injury and demanding that Mandi take me to the infirmary to end this and put them out of their misery.

"Why don't we just pick teams and start playing?" Hayden asked us all. And I never thought I'd feel this way, but I was glad to hear her voice. I'd rather do anything than watch Mandi and this guy talk about their mutual love of hanging out. I followed the girls at a slight jog to the far side of the court.

"OK, so should we pick team captains and then choose teams?" Sylvie asked as she bent down to grab the ball.

"We already wasted enough time watching those two."

Hayden pointed at the counselors. "Let's just do it you two versus us three. That's how it was going to wind up anyway."

She was right and we didn't complain. I was just glad to be playing with Sylvie. But after the first serve, it was clear that it was really just Sylvie versus the tremendous tres. She was running and spiking and setting and calling "Mine!" all over our side of the net. I tried to be useful by swatting away mosquitoes.

About four serves in, Aiden hit the ball and it was like a cannon launched straight at me. My immediate instinct was to duck from the large object flying toward my cranium. But instead, I very consciously decided to be a good teammate to Sylvie and try to play the game. I yelled, "I got it, mine," because that was what she did whenever she was about to touch the ball. Only as the ball got closer to me, I changed my mind. "No, wait, maybe you should get it." I turned to look at her to see if she heard me and promptly got hit in the side of the head with the ball. And while I'd love to blame the head trauma on Aiden's killer serve that was intended to send me to the ER, I can guarantee that my cranial swelling was completely unplanned for the trio. Me and my lack of hand-eye coordination and reflexes were one hundred percent at fault. That's not to say they still didn't enjoy seeing me eat the ball.

Somehow from that head bonk, I got a piece of dirt in my eye and spent the rest of the game on the sideline, trying to blink it out. I also occasionally cheered for Sylvie, but to be honest, I was never really sure when she was scoring points or getting scored on.

Despite my beyond-lackluster performance, Sylvie

managed to hold her own, and by the end of the game, we were tied.

"Nice work, team!" I put my hand up for a high five. I couldn't support her on the court, but a little postgame rah-rah was definitely within my realm of athleticism.

Sylvie took a break from wiping her sweat-covered face with her sleeve and slapped my palm.

"Not only are you not on my trivia team, you're off my volleyball team if I ever try to go pro," she said between pants.

She had a point, but I did have some skills to offer.

"Fair enough. But here's something to consider. I'm really good at coming up with punny team names. Like, we could be the E! True Volleyball Stories or HitItOver-The.Net." I walked beside her as she headed to the water station in the middle of the field.

"Those are pretty good. OK, mind changed. You're back on the team."

"Sweet!" Vindicated, I fist-pumped and toasted her with my paper cup of water.

As we rejoined the group, Mandi was just saying goodbye to our volleyball noncoach.

"So I guess I'll see you later. I mean, just around camp. Not at any time or place in specific, just around. That would be like a date, and I didn't mean that because we don't have a date set up. And even if we did, where would we go, the mess hall? That would be weird. Romantic table for two, please. Not! . . ." And it went on and on.

"I think she needs to be enrolled in Laney's School of Love too," Sylvie whispered to me, her face scrunched in horror over the kamikaze flirting going on just a few feet away.

"Negative. Some things are far beyond help."

She nodded. "Well, I'm proud that you think I'm a save-able."

I smiled at her and wiped away a sweat bead that was about to drip down my face. I'd thought the same thing when she helped me up from the sand a few days ago. I was just glad to know that at least someone didn't think I belonged in the dirt.

Lucky for us and womankind in general, Mandi finally decided to get off the express train to eternal virginhood. "OK, well, we should probably head off."

"Bye, Sandy!" he called out, and waved. Even Aidan's mouth dropped open at that gaffe.

"It's Mandi with an *i*," she corrected him. I wanted to tell her to dream big but start small with him. Literacy would come, but she should probably focus on major consonant sounds before jumping into the wild and crazy world of vowels. She continued, "Well, I guess there's nothing left to say but 'Hit it, boys,'" she commanded to an imaginary band behind her. "*So long, farewell, auf Wiedersehen, goodbye.*" Her singing was slow and off-key, as usual. She was stepping backward as she sang and then once she hit the "cuckoo" section, she started hopping backward instead of stepping. After the hops, she turned around and started walking as if everything were normal and she hadn't just performed the weirdest thing I've witnessed since that Scientology video of Tom Cruise came out.

But I guess I shouldn't complain, because we were leaving the volleyball courts, which meant that our schedule of morning activity torture was already half over. Sylvie and I galloped after Mandi toward the archery tent. Hopefully, I wouldn't catch anything in the head there.

LP,

Sister, just got your letter. I think it's the first actual letter I received since we adopted that class of pen pals from Japan in grammar school. Weird. Anyway, you sound miserable. I wish there were something I could do to help. Is there? Let me know.

Here is pretty normal. Not a ton to report. Nose job d-day is tomorrow. I can't freaking wait. Well, not for the actual nose job, which is going to be heinously painful, but for the results. So excited. Stuff with Conrad is awful. He's being a total dick and I bet the only time he visits me during recupe is if he wants some of my pain meds. Beyond over him. Let's find me a new boyfriend when you get back and I'm deswelled and beautiful, OK?

Missing my BFF so freaking much,
K.

Chapter 12

We'd spent the entire past hour in the arts and crafts shed. Hayden and Co. were at the paint-splattered table, weaving embroidery floss and tiny beads into intricate friendship bracelets. From my point of view, it was actually kind of like a sweatshop with Hayden at the helm, barking orders and depriving her friends of sunlight and nutrients essential to healthy childhood development. OK, well, not really about the sun and nutrient deprivation, but these girls totally could develop carpal tunnel from the redos Hayden insisted on.

"What is this?" Her shrill voice snapped my attention from my crafting project and I looked up to see her yank the bracelet Aidan was braiding from her hands. "Didn't I decide red, purple, yellow, bead, bead, *then* blue? Am I just talking to myself here?" She shook her head at the premature blue stripe. This drama was actually almost as good as watching TV. I tried to scootch closer to hear more. "OK, you guys, I feel like I'm up here." She raised her hand up above her head and marked off an imaginary level. "And you two, you're down here." This time she marked a level closer to the table. "Please, come join me up here. Do I need to send you a formal Evite or will you guys just come on up?"

"H, come on. It's just one stitch. She can undo it," Aiden stepped in.

"You know what, don't bother. I'll just make this bracelet for myself. That's right. I'm going to make my own friendship bracelet because that's the kind of friends I have."

After a series of emotionally fraught huffs and whimpers from the trio, we all sank into a rather tense silence as we continued to work on our projects. If Sylvie got that pissed at me every time I effed something up, she'd be diagnosed with a rage problem. I was starting to realize how totally lucky I was that those three hadn't befriended me and I got a super-supportive buddy instead.

Sylvie and I, not so surprisingly, were not involved in the soap opera sweatshop. We were working on our own project. And equally not surprisingly, Sylvie was taking the lead on the project.

She was teaching me to tie-dye, a skill I hoped I'd never actually need to use again, so I wasn't paying that much attention to her technique. She would pinch and twist the fabric and then nod when she wanted me to wrap on a rubber band. Then she carefully dunked the two tightly wound and rubber-band-secured balls into buckets of dye.

She unbanded the fabric clumps, shook them out, and held them up for display.

"What do you think?" she asked.

I wanted to keep it together and do a Tim Gunn impression and be really throaty and all, "I see this garment, and I do see elements of greatness here. I just want you to bring them out. Make it work." But I couldn't. What she was holding up was just too amazing, and keeping in my utter awe would have been impossible. "Oh. My. God. How did you do that?" The entire world getting created in six days was not even close to how amazing Sylvie's crafting was. She had somehow dyed two pairs of shorts to read FART across the butts. It was like taking the Billboard Butts and multiplying their ridiculousness by a hundred, but then somehow dividing by zero or something so that it was the ultimate *anti*–Billboard Butts move.

"Yeah, I'm like a craftacular MacGyver. Give me some rubber bands and dye and I can turn any normal piece of clothing into a pale-pink-and-blue-spiraled work of art."

"No, don't sell yourself short here. These aren't just tie dye, these are like a political statement."

Sylvie gave me a look. "You know that just says *fart*, right? Not *universal health care*."

"OK, fine. Maybe not a political statement, but definitely a screw you to the man," I said, my hands waving around like I really had a point to prove.

"And by 'the man' you mean those three girls over there who might not weigh three hundred pounds all together and are currently in a heated debate about the color pink going before red in their friendship bracelets?"

"Yeah, exactly." I pretended that I had no idea how ridiculous I was being.

"OK, whatever. Let's go hang these to dry so we can wear them tomorrow and make our pointed political statements." She motioned her head toward the drying rack.

I was still so stunned by her arts and crafts acumen that I almost didn't see her fling my pair of statement shorts at me. Instinctively, I flinched, wanting to dodge the splattering dye. But then I remembered what I was wearing and stood full frontal to embrace the oncoming dye bomb. Wearing clothes that ugly was almost like having some sort of invincibility cloak. I could do anything without worrying about wrecking my overpriced duds. It was actually kind of liberating . . . minus the being held against my will in the middle of the woods part.

Anyway, by the time we had come back into the shed from hanging our shorts on the drying rack, our arts and crafts rotation was over. And to be honest, I was a little bummed. I liked arts and crafts. There were no balls flying toward my cranium, no water, and I got to sit down for most of it. It was pretty much like a trip to the spa compared to other activities.

Mandi stood at the head of the table smiling and clapping to get everyone's attention. "All righty, my girlies, let's clean up! It's time to head to the ropes course." My arts and crafts high—which I'm pretty sure was a natural high from enjoying myself, not from glue fumes—plummeted.

Sylvie and I had to wash our hands and empty our buckets in the sink. The other three were cleaning up their bracelet-making supplies as we shimmied past their table. Without even trying to eavesdrop, I could hear just how well their best-friend bonding session had gone.

"Great," Hayden said, sarcasm dripping from her tone like sticky drips from a rocket pop on a hot day. "So we didn't finish any of our bracelets. Now how are people going to know that we're best friends?"

"You could try being nice to each other. That might be a good clue," I said, in what I wanted to be a snarky side comment to Sylvie but turned out to be far louder and more confrontational than that. I gulped, realizing that I'd probably just opened a can of bitchface surprise.

"Yeah, right," Aidan answered, rolling her eyes at me with not an ounce of irony in her voice. "That's so not the point. People like totally wouldn't even be jealous of us for that."

Sylvie caught my eye and her mouth dropped open in an unsaid "I can't believe that really just happened."

"Unreal," I whispered back, and shook my head.

After an initial period of paralyzing shock from the trio of ridiculousness, Sylvie and I managed to finish our cleanup and marched out with the rest of the bunk toward the ropes course. As we strolled across camp, I could feel my stomach clenching with nerves. I was sure this activity was going to crank the camp awful up a few clicks. Until that point, everything at camp had been horrible because it was humiliating, but a ropes course sounded like it took the Timber torture up another level to where I would actually be afraid for my personal safety. I mean, I hated instructional swim, but I knew I wasn't going to drown in a shallow pool of peepee water. If anything, I was just going to get hepatitis from swallowing too much urine, and that was curable. Wait, it was, right?

Anyway, with the ropes course my well-being was in serious danger. I could totally see myself falling from my harness on the zip line because whatever synthetic material today's pair of freakalicious skirt/shorts were made out of was too slick, hitting my head on a million pinecone-tree branches on the way down, and then being attacked by wild Pennsylvanian boars. Sylvie would try and fend off the rabid animals, but even someone as good at nature and sports as she was had no chance against the infamously belligerent Pennsylvanian wildlife, and eventually, the only evidence left of me would be my teeth and the bead work from the floral decal on the pocket of my horrible T-shirt.

"Hey," Sylvie said, snapping her fingers in front of my face, "are you all right?"

"Oh yeah. Totally fine. Just flashing forward to my imminent death on the ropes course. No biggie." I tried to sound like I was making a joke, but I could hear the undeniable fear in my voice and I was sure that Sylvie did too.

She put her arm around my shoulders. "What are you talking about?"

I exhaled a deep breath, surprising myself with how scared I actually was. "Um, I don't know. Like I'm just picturing myself falling off the zip line or trapeze or tightrope, whatever the hell the ropes course is."

"Wait, this is about the ropes course?"

I nodded, frowning but trying to be brave, like a three-year-old about to get a shot at the doctor's. "If I don't make it out, I want you to have the rest of my bug spray, OK?"

Sylvie removed her arm from my shoulder so she could

turn to face me as we walked. "LP, if you haven't noticed, this is Timber Trails, not Club Med. They don't even have fans that work or a constant flow of hot water. There's no way this place would have whatever *American Gladiators* obstacle course you're imagining, OK? So you don't have to be afraid of that."

She was so right. Why had I psyched myself into a neurotic lather? This was just camp, not an astronaut testing program. Immediately, I felt my blood pressure drop from near-heart-attack levels and the half-frozen chicken nuggets I'd eaten for lunch stopped churning in my stomach.

"Thanks, Sylv." I centered myself, grateful to the evil lords of camp for allowing me at least one friend. "So nothing to be afraid of," I said.

"OK, well, not exactly *nothing* to be afraid of," Sylvie said, her face strained with the bad news she was about to deliver. "Just nothing *life-threatening* to be afraid of. But . . . well . . . I'd just say be afraid, be very afraid."

I immediately felt the lunchtime chicken nuggets begin their churn again.

"Wait, what? Tell me!" I begged, but we'd already arrived at the grassy clearing in the woods and joined the rest of our bunk, who were all attentively listening to a muscled man barking out instructions in a thick Eastern European accent.

"Here we are at ropes course." His yelling was so syncopated, it sounded like there should be a period after every single one of his words. "OK, what we do now is I assign partners and—"

I gulped and tuned out the rest of his speech. Sylvie looked over and gave me a wide-eyed nod. This was what I was supposed to be afraid of, very afraid of. And I was. Assigned partners? At that moment, I would have rather heard the words *flesh-eating wild Pennsylvanian boars*.

When I finally refocused on the Schwarzenegger impersonator, he was pointing to us two at a time and snapping, "You and you," indicating who was paired together. I saw him partner Sylvie with Mandi and Aiden with Aidan, and then time seemed to slow as he "you and you'd" Hayden and me together. I was beyond terrified at being Hayden's partner. Like more scared than I was when *My Boys* took that super-long hiatus and I thought that I'd never know who PJ asked to go on the Italy trip with her. Hayden let out a disgusted grunt and rolled her eyes to the point where she had to have seen her cerebral cortex. And honestly, I couldn't blame her. I felt like doing the same thing, it's just that my eyeballs weren't as flexible.

"OK, we're going to get started with the trust fall. You two"—a thick finger pointed at Hayden and me—"you demonstrate."

Now, I was certainly not a camp activities expert, but I'd seen enough episodes of *The Office* to know that a trust fall entailed closing your eyes and falling backward into another person's open arms, trusting that she would catch you before you hit the ground and shattered any vertebrae. And I also knew that I didn't trust Hayden not to dunk my toothbrush into the toilet, so I hid it in my cubby when I wasn't using it. Trusting her with my spinal cord's safety was so not an option.

"Um, I'm going to take a pass on this, guys." I raised my hands in surrender. "I get one pass a summer, right?"

The Timbernator continued like he hadn't heard me,

positioned Hayden's arms in a catch position, and showed her how to bend her knees on impact.

"Here's the thing about me that you probably don't know, I'm really attached to my spinal cord. Like, I'd say it's definitely up there on my top ten list of body parts." No one was listening to me but Sylvie, who was cracking up at my monologue. But the thing was, I wasn't trying to be funny. I was seriously scared. "And well, I travel a lot. And so like if I get injured and have to get a metal rod inserted, that'll just make the security check a complete nightmare for me. And I know that nobody here would wish longer security lines on even their worst enemy. So let's just skip the trust fall or play truth or dare or something equally as trust-building, but less head-trauma-causing."

"Now you cross your arms over your chest and fall backwards," the trust counselor ordered. Everyone had formed a circle around us and was waiting for the demo to begin. As I started to sputter out another reason that I was firmly against self-induced full-body casts, Mandi looked me in the eye and said, "Just do it." Then she marched over to me and bent down a little to get right in my face and say, "The longer you wait, the more time you're cutting out of everyone else's activities. And I'm sure that's not what you want to do to the rest of us, right?" She said all this with her typical perky voice, but I could tell by her tight grin and the crazy eyes that she was just a second away from breaking her nice-gal persona and totally freaking on me for being difficult.

"Yeah, come on," Aiden said.

"Just do it," Aidan added with no hint of enthusiasm or support in her voice.

This led to a round of repeating "Just do it's" from practically everyone standing in the circle. Sylvie's cries of "She doesn't have to if she doesn't want to, right?" were all but drowned out by the Nike-sponsored bullies yelling "Just do it."

I felt like I was in a super-dramatic scene from an after-school special about peer pressure, where they pan from face to face to all the characters faster and faster while these different voices are saying "Smoke pot, Johnny. Just try grass once. No one will know." Except for in my case, it wasn't free drugs they were pushing, it was a stupid trust fall.

Ignoring the cold-shoulder and comeback techniques I'd learned in my drug-awareness program, I gave in. "Fine! What's a lifetime in a wheelchair anyway?"

I turned around to make sure Hayden was in proper catching stance, and then for the first time in my life—after surviving party after party of just saying no to powders, pills, and cigarettes—I succumbed to the pressure of my peers. I closed my eyes and rocked back.

And I fell for five terrifying minutes—well, it *felt* like five minutes but was probably more like point five seconds—convinced I was either going to puke or lose the function of my legs in nanoseconds. But finally, I felt the impact of my back hitting Hayden's boney chest.

"See, aren't you glad you did it?" I opened my eyes to a mural of blackheads, and when I could finally focus, I realized that it was Mandi's face at point-blank range. She pulled back and smiled at me. I wanted to take her clogged-pored face and kiss it, I was so freaking pumped to be alive with all my limbs in working order.

I let Hayden trust push me off her and stumbled around

in the grass from the force. "On a scale of one to glad I did it, I'd rank this somewhere in the triple-digit negatives," I said once I'd regained my footing.

I watched as the rest of the pairs fell into each other, glad to be vertical. Then the ropes course counselor led us to two trees that had been looped together with twine several times and at bizarre angles so it looked like there was a magnified spiderweb hanging between the trunks.

We stood in a semicircle. "Now you have to figure out how to get every bunkmate through the web and to the other side without touching the ropes with your body or using the same path twice," the ropes guy instructed through his accent. He sounded a lot like the Count from *Sesame Street*. I so wished I were watching TV just then. Even PBS would have been better than this.

Mandi cut into the web instruction. "Actually, since someone—and I don't want to point fingers here, so I won't—was a slowpoke on the trust fall"—immediately, Aidan pointed her finger at me. I had a finger that I wanted to point back at her, but I stopped myself—"we don't have time for the web o' bonding. We need to head back and shower up!"

I was so focused on how awesome a shower and some predinner resting sounded that tuning out the evil glares and groans from the Billboard Butts and the ropes guy barely took any effort.

I exited the shower with one goal in mind: sleep. I flopped myself on my cot and closed my eyes for a power nap, but what must have been just ten minutes later I was thumped awake by Sylvie on her way back from the shower.

I opened my eyes and saw her about to pull a brush through her head of wet curls.

"No!" I shouted. Sylvie turned to me looking concerned. The rest of the girls couldn't hear the shrill sound of my panic over their hair dryers. "You can't brush curls!"

"What?" Sylvie asked, the brush still dangerously close to her scalp.

"Just put the brush down and we can talk." I felt like I was a hostage negotiator. "Put it down and step away. Your hair has never done anything to deserve this. It's completely innocent here."

She dropped the brush onto her bed and I breathed deeply in relief.

"OK, when you brush your curls, you separate them."

"Well, what do I do, not brush my hair? That's gross! It'll be a bird's nest."

"There's nothing gross about it. You just need to comb it in the shower. And believe me, a bird's nest would be a step up from where you are now, Macy Gray." Harsh, I know, but if there's anything I've learned from self-improvement reality television, it's that tough love is the only way. "Wait right there, I'll be back."

I ran into the bathroom and squeezed out a palmful of gel from whoever's bath caddy was left in one of the shower stalls and zipped back to Sylvie's bed. I sat down and she plopped herself cross-legged in front of me.

"OK, I'm just going to work this through. You're going to look so super hot." I said, lathering the gel between my hands and then spreading it through her hair. I felt like Michelangelo, sculpting her into awesome hotness.

As I finger-molded her curls into place, I started to worry

about my promise to find Sylvie a guy this summer. I mean, even with all the plucking and frizz-taming, there was still a pretty major issue with my quest.

"Um, Sylv. Just doing some forward thinking about Mission: Manquest. Are we ever going to interact with a single male specimen at Timber Trails over the age of seven? I know they're here. I've seen a few bunks of boys walking from activity to activity, but we can't really build a relationship on walk-bys, you know? Well, I guess there are the guy counselors, but they seem way off-limits. And I did see that weird maintenance guy who came around to fix the toilet after the girls in the bunk next door flushed all the tampons and had that whole gross backup. But he looked like someone who probably has a criminal record that should prevent him from working this close to kids. Not my ideal mate for you." I jumped off the bed and swung around to take a look at my work from the front and started fixing the face-framing curls. "I mean, I'm good. But what do you expect? Me to Geppetto some real live boys at arts and crafts? You know how bad I am with Popsicle sticks."

She laughed and pulled her head away, done with primping for the moment.

"Oh right, newbie, you don't know about boy/girl interaction here at the T-squared," she said with her eyebrows raised.

"Please, enlighten me, O Camp Elder."

"OK, well, as you've probably figured out by now, they like to keep us pretty separate. You know, because teen pregnancy isn't an activity on our schedule." I had been so focused on myself and the severity of my surrounding awfulness that until Sylvie's manhunt, I barely cared I wasn't

170

seeing any boys my own age. It was totally like when a chick from those Lifetime movies gets really depressed after she's lost her baby/husband/brother/boyfriend/all of the above and then she doesn't notice that she hasn't been eating or showering until a week later when her best friend barges in and insists on helping her piece her life back together.

"Anyway," Sylvie continued, "they make sure we never see each other. Like the older girls have instructional swim with the younger boys."

"Oh, I'm well aware of that," I interjected, thinking about my swim group. And in theory, that pretty much kept the boys and the girls separate during instructional swim. The older girls would be in the higher levels, and the younger boys would be in the lower levels. There was a little overlap in some of the middle levels, and obviously I was the only overlap in level one, but for the most part it was sex segregation.

"And the older boys have swim with the little girls after us, so we're not distracted by flirting or whatever during our lessons. And even with eating, we eat at the same time in the mess hall, but the guys have another entrance and we're in different rooms."

I was less than impressed with this lack of guy time. "So basically this is a two-for-one combo deal. A camp and a convent for the price of one?" I asked flatly.

"Well," she sighed, "kind of. We have dances every so often with the boys and there's the occasional free time where we're both on the fields sometimes. But yeah, that's pretty much it. Not a lot of coed interaction to work with."

"Dances? That sounds promising," I murmured as I brushed a flyaway off her face. I knew it would annoy her, but

I couldn't help myself. "What do you normally wear? Are they formal?" Now that her frizz was under control, I could totally do a sleek updo and pin in some flowers that would be very Sarah Jessica Parker glam.

"Ugh." She sounded grossed out and exhausted. "You'll see. The dances are totally lame. So not anything to get excited about. They're boring and just not a big deal at all."

Not a big deal? This was about as much of not a big deal as ticket sales for a Jonas Brothers concert. This was ha-ha-huge.

"Actually, it kind of does sound like a big deal. Basically, there are set times when boys can talk to girls and they need to carpe diem then or never, right?" Sylvie nodded. "That's totally going to be the kick in the booty these guys are going to need so we can get you some booty."

She laughed as she pulled her hair into a pony. I wanted to kick her in the booty for trashing the past fifteen minutes of my hard hair work.

Dear Perez,

 Woof, woof. I miss you, baby. Tell Mom to give
you a doggy treat from me, OK? Also tell her that
camp is so terrible that I've restarted my silent
treatment.

Imagine me scratching your belly,
Your Mommy

Chapter 13

After several more days packed with self-esteem-demolishing athletic activities, more time at instructional swim than Michael Phelps probably spends in a pool, and not a single s'more, the big announcement came.

We were all sitting at dinner, gnawing our way through unidentifiable hunks of protein and vegetation, when the camp director—a guy with a potbelly and white beard who answered my childhood question of what Santa does in the summer—got up to make the evening activity announcement. It was actually weird to see him. There are so few grown-ups at this place, normally the oldest person I see in a day is still in high school, so that made him look even older.

Now, typically, he gets up, coughs into the microphone several times, announces whatever banal activity is on the books for that night, and the camp crowd goes wild. Seriously, from the reaction, you'd think he just announced that there would be a kissing booth featuring the *Gossip Girl* guys and we'd all just been given a turn to mack on them. But it was normally something like moonlight kickball.

So when he made the evening announcement that night and I was too busy picking the stringy spinach/pureed broccoli/green hay from between my teeth to pay attention, I didn't really react when the girls around me started up with the whooping, fist-pumping, and high-fiving. I actually motioned for Sylvie to pass the salt.

"I can't believe you're not freaking over this," she said, setting the salt and pepper next to my plate.

"What would I be freaking about?" I gave up on the table flossing and spoke with my mouth full of unpluckable greenness. I probably looked like a zombie that had chewed itself out of its own grave. "Did he say we were going to play that totally lame version of kickball where you run backwards around the bases? 'Cause that's a twisted ankle waiting to happen. Or remember that rainy day when we got to watch *Lion King*? Do you think we could do that again? I effing love that Elton John song." I started humming to myself, crescendo-ing into a full-volume "CAN YOU FEEL THE LOVE TONIGHT?" No one but Sylvie could hear my musical stylings over their continued evening-activity frenzy.

"Let's do us both a favor and have you promise never to sing again." She was wincing.

"Not a promise I can keep, my friend, especially when we're talking about old-school Disney. I love me some soft rock love songs." I cleared my throat and closed my eyes to start up an emotive rendition of "Beauty and the Beast." "*Tale as old as time, song as old as rhyme,*" I belted with my husky alto voice, hitting almost none of the right notes.

"I always thought that song wasn't initially written with enough flat notes. I'm so glad you're adding them now." She cupped her hands around her ears to block me out.

I decided to conclude my show by hitting the highest note I could and dramatically shimmying my fingers jazz-hand style. "I know what you're thinking," I said.

"That I wish I'd been born deaf?" Sylvie asked.

I pretended not to hear that. "Why is Laney at this camp and not at a program for musical theater prodigies?"

"It's like you read my mind." Sylvie shoved a small piece of beef/pork/dog into her mouth. "But seriously, did you not hear what our activity is tonight?"

I shook my head.

"The dance," she said slowly, letting it soak in. She grimaced as she choked down her bite of question-mark meat.

"Wait, what? The dance?" My mouth was hanging open in disbelief. "Like they're going to let us see boys tonight? Boys who wouldn't list boogies as their main turn-on?" I couldn't believe this was all the warning they gave us. There was so much more prep work to do with Sylvie, and actually with me too. Looking at my legs, you'd think the last time I shaved was back when *Make Me a Supermodel* was on the air.

"Right, for these boys, boogies are just a secondary and sometimes even third-tier interest." By now the yelping from all the girls had cooled to a buzzing frenzy, and everyone was focused on finishing their food and clearing their tables as quickly as possible.

"Seriously, Sylv. This is a big deal. This is our chance." I put my fork down, figuring that I would go through the bottom of my duffel bag for any leftover Tic Tacs or chunks of lint that looked edible if I got hungry later. "We haven't even gone over any dance moves yet. Or how to introduce yourself. Do you think there'll be enough sunlight after dinner to get you a little bit of a tan? Or maybe we should go to arts and crafts and see if they have an airbrush and some light brown paint." My mind was moving even faster than my mouth. We hadn't gone over clothing or eye contact at all. And I wondered how I would do her hair. I didn't want to do anything too avant-garde. Maybe a french twist with some curls hanging down in the front? That seemed suburban enough. It was always how they wore their hair for fancy stuff on *One Tree Hill*.

"Take a few deep breaths, sister. You sound like one of those beauty pageant stage moms." She gave me her plate to scrape off onto mine and pass down to Mandi for stacking.

"You're right," I said over the squishing of food flopping from plate to plate. "No fake tanning. We need to spend all the time we have focusing on dance moves."

She nodded. "And what about personality? When do we focus on that?" She was joking, but it kind of was a valid point.

"When boys start calling boobs 'personality,' we'll start focusing on personality." I was only half joking. "But seriously, folks, we don't have any worries there. Your personality is awesome." She nodded, taking the compliment.

Everyone in the entire mess hall passed on the curdled chocolate milk they were calling pudding and rushed through the table-cleaning process so they could sprint back to the bunks en masse to prep for the dance.

As soon as we stepped into our shack, we were frantic full throttle. I ran over to my cubby, practically hurdling over each member of the trio of terror, I was moving so quickly. They were fluttering around their side of the bunk, trading, borrowing, trying on, and shrieking. I tore through my shelves and then Sylvie's, searching for something for her to wear. But my selection of DayGlo ensembles left more than a little to be desired, and Sylvie's collection of gym shorts, overalls, and polo shirts wouldn't even count as dress-up gear for Ellen DeGeneres. I finally decided on giving her the tank and skirt I wore on the bus down to camp.

"It's a little rank, but it's the best we can do. Our other choices would either blind your beau or give the impression that you're a five-year-old questioning her sexuality." I threw the outfit over to her bed.

She held up the crinkled top with just her fingertips. "Really? The overall shorts make me look like a lesbian toddler?" I nodded. "And an outfit that is a little stinky would be more attractive?"

"A straitjacket would actually be more attractive to a man than the overalls. Trust me." This cruel-to-be-kind bit was getting easier by the second. I so should be Simon's understudy for the next season of *Idol*.

She rolled her eyes, I assumed at the physical focus of the male half of our species, but I guess it could have also been at me. Regardless of whom she was judging with the eyeball somersaults, she still put on my clothes.

As she tugged my tank down, I asked Mandi if we could borrow her makeup because of course all I had was the small jar of Duane Reade–brand petroleum jelly that my mom packed. Mandi's sparkly pink spectrum wasn't typically the color palette I'd choose, but the only other makeup in the bunk was the mountain of Cover Girl and Maybelline the Billboard Butts had pooled together and piled on Hayden's bed. They certainly had a better color selection than Mandi, and I did think about asking to borrow a few things of theirs, but then I realized that Hayden's not dropping me in the trust fall earlier that week had probably filled my quota of Hayden favors for the summer. A few swipes of Define-A-Lash would definitely push her over the edge.

I pawed through all of Mandi's compacts and lipstick tubes and I found only three shades that wouldn't make Sylvie look like a conversation heart.

"OK," I said as I started applying her base. "Let's talk about dancing." I dropped the foundation sponge and held her chin carefully as I spackled on undereye concealer. Sylvie made a move to nod or speak or somehow express herself, but I shook my head and grabbed her chin a little tighter. "No moving or else I'm going to conceal your inner ear," I warned her. "All right, so the thing with dancing is basically just follow his lead. Like if he's a side-to-side foot-tapping guy, don't go all double spin, back-handspring, moonwalk on him. Keep it mellow. But if he's more—"

But I wasn't able to finish my sentence because I was abruptly cut off by Aiden and Aidan's yelping. If I weren't more acclimated to this for-dogs'-ears-only screeching, I would have flipped into if-you-see-something-say-something mode and made moves to call the authorities. By this point in the summer, the girls had not only beaten me into being too afraid to ask for a wand of drugstore mascara, they had also worn down my ability to assess cues for emergency.

"You. Look. Fan. Tas. Tic," Aiden said, drawing out every syllable and then letting her mouth hang open to display shock and awe at the aforementioned fantasticness. It also displayed that she hadn't flossed after dinner.

I couldn't help myself. I turned away from Sylvie to see what was so fantastic. It was Hayden, of course, who was just emerging from the bathroom. She had her hair in a high pony and was wearing a plain white T-shirt, terry-cloth shorts that I'm sure said something vaguely alluding to promiscuity on the butt, and ankle socks and sneakers. She was also weirdly shimmery and her acne bumps reflected the light in a bizarre way. All in all, I'd say the look was Disco Ball Goes to the Gym.

"Really?" she said, not sounding at all like she didn't believe her friend's compliment. "You don't think this is too much body glitter?"

I felt like I was committing a sin by not hosing her down and washing that glitter off, it was so hideous.

"Too much body glitter?" Aidan asked as she flipped off her hair dryer. "As if that were even possible!"

I actually surprised myself by not gagging. Though I'm not sure if this was something to be proud or ashamed of.

I got back to work on Sylvie, and just as I was dabbing the final coat of gloss on her pout, Mandi made the announcement that it was time to head off to the dance. It hit me that I had zero time left to prep myself. With Sylvie in my one normal outfit, I was stuck in something billowy and blindingly bright. And no amount of cosmetics would help my face when my skin was reflecting the neon green of my shirt. Strangely, though, I realized that I didn't care. It was Sylvie's night tonight. Sacrificing my looks for others? I was like Stacy London and Mother Teresa all wrapped into one. I grabbed a sweatshirt and tied it around my waist and did something I never thought I would do without a gun to my head: I set off to a party sans makeup.

As I crossed the camp with Sylvie, I almost laughed out loud. Back home, I would barely cross the hall to the bathroom without makeup. The sad part was my bold move was already backfiring. I wanted this experience to be empowering, leaving me feeling fresh-faced and liberated. But it really just made me feel large-pored and masculine. And the huffing and puffing wasn't helping my current self-image either.

"We're going to a dance, right?" I asked, panting. "Because this feels weirdly similar to last week's hike." We had been walking for at least ten minutes, a good chunk of it up a hill laden with roots that I kept tripping over. I really wished we could hop into a cab—and please note that I just said "cab," not "limo" or "car service." This nature stuff was totally turning me more granola.

"We're almost at the rec hall," she assured me. She had been tugging at the top I'd loaned her the entire walk. "Are you sure this isn't too tight? I feel a little skanky."

How was I going to explain to her that a little bit of skank could go a long way?

"That's the point," I said slowly, trying to avoid an asthma attack. "If you keep stretching it out like that, the armholes are going to get huge and your bra is going to be exposed for all of Timber to see. And then we're really talking skanky." She immediately dropped her hands to her sides.

"And you did my makeup so it looks natural, right? Not like that Raven-Symoné teen drag queen look?"

"Yes, you look gorgeous. Freaking out now is just going to make you sweaty and the makeup is going to smear off. So just"—I did some deep breathing to demonstrate—"calm down." I rubbed her back as she breathed a bit, but even as I was trying to pacify her, I was kind of freaking out myself. This night could be huge for her.

We slowly approached the rec hall and Sylvie stopped at the stairs, spit out her retainer, and shoved it in the pocket of my skirt while the rest of the girls streamed past us in a frenzied mob to get into the dance. I watched anxiously as Sylvie looked up at the door. "Oh my God," she whispered. "He's here." Every part of her skin that wasn't covered by the tank and mini suddenly turned a blotchy pink.

My body tensed too, in what must have been sympathy nerves.

"He who?" I glanced up at the doorway, which was now crowded with girls pushing their way in, but couldn't see anything.

"*He* the guy I've had a crush on for the past five summers." I watched as the skin blotches grew and melted into each other, making it look like she was wearing a hot-pink wet suit.

"Whoa, whoa, whoa." I waved my hands around like a maniac, almost hitting her, we were standing so close. "You never mentioned there was a *specific* guy in mind for this quest." I was sure that I had asked her if she liked anyone at some point. I wracked my brain but couldn't remember ever inquiring.

"Does that change anything?" She cocked her head.

"Yeah, totally. Put your retainer back in and let's run over to the bunk and wash off the makeup and change you into your OshKosh B'Goshes. I didn't know it was one particular guy."

She turned around and crouched down, like a sprinter waiting for the gun. "Really?" she asked, about to propel herself back to the bunk.

"No, not really. I'm a hundred percent kidding." She sighed in total aggravation. Then I sighed because by her willingness to bolt to the showers and into a comfy pair of overalls, I could tell that she really hadn't appreciated any of the makeover. "I just didn't know you liked somebody," I said kind of quietly.

"Yeah, well, I didn't say anything because I didn't know if he was here this summer."

I shook my head at the sex segregation rules. So effing ridiculous.

Then I started up the stairs and waved her to come with me. "Well, come on. Let's go talk to him."

She rushed up next to me as we entered the rec hall and pointed across the room. "There, that's him. Eli Sternman." Her voice sounded softer when she said his name.

At first, I couldn't even see where she was pointing. I was too distracted by the construction-paper chaos that had apparently turned the brown and dusty rec hall into a party. It was still brown and dusty but was now festooned with fluorescent cut-out stars attached to the rafters with yarn, and there was a huge banner hanging across the stage that read UNDER THE STARS. This five-year-old-with-safety-scissors motif was all it took to send the camp's constituency a-grooving. Everyone was dancing, and I saw Mandi across the dance floor, beckoning us to come join her by pointing at us and mouthing along with the music, *"You can be my black Kate Moss tonight."*

I shook my head a determined no and then followed Sylvie's point. There, past a shimmying Aidan, was the object of Sylvie's desire. And if I didn't know any better, I would have thought this guy was an extra from *Revenge of the Uber-Nerds: When Wedgies Attack.* I was struck speechless and tried my hardest not to show any alarm on my face.

"So, should I just like go up and start dancing with him, you know, like you said? Following his lead?" Sylvie asked, adorably unaware of the fact that I was in elastic-waist-denim shock. Yes, that's right, elastic-waist denim. Stone-washed, to add insult to eyesore.

Suddenly, the *Legally Blonde* coaching sessions I'd been leading seemed rather pointless. I mean, to any of the other oogie-cookie-playing Timber hombres at this dance, a tight tank and some hair flips would be all the come-hithering they'd need. But even from across the room, I could see that this Eli Sternman character wasn't exactly the horniest rhino in the zoo.

And looking at him—at that moment cleaning his glasses on the bottom of his shirt while doing some sort of tongue gymnastics with his retainer—he seemed to be the same kind of clueless mega-dork Sylvie was. And I meant that in the most loving way possible. So in theory, this made them perfect for each other. But in practice, this totally made my summer-loving project about as easy as proving Suri's paternity.

I'm not normally one to give up, though—hell, I'd still be trying to rock the mega-flared jewel-tone jeans *Glamour* said were the thing last spring if Kennedy hadn't forced me to give them to charity. But before I could create plan dork point oh, I was distracted by a total blast from the past. And by the past, I mean just weeks before when I was in New York. However, if you looked at the blisters on my feet or the bug bites on my legs, I swear you'd think it was the upwards of two and a half years ago. Anyway, standing a few feet away from the object of Sylvie's adorkation was Ryan Bellsinger. Yes, Ryan Bellsinger. The unwanted cousin to the private-school party king of New York, the constant smudge on the shine that was the upper crust of the Manhattan underaged, the only person who touched the snack table at any of Conrad's parties, and the not-so-affectionately named Fag Face. That Ryan Bellsinger.

"Stay right here." I turned back to Sylvie. "Don't dance, don't even tap your foot. I'll be right back. I just need to say hi to someone." I held her eye contact for a second, just to let her know how serious I was about the dancing moratorium.

Then I turned and barreled toward him. "Ryan? Ryan!" I screamed from too far away for him to hear.

I sprinted past a twelve-year-old couple grinding up on each other so intensely, I almost stopped to ask if she'd been vaccinated for HPV. But I didn't have time for a stranger's health issues when I was this overjoyed to see someone from my life B.C. (before camp).

As I pushed my way through to him, I couldn't help but fantasize about him marching up to the Billboard trio and telling them how cool I was in the real world.

"*Yeah, Laney's a pretty big deal at home.*" I'd puff up my chest as he vouched for my NYC cred. "*Like she's part of the bitchy, mean girls at home. And they're way meaner and bitchier than you could even dream of being.*" Hold up, that wasn't exactly how I wanted that fantasy to go.

But I didn't have time to daydream something else, as I was just arriving at Ryan's back.

"Hey, Ryan!" I tapped on a T-shirted shoulder. "What are you doing here?" I was grinning like a nerd and totally acting way more excited than was cool, but I really couldn't hide how pumped I was to see him.

Ryan turned around and looked at me, not even feigning recognition. At first I was a little embarrassed. I mean, we've been running in the same social circle—well, technically, I've been running *in* the circle, he's been satelliting *around* it—since preschool. Then I remembered what I was wearing—baggy floral capris and a hot-green T-shirt with matching floral cuffs—and then, more horrifyingly, what I wasn't wearing—makeup—and got way embarrassed.

"It's me, Laney," I said, quickly moving my fingers up to pinch some makeshift blush into my cheeks.

"Laney *Parker?*" he asked, his face crinkling in total disbelief. He looked me up and down, taking in my horrific ensemble and then focusing on the lace detailing around the neck of my T-shirt. "Wow, I didn't recognize you for a second there."

"I'll take that as a compliment," I said, biting my bottom lip and waiting for him to start the conversation. Despite my excitement, I was still in camp awkward mode and couldn't think of anything normal to say. This place was like kryptonite for my cool.

"So . . ." He drew out the vowel so his mouth was in a tight O.

"So why am I here in the middle of the rec hall dance dressed like Dora the Explorer instead of in New York personifying everything you probably hate about the New York social scene?"

He chuckled a little, shoving his hands into the pockets of his jeans. "Yeah. That's exactly what I meant by 'so.'"

I laughed a little and glanced down at my outfit, focusing on my summer "dress shoes"—aqua socks. "Yeah, I'm kind of wondering the same thing." I looked back up at him. "Well, without getting too dramatic here, my evil nonstepfather brainwashed my mother and they're pretty much holding me here against my will for the rest of the summer." I took a deep breath that I hoped made me sound like a helpless victim. "Oh"—I looked to the side to seem even more forlorn—"and my mom packed for me, to add to this crisis."

That was all it took for his chuckles to turn into full-on rolling laughter. "You know, there are starving children in Africa who are less histrionic about their situations," he managed to get out between laughs. "Hilarious."

"OK, I'm no joke expert here, but I'd say this camp situation clocks in at several notches below hilarious." I crossed my arms in front of me. "Like at tragic."

"You're right, you're right. This isn't quite hilarious; probably just above entertaining but below actually funny." He finished laughing. "OK, so let me guess. You hate nature. You hate it here. You hate the people. And you have no friends."

Three out of four ain't bad. He was probably more accurate than most psychics.

The music changed to a slow song and all the grinding couples slowed down to deliberate humping. "Yes. Yes. Yes.

And no," I answered. "I have *one* friend." I said it with an insane amount of pride. Like how a normal person might say "I have one island nation in the South Pacific named after me." "And she's over there." I pointed at Sylvie, who waved back, proving that we did indeed have a deep and meaningful connection.

"Oh, Sylvie Manger? She's great." He waved at her too.

"You know her?" Yet another Sylvie secret that I was discovering tonight. I felt like a shocked fiancée on *The Moment of Truth* when she found out that the man she was about to marry was sleeping with her sister. Though at least Sylvie's reveals weren't really hurtful, life-altering, or publicly humiliating. And I wasn't sure how she would have known that I even knew Ryan to tell me that she knew him as well. But still.

"Of course I do. I've been going to Timber for years. You just kind of know everybody after a while. It's like a family." Yeah, like a horrible dysfunctional family that ends up on that *Supernanny* show where the nanny has to literally stop the kids from killing each other and spends most of the time explaining to the mother why empty bleach bottles aren't good teething rings.

"Well, if you know everyone, do you know that guy?" I nodded toward Sylvie's man.

"Who? Eli? Yeah. That guy is awesome!" he exclaimed. We both looked over at Eli, who had his eyes closed and was sucking on an asthma inhaler. He didn't seem to notice our stares. "Well, he's weird. But awesome still. I mean, 'cool' doesn't make someone actually cool, you know?"

I waited for a "The more you know" shooting star to appear above his head. But then I looked back over at Sylvie, who was pretty consumed with sucking on a lock of her own hair. I kind of wanted her to stop. I'd put so much curl gel in it, she could be getting drunk from the alcohol content.

I thought about how much better my life had become since meeting this retainered, frizzy-haired, Sudoku fiend. She might have been a fashion *don't*, but if *Glamour* had a page on friendship how-to's, her picture would totally have been in the *do's*. "Yeah, I know."

"That's what I love about this place." He motioned around the dance. "Not the rec hall specifically, but camp. Here, friendships are based on stuff that counts, not the bull-shit that matters in New York. Like how much your mom makes or where you got blackout drunk last weekend."

Or that you shaved your eyebrows off in the late nineties, I wanted to add. But considering that offending him would cut my friend count down by fifty percent, I decided to save that little piece of history for another time.

"So I was kind of thinking of getting two of these prime examples of uncool being the new black together." I explained Project Sylvie Sucks Face to Ryan.

"Uh, so basically, you're trying to live a romantic comedy?" he asked skeptically. Well, that made this whole thing sound really lame. This wasn't some stupid movie about getting Hugh Grant to change his womanizing ways and settle down. This was about helping someone get a little more fun out of her summer, the way she'd been helping me.

"Hey, Captain Buzzkill, why are you here? I didn't think you were invited." I rolled my eyes at him, but there was something so sweet about the way Ryan was looking at me that I knew he wasn't really trying to put me or the plan down.

He smiled. "Well, every party has a pooper, right?"

I nodded. "Yeah, you're right. But if there's anyone who's not having fun at this dance"—I made a big show of looking around the rec hall at all the couples connected at the grundle—"it's me. The pooper position has already been filled, so you'll have to find another role . . . like coconspirator in crushapalooza?" I paused for a minute, letting my pitch linger in the air. "And I'm totally not doing this to relive some old Olsen twins movie. I'm doing it because Sylvie has been so great to me. She reached out and literally picked me up and dusted me off. Well, I guess if we're going to be literal about the meaning of literal, I dusted myself off. But whatever. She took a risk and has made me whole again instead of just the shell of the fifteen-year-old formerly known as Laney that I was the first few days of camp. And I don't know how to weave friendship bracelets, so I feel like this is the one thing I can do for her this summer after all the stuff that she's done for me." I surprised myself with how emotional I was getting. I took a deep steadying breath. Tears around this much construction paper would probably turn into a papier-mâché mess.

Ryan was looking at me with a wrinkled forehead. He was clearly giving the situation a ton of thought. "When you put it that way, it makes sense," he said slowly. "All right, I'm in."

I was tempted to squeal and jump up and down and give him a spitty kiss on his cheek. Instead, I just left it at a tasteful fist pump. "Really? Sweet!" With Ryan on my side, getting Eli and Sylvie together seemed a lot more possible.

As I was about to launch into mission planning 007 style, I noticed that just about every pair of female eyes in the rec hall were focused on me.

I wanted to scream, "What? What? Is it because I'm not wearing butt shorts? Yeah, well, stare all you want at this illiterate butt! I don't care." But I thought I should check to make sure that I wasn't dragging toilet paper from my heel or anything. It had been my turn to clean the bathroom floor that morning, and I'd done a totally half-assed—wait, even worse, quarter-assed—job of it.

When I twisted around to check my hindquarters for TP, I realized that the girls weren't glaring at me. They were actually *gazing* at Ryan—half gaga-eyed, half fiercely flirting, but all definitely at Ryan.

I did a sitcom double take, whipping my head from their eyes to Ryan's face, Ryan's face to the sea of captivated campers.

"Is that one of Kennedy and your dance moves?" I heard him ask. My head whips paused long enough to give him a confused look. "That head-shaking thing. Is that one of those dance moves that Kennedy and you do?"

I had to admit Kennedy and I were quite the dancing queens, especially when anything old-school Kelly was involved. And I guess we *did* have some signature moves, but this fast-forward neck stretch thing I was doing? Totally insulting that he could think this was Lannedy choreography. But of course I couldn't say, "No, this isn't a dance move, stupid. I'm self-inflicting whiplash because I can't even fathom girls liking you. No, no, *liking* isn't the right word. *Pining*. I can't imagine girls pining for you. But they seem to be doing exactly that, and I'm shocked." So I just gave a vague "Yeah" and allowed myself to get incredibly awkward.

"Well . . . ," he started, to fill the silence. "Looks like the dance is kind of wrapping up. So I'm going to get in some last-minute grooving while I can." He shook it a little to demonstrate. I had to remind myself that geek was the new chic to avoid outright laughing at his moves. "Anyway, so I'm totally into the Sylvie and Eli set-up. It's about time my man got some attention." He raised his hand for a high five. "Talk to you later."

We slapped palms, and when I was still shaking out the pain from my hand—brother had a mean high five—he had already disappeared into the sea of preteens throbbing to the beat. At which time I realized I was standing in the middle of the dance floor looking like a lonely loser, so I quickly scampered back to Sylvie.

"You know Ryan Bellsinger?" Her face and tone registered pure shock, but in a good way, not in a predator-caught-on-*Dateline* way.

"Um, yeah. New York's a small place. Well, I mean, it's a big place really, but a small place in terms of who you know." I was stumbling over my words, still in awky mode from how weirded out I was by Ryan's summer social status upgrade. "What's his deal? Is he like the Prince William of Timber Trails?"

"Pretty much."

I scratched my head. This place was so bizarro world.

And then the announcement came via megaphone that the dance was over. The bearded camp director yelled into his megaphone necklace, "Ladies and gentlemen—and you've all been gentlemen, correct?" Nods came from the crowd that not thirty seconds ago had been weaved together by their upper thighs. "Tonight's dance is over. Please find your counselors and head back to your bunks to rest up for another Timberrific day tomorrow." The enthusiasm in his voice would have been contagious if I didn't know he was talking about a day of bug bites, instructional swim, and some sport that involved getting bonked in the head.

Sylvie exhaled a loud sigh as the masses of campers migrated toward the door. "I guess this was a failure." She fingered the recently plucked middle-brow section. "Even with perfectly arched eyebrows, I'm probably not going to get Eli."

My heart broke hearing her say this. How could she possibly think that she had anything to do with tonight's Eli-free ending?

I rubbed her shoulder, trying to comfort her. "What are you talking about? Yeah, tonight wasn't the honey trap we thought it'd be, but that's not because of you at all. The failure is all me." The crowd pushed us to the door and we merged with the masses as we made our way back to the cabin. "I totally misjudged the situation. The boobalicious top and the gallons of makeup and the defrizzed hair aren't going to matter to Eli. He doesn't seem like that kind of guy. All we really need to make this happen is to get the two of you to spend more time together. Don't you think?"

She nodded, and we walked in silence until we reached the never-ending staircase that led to our summer holding cell. I prepared myself for some mild hyperventilation as Sylvie started bounding upward.

"Well, I guess that means that I can wear my retainer again, right?" She plucked it from her pocket, shoved it back into her mouth, and grinned.

I nodded as I huffed up the stairs behind her. "But still"— puff, puff—"no"—puff, puff, dry retching—"unibrow."

"Fine," she said lightly, happy with the trade-off. "How cute was Eli, though? He's like a little nutty professor—super smart, but no clue. You know, with his high black socks and jean shorts." I let her wax dorky the rest of the way up the stairs. And then along the path to the bunk. And as we entered the cabin. And as we changed into our sleeping gear.

Fifteen minutes later, with only a one-hundred-twenty-second pause to brush her teeth, Sylvie finally ended her supercrush monologue.

"Good night, Laney. Thank you for everything tonight. Even though I might have developed some sort of rash from the foundation," she said as she strapped on her headgear.

"You're welcome. Good night, Sylv," I said as Mandi clicked off the lights and left the bunk. Lying in bed, I went over the evening and smiled to myself in the dark, thinking back on what Ryan said about what was really important. Maybe camp did have its merits—and more than just weaning me off a nasty caffeine addiction.

Exhausted, I closed my eyes, ready for REM, but the other side of the bunk was in a full-force gossip frenzy.

"Seriously, what was *she* doing talking to Ryan Bellsinger?" Hayden whispered to her friends loudly enough not just for those two, but for Sylvie and me to hear without even straining.

"Yeah, I've been lusting after that hunk of hunk since like I was eight," Aiden answered, not at all whispering. To use the word *lust* when referring to your eight-year-old self was creepy in the most disturbing of ways.

"Ew, that's pedophilia," Aidan retorted. The fact that Aidan and I were on somewhat of the same thought pattern was highly worrisome.

I opened my eyes and looked over at Sylvie. Even in the dark, I could see through the opening in her orthodonture muzzle that she was smiling and choking back giggles.

"He's so hot, I don't even care if it's illegal."

"God, you're so slutty," Hayden yelled from her bed.

"Yeah, I'm slutty. Slutty like a fox," came Aiden's reply. I could feel vibrations coming from Sylvie's bed. She was trembling from holding back her laughter.

Hayden lowered her voice by about a tenth of a decibel and said, "And how could he like Laney when I was like standing on the other side of the rec hall dying to give him my number if he would just ask?"

Keep in mind, there was about three feet separating their conversation from the foot of my bed . . . and actually from my foot up their asses too.

"Your number? But you don't have a cell here," Aidan interjected.

"God, not everything I say is literal. That was, like, a metaphor. I just meant that I would totally hit dat."

Dat? When had Hayden switched places with Soulja Boy?

I guess Ryan's idea of camp bringing out the cool in everybody was limited to just the boys' side.

Ken,

You have to save me! Actually, I've made one friend, so it's getting a little better here. But it's still like Brokedown Palace (the prison part, not the vacation part). Like I'm not allowed to do anything but clean the toilets and play sports. And I'm pretty sure I've contracted malaria from all the bug bites I have. Chronic boredom is a symptom of malaria, right?

Oh, and at the camp dance (don't ask, because you'd vomit if I gave you any more details) I saw Ryan Bellsinger. He goes to camp here too. I was weirdly pumped to hang with him. That's probably another symptom of malaria, right?

Tell Diet Coke and air-conditioning that I miss them dearly.

> You know you miss me,
> Laney P.
> PS—Send pics of the NJ! I cannot wait to see!

Chapter 14

Aside from some occasional tweezing, my plan of turning Sylvie into Frankenbabe was off. As disappointing as I found that, I was still looking forward to watching this geek love grow. The only thing was, there wasn't much to watch.

I had tons of ideas for fun campy dates to send Eli and Sylvie on—paddling around the lake to the background of light opera music, cuddling up next to a bonfire while humming "Kumbaya," her trust-falling back into his waiting embrace. Wait, his one-hundred-two-pound frame probably wouldn't be able to support her, she'd come crashing down onto the rocky forest floor, there'd be major head trauma, and suddenly their date would be in the ER. And with an open head wound, I doubted frenching was a medically advisable activity. Scratch that plan.

Whatever. It didn't matter, because as much as I wanted to play matchmaker, we were still at camp and still barely ever seeing the boys. This complete lack of guy interaction was a major kink in my plan, and I needed to figure something out stat.

"Are you OK?" Sylvie asked, peeling off her shorts, about to head off to the side of the pool that was more than ankle deep.

I undazed from my matchmaker fantasies. "What? Oh, I mean, yeah. I'm OK. I'm great. It's instructional swim, my favorite hour of the day next to cleanup. Why wouldn't I be OK?" I stretched my lips into a big fake smile.

"That's my girl. Always with the winning attitude," she sassed back, and then walked over to her level-one-thousand swim group.

I trudged over to Mandi and the tots in level one.

"Oh good. Laney's here. So now we can set off," she said, pulling on a cuff of her obscenely short shorts. They were terry cloth; pink, obviously. And not like any fabric looks good when its stretched two sizes too small over a butt, but terry cloth, with its little loops stretched out and holding on for dear life, was especially offensive.

"Yeah, let's go!" Brandt cheered, and the rest of the boys exploded into a six-year-old ruckus, yelling taglines from cartoons and squealing. As much as I wanted to separate myself from these ankle-biting peepee machines, I was actually starting to like the little ones in my group. I still despised instructional swim with every ounce of my being, but you'd have to be Cruella De Vil to hate a bunch of six- and seven-year-olds.

"Go where?" The edge of the pool was all of five feet away, and these boys were way more excited than they normally were to splash around and practice holding their noses.

"Level-one field trip!" She said it with the unbridled enthusiasm you hear when you watch those suburban teen movies and a football player yells, "Keg stand!" "We're going to the lake for swim today!" I thought back to my last (and first) time on the lake with the canoes and sighed.

The boys reupped their freakout, cheering and fist-pumping, and Mandi herded them into a line and pied-piped us out of the pool area.

We marched past the higher groups on our way out the pool gates, and they all watched us. It was kind of like stomping it out on the catwalk with all those eyes on me, but like instead of haute couture, I was just showcasing a Speedo wedgie and my own sense of self-loathing. But, you know. Tomato, tomah-crying-myself-to-sleep, right?

"Oh look, all the water babies are heading to the lake. How cute!" Aiden yelled from the diving board down to Hayden and Aidan.

"Don't call them water babies," Hayden hollered back from the second rung of the diving board ladder. I thought she was going to defend her brother, but her point had nothing to do with familial piety. "Because we're like soooo many levels above them, that would make us like water grandmas."

Aidan, who was waiting her turn on the concrete

agreed. "Yeah, why don't you call them water fetuses? Then we'd at least be water MILFs."

And this maybe was a historic first: Hayden and I both rolled our eyes at the same thing. Then she swan-dove into the pool and I trudged away at the end of my water embryo pack out the gate and up the dirt path to the lake. I instantly felt better as soon as I had left the pool area and was off their evil radar.

"Fishies eat your toes in the lake," Brandt belted out. "Nibble, nibble, nibble."

My digits were going to be a fish meal? The relief of leaving the pool area vanished and I wished I were back in the chlorinated waters. I hustled to catch up to him. "Like piranhas? Or leeches? Are you telling me there are flesh-eating creatures in the lake?"

He nodded.

Despite the blazing heat of the midmorning sun, I felt goose bumps push their way up to my skin, and my guts felt like they all turned inside out. They couldn't really put us in a lake with carnivorous fish, could they? I mean, this was camp, not *Survivor*. Actually, when I gave that some thought, I realized that the only real difference between the two was that there was no cash prize at the end of camp.

The rest of the march to the lake, I was silent, too afraid to ask any more questions.

When we reached the water, Mandi wasted no time. "All right, boys and Laney, into the lake!"

I dragged my feet prepping to get water-ready. If the fear of the toe-biting fish wasn't enough to make me try to avoid the lake, the smell of the lake was. The odor was a totally rancid mix of New York–sewer fishiness and the thick, gross, sweet smell of the Dumpsters outside the Food Emporium.

Boating on it was bad enough, but actually submerging my body in it was vomitous to the max.

All of the boys raced into the large puddle of algae and slime Mandi was referring to as the lake. "*Errybody in the lake get swimmin'*," she rapped, and then giggled. 50 Cent was probably rolling in his grave. Wait, was he one of the dead ones or not?

"Seriously, Mandi. I think I need to sit this one out," I whined, saber-toothed goldfish swimming in my imagination. I was going to have to fake some sort of medical issuse to get out of this.

But Mandi called my bluff before I could even open my mouth to start it. "Honey, is it lady problems? I'm starting to think that something's going around the bunk. Have you all been sharing bathing suits or something? I want you to see the nurse."

I'd heard stories about the nurse. Apparently, she was so old that back when she went to school I'd bet they were teaching leeching as a medical procedure. Going to her would totally defeat the point of sitting out, so I gave up.

"No, not lady problems. I'm fine." I sighed, then stomped my neon green Speedo into the icy stink puddle and paddled myself toward the group of boys who were already treading water a few feet out. If I didn't make it back alive, I was totally going to kill my mom for sending me here. God, I wasn't even making sense.

Brandt hollered loudly enough for me to hear over their splashing, "We all made the lake warmer for you!"

I wasn't sure what he meant until I got closer to the gaggle of splashing boys and the water around me suddenly became more tolerable and then even warm.

"Wow, you guys really did turn the water warm. How'd you do it?" I asked, honestly amazed at how they could make the lake feel like a heated pool and kind of touched that they would do something like this for me.

"We all peed!" Brandt shrieked.

Suddenly, I found myself wondering what temperature vomit would turn the water.

"Would you hurry up?" I had to practically drag Sylvie back to the bunk post–instructional swim. "Why are you moving so slowly?" I was so anxious to get my hustle on, I hadn't even taken the time to dry off the fishy urine water. When I cocked my head to give her a wide-eyed "hurry your hiney" look, drips from my hair splashed onto her. I should have felt bad about the diseased water getting on her, but I was too focused on rushing.

"Me, slow? You, hyped to do something at camp?" She stopped in the middle of the path. "What's wrong with you?" She gasped. "Did you swipe some of Mandi's caffeine pills? Is that why you're in Energizer Bunny mode?" Stopping for questions—this was completely unacceptable.

I grabbed her hand and yanked her down the path. "No! But nice to know you'd think that I'd swipe scrips." She tilted her head to the side and gave me a look. "OK, yeah, fine. Shopping in medicine cabinets is totally something my friends have done, but never me. I'm totally against that stuff. And of course that's not what's going on now. I want us to rush up so we can rush back down super fast. If we're early enough, don't you think there's a chance we could catch the boys before they head into their side of the mess hall for lunch? I mean, we have to try something to get you time with Eli."

I was sure I wasn't the only girl at camp who had figured out this trick. Though considering that Sylvie was clueless and the Billboards had the critical thinking skills of a pet rock, maybe I was. By the time we had reached the staircase to the bunk, Sylvie was struggling to keep up with me. I galloped up the steps two at a time, yanking her by the hand behind me.

"Who knew you could move like this? Why didn't you show this kind of hustle when I picked you for my team in softball?" she panted.

"I only exert this kind of energy when we're talking about rounding a different set of bases." I winked and then rolled my eyes at myself. That was such a creepy uncle thing to say.

"I don't know whether I should be grateful or grossed out, but I'm going with it." She continued her ascent a few steps behind me.

When we reached the top, I wanted to do a *Rocky* celebration dance, but the stopwatch of love would not allow for that.

We ran into the bunk and threw our wet towels down.

"OK, ready?" I commanded more than asked. If we were going to make this casual rendezvous happen, we only had time to turn around and hightail it back out there.

"You don't want to shower the lake stank off?" She sat down on her bed to change her shoes. Leisurely, I might add.

I took a whiff of my skin and recoiled at my own stench.

"No, we don't have time. Let's go. And forget the shoes. Your soccer cleats are fine."

She was eyeing me with that overconcerned look the families on *Intervention* always have when they're talking about the addict. "I'm really worried about you and I'm really not wearing my soccer cleats to lunch," Sylvie said.

Since when did she care about footwear fashion? I stood, tapping my foot while Sylvie unlaced her shoes and stepped into some water sandals. She got up slowly. "Now I'm ready, Herbie Fully Loaded. Take me wherever you're so set on going." Again I took her by the hand and dragged her out of the bunk.

We flew down the stairs and ran to the field near the mess hall where the early birds congregated before the meal bell rang. I was winded when I arrived. I'm pretty sure I hadn't worked out that hard since the one time last year when Kennedy made me go to the gym with her. She set my treadmill to 8.0 mph and thought that her cheering me on would be enough to get me to run that fast. I wound up hitting the emergency stop after three minutes and running at about 10.3 mph to the bathroom to puke. I've sworn off cardio and voluntary sweating ever since.

"Well, look who's excited for lunch." Ryan walked toward us, Eli by his side.

Perfect! The plan was working! This made the fact that I still smelled like a smoked salmon platter almost worth it.

"Yeah." I shrugged. "I have a thing for chicken nuggets with the middle still frozen, so I dragged Sylvie with me so we would be first at the table. I didn't want to chance them defrosting." I casually moved my eye contact over to Eli. "I'm not sure that we've met. I'm Laney Parker. It's my first year at Timber." I stuck my hand out for the shaking, excited to finally meet the guy I'd been aiding and abetting an obsession of.

"A pleasure to make your acquaintance, Laney Parker."

His voice was nasally and squeaky. "You'll have to excuse me, though, from shaking your hand. I'm a little congested and I'm not sure if it's from allergies or a summer cold. So just want to play it safe to make sure I don't infect you. That would not be the beginning of a beautiful friendship."

Sylvie chuckled, and I seized this perfect geek opportunity.

"Sylv, don't you have allergies? I wonder if you two are allergic to the same things?" Wait—what was I thinking? I mean, was there a worse topic of conversation to initiate flirting? Maybe bringing up my mom's hysterectomy.

"Well, should we start with the pet danders and see where we match up?" Eli already had his fingers out to count the things he was allergic to. "Mammals: Dogs, cats, gerbils . . ."

I looked at Ryan and mouthed a silent "Wow!" He nodded and then took a step to the side. I followed him, inching myself over to give the two lovebirds some space. Though I probably shouldn't call them birds. I'm sure Eli was about to list feathers as an allergy.

"So . . ." I craned my neck to look Ryan in the eye. I'd never realized how tall he was. Although, I guess I never wore flats in the real world. I'd also never realized how nervous I got when I talked to him. Although, I guess I never really talked to him in the real world.

"So," he responded, running his fingers through his messy brown waves.

"Um." I was fumbling for conversation topics. Back to the meeting-new-people and making-new-friends skills I totally lacked from being in my bubble of beautiful people for too long. Ryan wasn't technically new, but he was definitely not a real friend yet. And I wasn't sure how to even start down that path. "What are *your* allergies?" Ugh, seriously? Why did I lead with that? I couldn't have felt more like a doofus.

He paused for a second, and his mouth twitched into a shy smile. It was actually kind of cute. "Don't really have any. Are you OK here? Camp can be brutal when you're new. Especially at your age."

My age? What the crap did that mean? I was fifteen, not a freaking Golden Girl. Before I let myself get all oh-no-you-didn't on him, I saw that smile and realized that he really was just checking on how I was doing in an uncomfortable scene. Way nicer than letting me sit in the corner and eat baby carrots and bean dip . . . metaphorically speaking. Of course, I'd have been all over the bean dip if there were any.

"It hasn't been easy. Thank God for Sylv. Without her, I don't know how I'd deal. I'd probably spend all my time trying to break out. Like a female Wentworth Miller."

"Would you get the body tattoos for the full *Prison Break* effect?" he asked, his eyes crinkling with amusement.

Finally! A normal conversation flow.

"Obvs. My escape strategy would be to plunder all the supplies in the arts and crafts shed, either tatt myself crazy or maybe brand myself with some gimp inlay or something, and then head out into the great naturey yonder and walk until I hit Park and Eightieth."

It actually wasn't the worst plan in the world. I silently contemplated the possibility of it being successful.

He nodded in assent. "Quite the plan." And then he put his hand on my shoulder, which surprised me. What surprised me even more was that I didn't mind it at all. "You have Sylvie, which is great, but know that now you also have me. So if you need anything, try and find me before you start welding craft supplies to your extremities, OK?"

"OK," I agreed through a soft giggle. "That's really nice of you, Ryan." His hand was heavy on my shoulder, and warm too, even compared to the heat of the noon sun. It shocked me how much I liked being touched by him. I was also shocked by how much I was crotch sweating in the acrylic fabrics of my bathing suit and shorts, but that's neither here nor there.

Then the bell rang, announcing that the tasteless industrial-quantity meals were about to hit the sticky tables.

"Hey, Eli, let's go, man. I want to get a good seat." Ryan dropped his hand off my shoulder and I missed it the second it was gone. Eli waved bye to Sylvie and the guys started off toward the boys' entrance to the mess hall.

"Bye, Laney." Ryan waved.

"Bye, Ryan! I liked your hand on my shoulder." What? Why did I say that out loud? And why was there suddenly no filter between my brain and my mouth? "I mean, just bye, Ryan. Not the last part."

Thank Jesus, Allah, Buddha, and summertime breaks from Ritalin that Brandt and his posse came hurtling toward the mess hall just then, yelling like a tribe on the warpath off to battle their frozen meals. Their noise blocked my blurted confession from even hitting Ryan's ears.

Sylvie gave me a friendly nudge and I stumbled a step.

"Um, what was that, Captain Creepy?" she asked as we walked toward the mess hall. Apparently, she had managed to hear through the When ADD Attacks reenactment.

"Oh nothing. I mean, like I just said it." I was a runaway

train of nervous rambling. There was no stopping me. "I didn't mean it at all. It just came out. I wasn't even thinking it before. Plus it's an inside joke. A New York thing. Yeah, that's just something everyone says to each other in New York. No big deal. Let's not talk about it anymore. As in never again." How could Ryan "Fag Face" Bellsinger be riling me into this bumbling blabbermouth? "Let's talk about you. How did things go with Eli?" I spit out, obviously eager to switch subjects.

"Methinks she doth protest too much." She elbowed me a little to let me know she was kidding.

Before Sylvie could mock me anymore, Hayden poked her head into our conversation. "Yeah, methinks that too." She must have been walking behind us for a few minutes before wedging her greasy face between us. "Wait, 'doth protest' means 'wears ugly clothes,' right?"

I rolled my eyes. "Methinks you should invest in some Proactiv." I heard myself say it before I'd really even thought it. I guess this bout of not being able to filter myself had its ups. I mentally high-fived myself.

＊ ＊ ＊ ＊ ＊ ＊ ＊ ＊ ＊ ＊ ＊

How's my Laneybelle? Camp looks wonderful
from the pictures they post on their Web site. Did you
know that they do that? Post pictures of all of the
campers to a blog the parents subscribe to? That's right,
your mother reads a blog now! Very neat, huh? There
have only been a few pictures of you so far, though. In
one it looked like you had the word FART written on
your tush!?! Did you run out of the outfits I packed
you? Need me to send more? Just send the word and I'll
send the skorts!

Mark sends his love. We're off to a weekend yoga
retreat in Hudson, so if you don't hear from me by next
week, send help. I could have gotten stuck in compass
pose! LOL (laugh out loud) as they say, right?

Sending love and light your way,
Mom

＊ ＊ ＊ ＊ ＊ ＊ ＊ ＊ ＊ ＊ ＊

Chapter 15

"Are you up, Laney?" Mandi's sugary voice was booming from not even two feet above my head.

I rolled over, further burritoing myself into my blankets. "I very clearly said no when you yelled into my ear six minutes ago. Nothing has changed." Why do mornings even exist? No one really likes them.

Her flip-flopped foot slapped the floor. "Come on, it's the Fourth of July. Today's going to be so fun."

I lay as still as I could, playing dead in my bed, hoping she'd lose interest and find another sleeping camper to torment.

"There's no instructional swim today," she added, trying to tease me out from my covers.

I didn't know that underwater anguish followed the bank holiday schedule, but it was certainly a pleasant surprise. And enough to get me out of bed.

"Fine," I said, curling myself up into a seated position. "I'm up."

"She's aliiive!" Mandi stuck her arms out and zombie-walked herself into the bathroom. I couldn't decide if being half asleep made Mandi's impressions more or less painful.

I groggily oriented myself to my surroundings and noticed that Sylvie, who was already brushed, washed, and dressed, was sitting on the foot of my bed.

"And today's not just about no instructional swim." Her face broke into a smug smile.

"I know, I know. It's a day to celebrate our freedom. *'There ain't no doubt I love this land. God bless the USA and yaddah yaddah stand up next to you,'* I know." I made a move to exit my cocoon of warm goodness.

Sylvie waved her hand in front of her face. "OK, that can't be morning breath. Did you swallow a dying carcass or some sort of landfill before bed last night?" I puffed quickly into my hand and inhaled. I was almost knocked back into bed by my own rancidness. Over my gags I heard her continue on. "Anyway, I wasn't talking about any star-spangled pride, I was talking about boys. Tonight there are fireworks and we watch them with the boys."

OK, today was officially the best day of my summer so far and I hadn't even been awake for three minutes.

"Well, *that* really is something to celebrate." Suddenly, getting out of bed didn't seem difficult at all. I jumped out.

"All right," I said, standing hands on hips. I was totally enthused now, but was whispering so I wouldn't blow any of my fire breath near her. "We clearly need to spend all day obsessing and plotting. What does your schedule look like?"

She mimed thumb-rolling through a BlackBerry. "Well, I have a lunch appointment and then something this afterno— You know what? That can all be moved around. I'll have my assistant take care of it. So I'm free. Let the obsessing begin."

I laughed. "Great. Actually, wait, let me brush my teeth and then let's commence the unhealthy obsessing, plotting, and general behavior that typically leads to restraining orders."

She nodded in agreement and sat on her bed Sudokuing as I frantically ran around, trying to get ready and dressed as quickly as possible so Mandi wouldn't push me out of the bunk for breakfast before I could even slip on my elastic-waist shorts.

I managed to beat the Mandi timer and leave the bunk of my own volition and completely clothed.

I thumped down the staircase. "I can't wait for the class-action lawsuit against Timber when we all sue for reimbursement and emotional trauma involved in the arthroscopic knee surgery we're going to need from these freaking stairs."

"When did my best friend at camp turn into my grandmother?" Sylvie asked, laughing as we treaded off the final step.

It took a second to register what she had just said, and when I did, I was genuinely touched . . . by the "best friend" part, not the "grandmother" part.

"Best friend? Aww, I'm flattered." I said it like I was joking, but I really meant it.

"Best, only. Kind of interchangeable at this juncture in the summer," she clarified. I laughed and nodded. So true. And so sad. Sylvie continued, "All right, let's get back to planning for tonight. Do you think he's going to kiss me? I've never kissed a boy. Should we practice? I mean, not on each other. On a pillow. That's what they always do in Judy Blume books."

I could tell she was getting nervous from how quickly she was talking all of a sudden. But nerves or not, I was not having her tongue a down pillow.

"Deep breath," I commanded, and waited for her to exhale. "OK, first of all, does your library exist in a time warp or are you just reading all of your mom's books? Because learning how to kiss on a pillow is about as effective as learning how to act by watching *What I Like About You*. I promise, you'll know what to do when the time comes." She nodded with intensity. It reminded me of how I nod when I'm super into a lesson a teacher is giving. It felt like Sylvie should be taking notes. And then I laughed, imagining what the notes would look like.

Kissing pillows
   Not as helpful as most out-of-date teen lit would lead you to believe.
Jennie Garth
   Not talented
   Should have left her career where it belonged, in the nineties.

I was still half giggling when we arrived at our bunk's table. As I pulled out my plastic chair to sit, Hayden attacked. "What's so funny, Laney?" Technically, this was a normal question. But the way she spat it at me, you would have thought she was saying, "Why did you torture and then senselessly kill my two-day-old puppy, Laney?"

"Nothing's funny, Hayden. And it's definitely not your sad attempt at a french braid, if that's what you're worried about." I didn't know where my bitch-factor delta force was coming from. Maybe having an officially announced best/only friend at camp was building my confidence back up. And I guess by confidence I meant ability to throw down. Same diff, right?

Post–breakfast smackdown, the rest of the day was surprisingly normal. Well, I guess it wasn't *totally* normal, as without instructional swim, my lungs weren't waterlogged and my self-esteem wasn't pummeled by eleven a.m. But we still did a ton of activities.

In arts and crafts we made these brooches out of a dozen safety pins and seed beads that were supposed to look like an American flag. After nearly an hour of accidentally pricking myself and enough cussing to qualify me as a contestant in *Flavor of Love 4*, all I had to show was three beads on a safety pin that I couldn't manage to close. I looked around at all the other girls in my bunk. Even Aidan, who IQed at somewhere below your average houseplant, had managed to pin together a beaded flag. I found myself wondering how someone who aced trig without breaking a sweat could not figure out how to do a craft project intended for a nine-year-old. I guess getting through a day with my self-esteem intact was too much to ask around this place.

Later in the afternoon, we played a game of soccer against another girls' bunk. The shirtless (and apparently brainless) soccer counselor split us into teams.

"All right, all right. You guys"—he pointed to the other bunk—"can be the Indians. And let's call you guys"—now he was gesturing toward us—"Columbus and His Merry Men. Special team names. You know, for Independence Day."

Sylvie and I looked at each other, somehow managing not to crack up. You didn't need to take AP American history to know that this guy must have been high since potty training to not know the story of the Fourth of July.

By dinnertime, the entire female population of Timber had worked themselves into a lather of nerves and tension over the impending coed activities of the evening. And I was definitely part of the tizzy. I couldn't help but get amped for Sylvie's night to come. Conversations were stilted, minds wandered, anxious perspiration was at an all-time high. OK, maybe that last one was just me and maybe I forgot the deodorant postshower. But still, you get the picture. The mess hall emanated stress. The actual meal was just as gross as always—a mélange of meat scraps, cream of bland soup, and noodles served by the ladleful—but I found myself even more disgusted than usual. The girls were all on the freak because we were going to be mingling with the boys tonight. Now I understood why the dance was a last-minute announcement. If we'd been given any more time than that to think about it, the infirmary would need more than just a nurse, it would need a psychiatrist with a pad of Xanax prescriptions. The sex separation might prevent a teen pregnancy outbreak, but mental breaks, I think it could actually cause them.

I stuffed as much of the roast into my stomach as my gag reflex would permit and then leaned back in my chair and turned to Sylvie.

"So are there going to be fireworks tonight or what?" I thought I was just asking Sylvie, but apparently not.

"You mean between Ryan Bellsinger and me? Yes," Hayden said, inserting herself into the conversation.

"No, that's not at all what I mean, Hayden." I mushed my leftovers with my fork.

"Yeah, H. She probably meant with me," Aidan said as she reached into her shirt and adjusted whatever combination of crepe paper and newsprint she'd papier-mâchéd into lumpy falsies. O arts and crafts shed, you supply the stuff of miracles. "Ryan's so into me."

I rolled my eyes.

"Nope. I actually meant *literal* fireworks."

"Oh," one of the three sighed—I couldn't decipher whose animal sound was whose—then the table went silent, all probably in Ryan-induced daydreams. Camp was like Ryan's second life. Like when those gaming geeks make these slamming avatars that dress cool and are good at sports and don't look like the kind of people who understand binary code. He'd totally re-created himself here. He was cuter and more popular and cooler. I had to admit that even I was a little under his spell.

The static of the microphone turning on cut through the mess hall, and the camp director's amplified throat-clearing interrupted the Ryan Bellsinger three-way fantasy going on across the table. "Attention, attention, all Timber Trailers." Bizarro Santa waited for the mess hall to silence itself. "First of all, Happy Fourth of July to you and yours. And second of all, as you know, we're planning fireworks for this evening. And don't worry, we have a fire marshal standing by. So things'll go more smoothly this year than last. You know how the expression goes, start a forest fire once, shame on you, start a forest fire twice, you get imprisoned for arson." He laughed, although it sounded more like a judicial warning than a joke. "So I'll excuse you all back to your bunks—"

I saw his mouth continue moving, but whatever he was saying was just a gurgle under the sonic booming of chairs scraping back and the stampeding of flip-flops out the door. The rush to get prepped for a coed activity was more intense than the running of the bulls. And probably more likely to trample an innocent bystander. Even though I wasn't quite as manic as the rest of the Timber gals, I was still totally part of the boy-crazy frenzy.

But because I was slightly distracted trying to come up with puns on Independence Day, like In Da Pants Day, for Sylvie's big night, the two of us were moving at less than a full sprint on our way out of the mess hall. So of course we were the last to arrive at the bunk. The trio and Mandi were already in prep mode. And it was nice to see the patriotism the gang was displaying. They were all dressing in red, white, and body glitter—the cosmetic of freedom.

I sat on my bed, grabbed a sweatshirt from my cubby, and balled it up to take with me to the fireworks. That was pretty much all the prepping I was planning on for this holiday. As much as I would have loved to give Sylvie another hot-tastic makeover, Eli was not the kind of guy who cared about looks or ill-fitting overalls. So I kept my mouth shut about incor-porating leave-in conditioner and an eyelash curler into her daily regimen, even though they would have made a world of difference. My mission was really to just get them to spend time together. And I had to keep my eyes on the prize, not on her frizz.

Hayden called out to her cohorts, much louder than necessary, but she was under the blow-dryer and couldn't gauge the volume of her own voice. "Hey, A-squared."

I was actually very impressed that she understood the concept of exponents. I looked over to see if she was reading off some sort of algebra cheat sheet and saw that she was bent over, blow-drying the underside of her hair. I think she was trying to straighten her mop of grease and tangles, but all she was really doing was frizzifying it. If only she hadn't been such a bitchface to me, I could have rocked her world by introducing her to a round brush.

"I've got an awesome idea," she belted across the bunk.

"Stuffing our bras with pudding in Ziploc baggies?" Aidan screamed her guess with enthusiasm.

"What?" Hayden clicked off her dryer.

"Do you want to put pudding in our bras to make our boobs look bigger?" Aidan said, more slowly this time so her friend could hear.

"Um, no," Hayden spit back at her.

Was it wrong that this conversation wasn't grossing me out but making me a little hungry?

"Yeah, I didn't think so," Aidan said, clearly embarrassed. "I just said it. Twice. I mean, I didn't really think it. Or I did think it, but only before I said it, not after." Her babbling continued until Hayden cut her off.

"How about we change our outfits so the bunk is dressed exactly alike tonight?" Even though the hair dryer was off, she was still shouting. The whole bunk and probably the bunks on either side of us could hear her loud and clear.

The Aide/ans loved the idea and expressed this with high-pitched screaming. I wasn't sure why they were so pumped about this. I thought they dressed the same every single day. I must not get the nuances of butt shorts.

"Sure." Wait, was that Sylvie's voice? I turned around and confirmed that it was indeed my best—fine, only—camp friend sororitizing with the enemy. "How about we all wear sweats or something comfortable?" It had to be a sudden onset of amnesia, right? There was no way she could have remembered where she was and who she was talking to.

The Den/Dan Clan took it upon themselves to snap her out of it. "By 'the whole bunk,' I meant"—Hayden pointed to her fellow clique members—"us. Definitely not you girls."

I could see Sylvie's face melting into a frown. And while a full-on makeover had clearly been proven unnecessary for wooing her man-caller of choice, an undamaged self-esteem was still crucial. It's a fact that nothing is sexier than a woman with a sense of self. And nothing is more repulsive than self-loathing. Well, a body odor problem probably is, but let's stick to the topic at hand, shall we?

Hayden's slam was like my Bat signal. And even though I was completely baffled by why Sylvie had taken a dip in enemy waters, I knew it was my duty to rescue her. So I threw on a figurative cape and swooped in for the save. "Good one, Sylv!" I laughed and held up my hand for a high five. She slapped me back, slowly and completely confused. "You totally had them believing that we would want to dress like them. I mean, the butt labeling? Puh-leeze. The only labels we wear are designer, and they're on the *inside* of our clothes." I stood with my hand on my hip, trying my best to look fearless and heroic.

It was only after the rant that I realized how ridiculous I sounded talking about Sylvie's and my designer clothing. She was sitting on her bed in a pair of those pants that you can zip off into shorts. I was standing above her trying to exude Tyra amounts of confidence in my orange shorts, which I'd cuffed up to display their pink lining—the extra color felt festive for the holiday.

Hayden et al didn't seem to notice our pot-calling-the-kettle factor. We got a stammered "Yeah, well, um, well, whatever" and then a cold shoulder. But I did see Hayden slip off her HOTTIE butt shorts and put on a butt-free—well, a butt-*slogan*-free—pair before we left the bunk.

"You OK?" I joined Sylvie on her cot, the scanty piece of foam and tin foil bending under our weight.

"Yeah, I don't know what I was thinking," she said, sounding totally dejected. She shook her head and her glasses rattled a little.

"I know what you were thinking about," I singsonged like a first grader on the playground, trying to cheer her up. Then I twisted around and hugged my hands around my back so I looked like I was making out and whispered softly enough that team evil couldn't hear, "Oh, Eli! You know what they say about a man with a big inhaler, don't you? I love the musky smell of your allergen-free bug spray. Is it just me or are your glasses fogging up?"

"That's it. I'm letting you drown next time you fall out of the canoe." She crossed her arms and managed to act stuffy and indignant for all of point eight seconds before joining me in a giggle fit.

"Seriously, though, what were you thinking when you wanted to join forces with the wicked witches of the other side of the bunk?" I asked, thoroughly confused.

She sighed and opened her eyes wide to show how shocked she was herself. "I have no idea." A second went by as she contemplated her actions. I sat quietly, letting her think. "I guess I was kind of flashing back to home. Like on my field hockey team, we always dress the same for school on a game day, and when I heard Hayden ask, I totally just reflex responded like when my captain asks that question after practice. So weird."

"Yeah." I nodded, taking in her explanation. "Weird that you just replied like that without thinking. And even weirder that you wear sweatpants to school."

She laughed, but I was totally for real.

"Everyone in America wears sweatpants to school occasionally. You and your *Project Runway* High are the anomaly."

I crinkled my nose at the thought, but agreed to disagree. And it was the perfect time to end the convo, because Mandi was ushering us out of the bunk with her usual sense of urgency.

"Hurry, hurry," she cheered as she corralled us through the door. "We don't want to miss a second of the Fourth of July–evening fun!"

As soon as we set foot into the clearing in the woods, I heard a loud "Laney, Laney, over here!" and saw Ryan waving his hands. I was relieved to see him right away, because I thought with so many people and so much darkness, there was a chance I could have wasted the entire night trying to find those boys. I started to run to him, total Celine-Dion-music-video style with open arms and my hair billowing in the background and a white lacy dress and a meadow of flowers between us—OK, totally not like that, but that was kind of how I envisioned myself as I tried to push through my fellow campers. I barely made it three steps into my soft-rock delusion when Mandi put her arm out like a closing gate in front of me.

"Girls to the left and boys to the right." She gestured like a flight attendant pointing out the emergency exits.

Well, this was a literal roadblock on the path of summer love.

"But I want to say hi to my Ryan. I mean, not *my* Ryan. My *friend* Ryan. My *just-friend* Ryan." Why was I awkying out in front of Mandi?

Her face was completely devoid of sympathy for me or my sudden bout of social anxiety. "Your Ryan is just going to have to wait until the next dance to say hi. Girls to this side and boys to that side," she commanded. I hated when Mandi got like this. It was like she had two modes—cheerleader Mandi and RoboBitch Mandi—and she switched from one to the other the second you pushed back on her. And I might not have learned the breaststroke during my torturous hours of instructional swim, but I had learned not to fight with RoboBitch Mandi. You never won.

I glumly made my way back to the line and started the trudge to our bunk's designated bench. Again Ryan yelled out my name. I turned, about to yell back that I wasn't allowed to talk to him, but then saw that he was doing a complicated series of hand motions. It was like air-traffic control meets the hokey-pokey.

I had no idea what he wanted and threw up my arms, palms up, in the international sign for "WTF?"

Sylvie leaned over and whispered, "He's trying to tell you to get me to sit on the inside end of our bench and he'll get Eli to sit on the inside end of his bench and aside from a gaping aisle, it'll be like Eli and I are sitting next to each other."

"You got all that from the hand jive?" I was astonished, but still proceeded with the plan, shuffling in front of the Billboard Butts and squeezing our tushies onto the end of the bench. Ryan did the same thing with his romance protégé, and the couple was nearly sitting next to each other. Circumstances considered, this was a success.

Mandi had apparently been watching the entire sign-language exchange. She came over and stood next to Sylvie, blocking whatever chance she had of talking to or even looking at Eli. I couldn't freaking believe it. Even for Robo-Bitch, this was obscenely nasty. "What a perfect place to see the fireworks!" she said, widening her stance and digging in for the remainder of the evening. I wanted to scream, I was so frustrated with my foiled plan. But that would have probably just stirred the beast even more, so I just stewed.

Before I could snark something into Sylvie's ear about the lockdown-level anti-coed security, the first crack of the fireworks exploded. I looked up to see a small spark in the sky. For the next five minutes, a series of pops and bangs sounded, but not much of anything burst in midair.

"Is this it?" I asked Sylvie.

She nodded, her eyes rolling.

Honestly, the time Conrad tried to light one of his farts on fire—yes, this was who I could potentially be best-friend-in-laws with in about ten short years—and just wound up burning a hole in his Sevens was a more spectacular show than this display of patriotism and blatant disregard for forest-fire regulations.

To Whom It May Concern (cough, cough, MOM):

Please unsubscribe me from your mailings pertaining to sending me more skorts. Know that I interpret these skorts offers as threats and find them offensive. If I receive any further offers, I will be reporting you to the system administrator.

Thanks in advance for your compliance,
Your estranged daughter

Chapter 16

"OK, so what's our next opportunity for some coed contact?" I asked as we clomped down the staircase on our way to the mess hall for lunch. "The Fourth wasn't exactly your opportunity for under-the-fireworks frenching or anything. We've gotta make it happen next time."

The counselor intervention had been devastating, but I wasn't discouraged. With another shot, we could totally make the love match happen.

"I don't know when next time will be," Sylvie said, sounding a bit concerned.

I stopped walking and looked her in the eyes, getting concerned myself.

"What do you mean? Isn't there something coming up? Like a square dance or a campwide butter-churning contest or some sort of bi-gendered stick-whittling jamboree or something?"

"You know that we're at camp, not Magic Kingdom's Frontierland, right?" I rolled my eyes at her sass. "And I really don't know. You heard that those thirteen-year-olds got caught sneaking over to the boys' side of camp last night. Sometimes they punish us all when crap like that happens and cancel dances and stuff."

We'd started walking again, but I was in panic mode now. Stressing and obsessing over Sylvie's crush life was the only part of camp that I actually enjoyed. Not to get too dramatic here, but I'd have had no reason to get up in the morning without the Sylvie/Eli love connection. OK, I just got too dramatic. But still, without that, a huge chunk would have been taken out of an already minuscule piece of my summer that I was enjoying. I was seriously pissed at the thirteen-year-olds' bunk.

"Ugh, are we the thirteen-year-olds' keepers? I think not. Why are we suffering for their bad behavior?" I whined.

"Bad behavior *and* stupidity," Sylvie added. "I mean, I'm no expert, but I would know to take my headlamp off while I was making out with a guy. Unless you're a miner, it would be a total mood killer. Plus, it's so obvious that you would get caught."

I almost stopped in my tracks again. "That did not seriously happen."

"Yeah, it did." She nodded furiously, her frizz bouncing

everywhere. "A girl in my swim group told me. Well, I kind of just overheard her telling her friend, but whatever, it for sure happened. Apparently, one of the twelve-year-old boys in the next bunk over saw the light bobbing up and down and using his deductive naturing skills thought he was getting flashed an SOS. So he rang his bunk's emergency bell, which of course triggered every bunk to ring their emergency bell. The two were caught by just about every counselor in the entire camp, all of whom arrived en masse to apply CPR. And then the most horrifying part is that the girl had to give an incredibly detailed account of the macking to the camp director and then call her parents and tell them what happened."

As awful and scarring as I was sure the whole parental play-by-play had been, I was still a smidge jealous that she got to use a phone.

"How could they be doing this to me?"

"Who's doing what to you?" a deep, smooth voice said from behind me.

I whipped my head around, almost blinding myself with my chlorine and perspiration dreads. "Oh, Ryan, hi." Immediately, my heart rate doubled. Then his lips curled into a completely cute smile and my heart's thumping picked up to about a million miles an hour. "I was just saying that I hoped the cross-gender bunk raid wouldn't mean that we couldn't see each other. We meaning Sylvie and me seeing Eli and you, obviously. Not just you and me. Weird that it sounded like that at first, right?" I took a big, audible gulp and swallowed about a pint of air that would probably come up as an embarrassing burp in a few short seconds.

"Nah, I don't think that'll happen. Plus, you're seeing us

now." He took a pause and looked at me with his dark brown eyes. "And by us, I do just mean me now. Eli was taking forever getting ready. Something about his boxers getting caught in his zipper and I was starving, but now, this." He pointed toward the mess hall and I saw the cluster of campers outside it.

"What's going on over there?" Sylvie asked, inserting herself into the convo.

"Yeah, is the mess hall giving out, like, um," I started, and then I stuttered for a bit. At least I couldn't blame this case of verbal malfunction on my Ryan-induced awkwardness. I just honestly couldn't think of one freaking thing the mess hall could be doling out that anyone, let alone a mob of anyones, would be interested in.

After I puttered out, Ryan jumped in. "There's like some sort of infestation in the kitchen and they said it's going to be fifteen minutes until it's cleaned up."

"What infestation only takes fifteen minutes to clean up?" I asked, feeling my stomach turn and knowing that my face was probably going a little green.

"Don't ask," both Sylvie and Ryan said. We stood silent for a few seconds, me trying to think of ways to get the Department of Health in to inspect this place and them probably thinking of some way to distract me.

Finally, Ryan broke the silence. "There's Eli!" he said as Eli approached the group. "Yo, man, you get your dick unstuck from your zipper?"

Eli shook his head. "This guy's hilarious." Eli pointed at Ryan and continued, "Give him a microphone and his own HBO special. Really, I feel guilty that we're the only ones getting to enjoy his genius sense of humor right now."

Geeky? Yes. Shit taker? No sir. I liked it. Ryan was so right—cool didn't really count for cool.

And furthering the point of Eli being the total anticool, I took a look at his shirt. It had a heavily orthodontured smile silk-screened on it and the words THE TIN GRIN IS IN in big bubble letters. If the letters had spelled out SYLVIE'S SOUL MATE, the shirt wouldn't have been a better indication of how made for each other those two were.

"Sweet shirt, Eli. You know, Sylvie has a pretty major headgear set that she sleeps in," I offered. In any other situation, this would be the equivalent of mentioning that she still had a peepee-guard sheet on her bed, but with Sylvie and Eli, I knew that dentalwear talk would be more romantic than candlelight and Joshua Radin—yes, I think his music is sexy and I'm not embarrassed to admit it. Well, not *that* embarrassed.

Sylvie switched her weight from one foot to another. "I do. I got it tightened before camp, which was killer, but now it's not that bad," she started in on her sweet-talking.

Ryan and I just stood by, mute, as they discussed the finer points of bite plates. I tried to think of something to say to him that wasn't related to Sylvie and Eli, but I couldn't come up with anything. I just stood there, arms swinging and tongue tied, until the bell announcing that whatever alien or insect that had invaded the mess hall had been eliminated.

"Well, I guess that means we have to say bye, guys," Sylvie said for the both of us, as I was still mute.

"Bye!" Eli said, and Ryan waved.

Then we split up to head to our separate entrances.

I continued my silence as we walked. "Is something wrong?" Sylvie asked, genuine concern in her tone.

I thought for a second. Something definitely didn't feel right, so I guessed that meant something was wrong.

"I don't know. I mean, I feel like I'm not myself around Ryan. And it's so weird. Like just then, I couldn't think of a single thing to say to him. And I've known him for practically my whole life and so there's no reason for this to be happening now."

"I can think of a reason." Sylvie eyed me slyly.

"Seriously, what is it? This needs to stop."

And I don't know what I was expecting her to say, because the options were limited. Either it was some weird spell that Hayden had managed to voodoo on me, or . . .

"You like Ryan."

"Do not!" I shrieked at the thought.

"OK, let's not get too fifth grade here, but you do too. It's obvious. The nervousness, the superinterest in seeing the boys, the stuttering. If we were in school and not at camp, you'd be writing his name in hearts on your notebook." She raised her eyebrows, impressed with her own diagnosis. "And I don't want to get cocky here, but I feel like maybe this student of love has become the teacher."

I wanted to yell "Do not!" again, but at this point we were sitting at our lunch table, surrounded by our bunk, and drawing attention to that convo topic would have been a really stupid move.

So I sat all through lunch nibbling on my cicada-n-rat quesadilla and stewing over this alleged crush . . . which was so not true. I mean, what was there to crush on? He was Ryan "Pity Invite" Bellsinger back in New York and I was Laney "Regular Invite" Parker. I mean, yeah, he was really nice and charming and super smart and witty. But Ryan? I don't know. It would be the story of the century back home.

I could just see it flying from cell to cell at a speed that would make *Gossip Girl* look like she was using dial-up. And if it did happen, Kennedy would probably rather listen to the audio of her deposition for her parents' divorce trial than me talking about making out with Ryan. And what's the point of making out if you can't g-chat about the particulars for hours afterward? I don't know, liking him just felt so impossible.

But then again, I thought Paris having any talent was impossible, and I still sometimes find myself humming "Stars Are Blind." So maybe anything's possible.

As we were clearing the lunch plates, the director hoisted his flab and beard over to the microphone. "Attention, Timber Trailers. I have a big announcement, so please be quiet."

I crossed my fingers, closed my eyes, and whispered, "The rest of camp is canceled. The rest of camp is canceled."

"Tomorrow is Timber Color War!"

This, like most of his announcements, meant nothing to me. I'd just wait for Sylvie to explain it later.

But as always after a postmeal announcement, the crowd went crazy. Every girl was acting like she had just won *American Idol*—fist-pumping, tearing up, thanking her family, her manager, and Jesus. It was nuts.

I shifted my chair to face Sylvie.

"Hey, walking camp Wikipedia." She raised her eyebrows, ready to enlighten me. "Two questions: what's a Color War and should I care?"

Sylvie rolled her eyes. "It's kind of the worst. I don't know why everybody always goes into heat the second they announce it. Basically, the entire camp gets split up into two teams, red and blue. And then the teams battle all day in sports and swimming. At the end of the day, there's a huge capture-the-flag game, and then the team that won the majority of the activities is named the winner, and that's quickly followed by a fifteen-minute diatribe explaining that we're all actually winners here at Timber, not just the real winners."

She clearly wasn't excited about this, and I wondered why, as it didn't seem any worse than a normal day.

"That doesn't sound that bad. I mean, there's no instructional swim, right?" I ducked to get out of the way of a very aggressive fist-pump from Aiden.

"Well, yeah, but it's worse than instructional swim. Like, there's face paint and cheering and you have to wear your bathing suit all day in case you're nominated for the water activities."

"Ha," I laughed. "I would never accept a nomination for water activities." I wagged my finger in the air to accent my point.

"No, it's not a choice. Like when they say 'water activity,' you say 'how wet?' It's like being in the army . . . but without buzz cuts."

This seriously frightened me. Unless the water activities were bobbing around in the shallow end, I was so obviously not going to be able to do them. And if they forced me, I was pretty sure I'd be facing a watery death.

Interrupting my chlorine-choking panic, Mandi offered our table these wise words, "Remember, you guys, tomorrow is about fun, not winning or losing. But in my ten years at Timber, I've been on the winning Color War team every year, and this year's going to be no different. So"—she paused to give us time to appreciate the level of her camp success—"you better hope you're on my team. I always make sure my team wins the spirit section. I swear I just fully got my voice back like two weeks before camp this year from how hoarse I was after last year's Color War."

"I seriously hope I'm not on her team," I whispered to Sylvie.

She nodded. "Yeah, you lose if you aren't on her team, but you kind of lose more if you are."

"Waaaaake up, Bunk Redwood!" Mandi sirened like the host of a cheesy morning show. "Up and at 'em! It's Color War today and I have our team assignments!"

I opened my eyes and then immediately shut them. "You have a.m. and p.m. mixed up, it's still pitch-dark outside," I said, assuming that Mandi was a clock radio I hadn't set correctly after the last power outage.

I felt my blanket get ripped off me. "No grump bunnies allowed this morning. It's Color War!" And then she started giggling uncontrollably, I think from overexcitement.

"What if I slept naked? Who'd be giggling all the way to the sexual harassment settlement then?" I grumbled to no one in particular, and got out of bed for the Color War assignment lineup.

Mandi went down the line, checking an official-looking spreadsheet, assigning each girl a team and tossing her a T-shirt in her color.

"Ladies, the Bunk Redwood Color War breakdown is . . ." She walked up to Hayden. "Red!"

Hayden caught the shirt Mandi tossed her way.

Mandi walked down the line. "Aiden, you're also red."

She took her shirt and then turned to hug Hayden. They were both so excited that they weren't even saying real words, just yelping into each other's ears as they jumped around in circles. Even if I'd won the lottery, I wouldn't be that excited this early in the a.m.

Aidan was next in line. "You're blue," Mandi announced. I could see the tears pooling at the bottom of her eyes, about to drip out. Her bottom lip pushed itself out as she frowned and tried to keep herself from fully crying. The other two-thirds of her trio was still too busy congratulating themselves on their mutual redness to console their friend. I kind of felt bad for her.

"And Miss Sylvie"—Mandi looked down at her sheet—"you're blue too."

Sylvie balled her shirt up and looked my way as Mandi sidestepped to stand right in front of me. "Laney is on the . . ." She paused, double-checking her sheet. I realized that I was so nervous to hear if I was on Sylvie's team or not that I actually wasn't breathing, so I took a deep breath to keep from passing out. "Red team!" she exclaimed.

My mouth dropped open as I caught the red tee she threw my way, my chin hitting the collar of my REAL MEN LOVE KITTENS night shirt. (Thanks, Mom.) I was going to be separated from Sylvie for an entire day? This was unimaginable. There were Siamese twins who spent less time together than Sylvie and me. There was no way I could get through a day here without her.

I didn't think that I could get any worse news, until Mandi made another announcement.

"And I'm on the red team. So you three are lucky ducks!" she exclaimed.

A full day without Sylvie and with Mandi? Anxiety

overload! I was seriously starting to sweat at the thought of it.

"I want to be on red," Aidan said, pouting.

"I'll switch with you." I said it as a reflex, not even thinking. I had snatched her shirt and given her mine before I'd even fully comprehended that I'd just saved myself from a day in the deepest depths of sunshiny athletic hell. It was like when you pull your hand away from a hot stove before your brain has even registered that it's hot. It's just your body's way of surviving.

Aidan was looking down at her new red shirt and smiling. She started to make a move to break into the Hayden and Aiden hug celebration, but Mandi's booming voice stopped her.

"Uh-uh. Trading's not allowed. A team is a team." Mandi's hand came toward me, trying to grab back the blue T-shirt I was clutching to my chest, but I flinched and jumped back, pulling it out of her reach.

"I will die if you put me on the red team. My knees will buckle and I'll keel over and cease living if you take this blue shirt from me. Do not test me, Mandi. It will happen," I threatened, my voice wobbling with separation anxiety.

"But it's a rule. No team switching. It's right here on the clipboard, I can show you."

I wanted to grab the clipboard from her hands and throw it and all of its stupid rules and team assignments into the lake.

"And rules can be broken," Sylvie jumped in. "Kind of like self-defense. Murder isn't allowed, but when it's self-defense and you had to do it to protect yourself, it's fine.

Laney's switching teams to save her life. Those are her choices: be on the blue team or die. I think you can bend the rules to save an innocent life here."

Hello, future prelaw major!

Mandi waffled for a full two seconds before deciding that sparing my life was worth a rule bend.

"Fine," she said, clearly irritated but also—judging from her expression—not really sure what to think about Sylvie's Elle Woods moment. "You can switch with Aidan."

I sighed and whispered a quick thank-you. I wasn't sure if it was to Mandi or to the gods of Timber Trails. The other girls squealed at uniting their trifecta in color warfare, and I returned to breathing at a normal pace.

I slipped out of my nightshirt and into the blue Timber T-shirt I had swapped Aidan for. It was a size XXL and came down to my knees, which made me look like I wasn't wearing any shorts. But considering my shorts situation, that was a plus.

Team uniforms on, we all left the bunk and leapt down the stairs together, looking like a pantsless brigade. We were just approaching the mess hall when I felt a tug on my sleeve. "No. This way," Sylvie said sleepily as she pulled me toward the far entrance to the building—the boys' entrance. "Blue sits in the boys' half today."

I stopped my morning shuffle. "You mean boys are involved in this camp-sanctified gang warfare?"

"Yeah. I said the entire camp. Boys, girls, counselors, the nurse, whatever monster that probably lives in the lake, *everyone* is involved in Color War." She rubbed an eye with the back of her hand, totally not realizing that this was the newsbreak of the summer. Now I was especially pumped to be on her team—I'd be able to help with some potential Eli contact. How could she not have let me in on this?

"You never said boys were going to be involved. Hello, that changes everything. I wish I'd known so we could have been planning."

I was flailing my hands, trying to make it clear that I needed warnings for these kind of coed events.

She pushed her eyebrows together and looked at me sternly. "Oh my God." Her voice was slow and a little mean. "You're turning into the al qaeda of crushes. Like what is there really to plot?" My stomach dropped. Was my only friend of the entire summer dumping on me?

She started walking toward the boys' entrance, leaving me with my arms crossed, waiting for an apology. About ten steps away she finally realized that I wasn't at her side and she turned around. "What?"

"Um, a terrorist comparison before eight in the morning? Totally not fair." I started to tap my foot. My feelings were hurt and I needed to hear something from her to make me feel better.

"Fine, I'm sorry." She sounded sincere and I forgave her immediately. "It's just that you're always so focused on the boys, and like, yeah, I want Eli, but I also want to do other things aside from strategizing our second-base domination."

All of a sudden, it made sense why she hadn't told me about the boys and Color War. She didn't want me to plan anything or help her out.

I took a breath. "Wow, OK, I guess I didn't realize that I'd become Osama bin Lovin'. I'll tone it down."

I was still confused about how exactly she wanted me to proceed. I mean, she didn't want me to give up on Eli and her forever, right? Just be a bit more mellow about it? This was so weird for me, because at home, there was no way that I could talk about Kennedy's love life enough, let alone too much. I figured that for the rest of the day, I'd not even mention Eli, and afterward I'd just kind of feel it out. If Paris and Nicole can go back to being friends after their massive friend divorce, Sylvie and I could get over this tiny bump. And I was pretty sure neither of us would end up with short, gross, tattooed rockers, so we would even have a happier ending than them.

Resolved to be silent on the topic of anything with a Y chromosome, I followed Sylvie into the mess hall and immediately saw Ryan sitting at a table in a blue shirt, gazing into a bowl of Cocoa Puff–residue milk. Obviously, I wanted to say something to Sylvie about him, but I didn't know whether the vow of guy silence applied just to Eli or to all boys, so I tried to be quiet. But my heartbeat became so loud at the sight of him and my sweat glands started producing so much perspiration that I was sure she was going to shush me. I decided not to acknowledge him and let Sylvie take the lead on how to handle this coed situation.

I followed her as she made a beeline right to his table and plucked two cereal boxes from the center of it, then plopped down across from him. I did the same . . . except I grabbed three cereal boxes.

"Hey, hey, ladies," Ryan greeted us, then wiped his mouth on his sleeve. I wanted to shake him and tell him to stop acting like such a boy, because Sylvie was so over guys today, but when I looked at her, she didn't seem to care. "So, this is lucky that we three are together. Eli's on red, though. Bummer."

He was making eye contact with Sylvie when he said that. I tried to get his attention and send him "Ixnay on the Lieay" vibes with my eyes. Obviously, that didn't work. I turned to Sylvie to see if she was going to blow up at him like she had at me, but there wasn't smoke coming out of her ears or anything.

"Yeah, I guess," she said. "Mostly because we're probably going to kick red's butts!"

"That's the team spirit!" He smiled. "LP, what about you? Got some blue energy?"

"Um." I tried to stall, thinking of what an appropriate sporty spirit thing to say was. I might know a lot about American history and iambic pentameter, but going to an elite private school that had nationally ranked fencing and equestrian teams didn't learn you much about proper athletic fan behavior. "Sack that quarterback!" I exclaimed, pumping my fist in the air. I thought I'd heard Ken's dad yell that at the TV once when he was watching some game.

They exchanged weird glances for a second before both of them burst into laughter.

"Hey, you guys. I'm trying. It's the effort that counts, right?" I whined, attempting to sound offended even though I was laughing at myself too.

"Effort?" Ryan managed to simmer his laugher down enough to get a sentence out. "You have a lot to learn about Color War if you think effort counts." That sounded rather menacing to me, but he and Sylvie started up their hysterical giggling all over again and I couldn't stop myself from joining—their laughter was contagious.

Before I could say something else hilariously unathletic,

a counselor got up and introduced himself as our team leader. We then watched his head turn disturbingly deep shades of burgundy as he yelled at us about how important a blue win was.

"See?" Ryan whispered my way. "The focus is on winning, not efforting." I nodded and got a little more nervous about the rest of the day. If we were getting this kind of speech during breakfast, I was afraid for how intense it was going to get when we were actually doing activities.

I had to wolf down my last bowl of Froot Loops to march out to the playing fields with my team. I wondered if competitive eating was one of the Color War battles. I could totally participate in that.

The Color War elves must have been busy the night before, because there were relay races galore set up on the fields. I got the hang of the Color War beat pretty fast—the tomato head counselor would call out an activity, watch the hands of our blue team pop up in the air, and pick out a volunteer to represent us in the next challenge.

"The bat-spin run!" Tomato Head hollered.

"That's when you put the base of the bat on the ground and bend your forehead down to rest on the handle, spin like ten times, and then run the race when you're really dizzy," Sylvie explained to me. I was splayed out on the grass, racing myself into getting the bronzest tan possible.

I lifted my head a bit and opened one eye to look at her. "So it's not lying here and getting tan? Then I'm not interested." I reclined back into my sun-soaking repose.

"You better volunteer for something. Everyone has to do at least one activity, and if you wait and don't volunteer, you're just going to have to do one of the shitty ones at the end of the day," Ryan's voice warned.

"I'm actually going to practice peaceful resistance, which can be really powerful. They can't make me do something I don't want to do. That's just not fair."

"Oh, but they *can* make you do something you don't want to do. That sentence is pretty much the summary of your entire summer," Ryan pointed out.

As I turned to give him a look, I heard Sylvie offer, "I'll go!"

I flipped my head and saw her bolting away. "Is she competing in something?"

"Yeah, the one-hundred-meter dash. She's crazy fast. We'll totally win with her."

A little surprised at her willingness to participate so early in the day, I sat myself up next to Ryan to watch Sylvie run. I looked around and saw that every female member of the blue team was shooting lasers of hate and jealousy my way because I was sitting next to Ryan. And instead of getting defensive or angry about it and shooting them all nasty looks back, I just felt super lucky that he wanted to hang with me.

"So, um, thanks for being so nice all the time and stuff. I know there are a hundred other people you could be sitting with right now." My stomach suddenly seized up with nerves. But I knew that I needed to get this last part out. I just wanted him to know that I appreciated how hugely awesome he'd been to me and how I knew that it was more than I deserved. "And like especially because I'm not the nicest person to you in New York."

"No biggie. You know, it's like the Golden Rule."

I crinkled my forehead. "She who makes the gold makes the rule?" That was always the golden rule in my house. Or at least, it was when I wanted to get triple pierces in both ears.

He chuckled a little. "You can take the girl out of the Upper East Side, but you can't take the Upper East Side out of the girl, huh?" He rubbed my back as he mocked me and I swear it was like his hand was electric, sending little shocks up and down my spine. OK, if a back rub made me feel like I'd just stuck a wet finger in a socket, then Sylvie was definitely right; I had a crush on Ryan. As weird as it was, fighting it wasn't going to do anything. I figured I might as well just roll with it. I really wanted to obsess over this revelation with Sylvie, but she was busy sprinting down the field. Even when she got back, I knew I should probably still stick to my decision to not discuss boys with her at all, because I wasn't sure which topics were discussable and which weren't. Ugh, what were we going to chat about that had nothing to do with testosterone at all . . . tampons and Ryan Seacrest? That would get boring fast.

"The Golden Rule is 'Do unto others as you would have done unto yourself,' " he clarified.

"So does that mean that you want to hang with me when we get back to New York?" I was trying to sound flirty to my newly admitted crush, but bringing up New York just felt awkward and foreign.

Plus, he didn't take the bait, which made me feel even more awkward. "Would it have to be with your crew? Because I don't think I could handle that."

I deflated a little when the words came out of his mouth, but I really couldn't blame him. He was right; him and me back home would be beyond bizarre. This crush was totally an outside-the-five-boroughs phenomenon, and the smart thing would probably be to just ignore it. But the thought of totally shutting him out once I got back to my real life majorly bummed me out.

Luckily, the rest of the day was intense enough that I barely had time to dwell on the viability of my crush. Ryan and Sylvie each volunteered for a million activities, and I got very serious about cheering for them. Sylvie totally dominated her sprinting, Ryan won a soccer kick competition and the Frisbee throw, and Sylvie kicked some red team butt again in a baseball-hitting competition, though she lost the pull-up-off. I remained planted, dominating my own triathlon of holding down the fort, working on my farmer's tan, and refusing to respond when asked, "We've got spirit, how about you?"

After a special lunch of all red and blue foods—I can't even fathom how much food coloring it took to turn all those hot dog buns blue—the competition moved poolside. Again Sylvie and Ryan volunteered themselves for tons of water activities, and I sat on the unmuddiest patch of grass by the pool cheering.

Finally, late in the afternoon, Ryan decided to take a break from swimming for a while and kept me company while Sylvie continued to compete in the water.

Honestly, it was hard to keep up with the conversation because I'd get distracted by how good he looked without his shirt on. He'd definitely be more popular at Conrad's parties if he came wearing only pants and shoes.

I managed to somehow be holding up my end of a convo about how we both secretly loved *The Suite Life of Zack &*

Cody even though we were way too old. When he said that Cody was his favorite, I freaked on him. He was my favorite too! What were the chances? (Technically, one in two, I know.)

"I lost," a sopping Sylvie said as she plopped down next to me.

"Confession: My TiVo is set to record every episode, and that's totally not the only Disney Channel show I'm into," I added quickly before acknowledging Sylvie. Ryan started cracking up and I turned to my friend. "Aw, honey," I said, "you're a winner to me. I mean, you didn't drown, and that's more than I could do in the water."

"All right, all right, all right," Tomato Head yelled, clapping his hands to get our attention as if screaming at about a jillion decibels wasn't enough. "We have one competition left, and from my records"—he pointed to his clipboard on the ground—"there's one person on the blue team who hasn't yet participated." And even though I was hoping it wouldn't be me, I knew it would be. Sylvie and Ryan had warned me that this would happen. I guess I just thought a natural disaster or something could possibly strike before I needed to participate. But willing a tsunami or earthquake was a lot more difficult than *Bruce Almighty* made it seem. "And that blue team member who must have been saving all her energy for the big finale, so she's certainly going to win, is . . ." Please don't say me. Please don't say me.

"Laney Parker." I would have rather heard anything else than my name then.

"The apocalypse is coming in ten seconds."

"Excuse me, ma'am, but I'm a producer for The Biggest Loser *and I think you'd be a great contestant for next season."*

245

"My friends and I are betting on this because none of us knows the answer. Are you a boy or a girl? It's just hard to tell because you have no boobs and a pretty prominent Adam's apple."

Seriously, *anything* but my name.

"I—I'm so sorry," I stammered, "but I can't participate. I'm doing this peaceful resistance thing, and I really would participate, but it's just against my beliefs." I was totally fumbling.

His tomato head shook, rejecting my excuse. "Get ready to race," he commanded.

I shook my head back at him and didn't get up from my towel. I figured that if I stood, there was a chance he could just push me into the pool, but it would be pretty impossible for him to actually bend down, pick me up, and throw me in.

He came close and stood over me, looking down, "You have no choice. You're swimming the next race."

By this point, the whole team was watching our showdown. I wanted to slither under my towel and disappear.

"Seriously, I'm sitting this out." I was trying to hold my ground, but I could hear my voice wavering like a weakling. After weeks of instructional swim, I couldn't do much more than the doggy paddle. And the thought of showcasing my swimming nonskills in front of the entire camp was nauseating. I just couldn't do it.

"The rules say that every member of the team has to participate at least once. If we don't follow the rules, we're disqualified and automatically lose." At this statement, the entirety of the blue team started to heckle me, yelling and screaming and bullying me into swimming.

After a lot of head shaking, I realized that losing the entire day's worth of activities would make me even less

popular than just tanking one. This was going to be mortifying, but I guessed no less unbearable than every other camp
activity I sucked at.

I threw up my hands. "Fine!" I stripped down to my suit,
muttering to myself about peacefully resisting with my fists
hitting someone's face, and made my way to the starting spot
on the pool's ledge.

I positioned myself in what I thought looked like a dive-
ready stance and glanced over at my red team competition.
It was Hayden. Perfect. There was no way this could be more
humiliating.

"Good luck," I said to her, not meaning it, but judging
from *Semi-Pro*, I gathered it was the right thing to say before
an athletic event.

"You keep your luck, 'cause you're the one who's going to
need it," she snotted back.

"Swimmers ready?" the referee asked.

We both nodded. I looked out over the wide expanse of
pool sparkling in the sunlight and waited for my cue.

"Set!" And then a loud, sharp whistle blew. Hayden
dove into the water, barely causing a splash as she skimmed
the surface and propelled herself forward.

I was totally frozen, standing there watching her swim,
until I heard the counselor yell from across the pool, "You
have to get in! Get in the freaking pool!" His head seemed
like it was on the verge of combustion. I nodded and looked
down at the water with my arms high above my head, trying
to psych myself into the first dive of my life. I took a deep
breath, my body pulsing with fear. I decided to somewhat alter
my passive resistance plan and go with passive-aggressive par-
ticipation. Exhaling slowly, I turned and walked the five

steps toward the metal ladder a few feet away. I looked over at my team and lifted my hands in a what-can-you-do shrug before slowly climbing into the cold water, rung by rung. Once I was completely submerged, I doggy-paddled my way out to my lane and stroked down toward the finish line. Before I was even an eighth of the way there, Hayden had already finished and the red team was celebrating with loud cheering. As I choked and gurgled and paddled my way across the pool, the blue team sat silent, shocked at either my lack of swimming skills or the amount of water I was able to swallow without exploding. I wasn't sure which.

I was about halfway into my personal swim through hell when I heard "Here we go, Laney, here we go." I looked up to see Sylvie and Ryan standing on the pool's ledge cheering me on. I'd love to say that this was all it took to get the blue team to rally and support me and soon the entire group was chanting my name and encouraging me to do the best I could, like the *Little Miss Sunshine* family with their fat daughter. But no, the next six minutes were just filled with my mouth making fart sounds as I choked and gulped for air and only two voices cheering me on. I'd also love to say that their encouragement inspired me to swim better and faster, but again no. I actually got worse toward the end, flipping on my back and floating, hoping that the remaining ripples from Hayden's wake would push me toward the wall.

I'm not sure how, but finally, I finished. My hand touched the cement of the ledge and I held on, so glad to be touching solid land that I stayed there until Ryan and Sylvie pulled me out.

"You came in second place, buddy!" Ryan put his hand on my shoulder, and of course it sent the tingles aflutter. But the "buddy" reminded me that we were totally in summer friends mode.

I was so winded I was dizzy, and there was a serious chance of puking in my near future from all the water in my belly.

Even in my near-critical condition, I managed to reply, "Second place? That doesn't make losing sound half bad. But you guys totally win the first-place spirit award in my heart." I gave them a super-cheesy smile.

"What's our prize, then?" Sylvie asked.

"Um, wet hugs and the privilege of letting me use your towels?"

"That's it? Then I don't even want to know what second gets," Ryan said, throwing his towel over my shoulders.

Kennedy, hello! Are you alive? I haven't heard from you in weeks and I'm getting worried. Should I send a letter to 911?

Not only are you my best friend, but you're pretty much my lifeline to the real world now. You can't ignore that kind of responsibility. Please send me a letter with the details of every freaking thing that has happened in the past few weeks and a long description of what a midafternoon nap feels like. I've totally forgotten.

Camp is still torture. Take pity on me.

Peace, Love, and Desperation,
Laney

Chapter 17

I thought the silver lining of the Color War debacle was that there was no way anything else Timber could be worse. I thought very wrong. There was something worse than publicly viewed humiliation in a pool that was more pee than chlorine: an entire camp gossiping about it after.

There was nowhere I could go to escape it. The trio of tactlessness obviously made the bunk an impossible place to be by bringing up the blue team loss every chance they got. I would get a weird stare on the fields whenever I passed another camper. And if it was more than one camper, the weird stare would be followed by whispering, finger pointing, and then a hushed laughter. Even my instructional swim group—who normally only chattered about cartoons and underwater bodily functions—brought it up.

"Mandi? Mandi?" Brandt asked through blue lips as we were all bobbing up and down in the freezing pool. Once Mandi focused her eyes on him, he continued. "Is there a swim level below one?"

"Nope, one is the beginning of the swim program," she explained. "Why are you asking, B-man?"

"Just because I feel really bad for Laney because she was so bad at swimming during Color War, and I don't want her to feel not as good as the rest of us in level one."

Are there undertows in pool water? Because I was praying for one to come and suck me down and drown me.

When the bell rang announcing the end of swim, I was the last person out of the pool. Hearing that even little Brandt had been exposed to the post–Color War fallout totally bummed me out. I wanted to put on a velour sweat suit, lie on a couch with a pint full of self-pity-flavored ice cream, and watch horrible daytime TV for the rest of my life.

I trudged over to my sad pile of clothes and stood above them, dripping. By the time I'd finally worked up the energy to actually bend over and pick up my towel to dry off, most of the other swimmers were on their way out the gate to their activities for the rest of the day. Mandi typically made the bunk wait, or at least slow down, so that we walked places in somewhat of a group. But I saw that she and the trio were already bouncing away, not waiting for me and my patheticness to get ready.

Sylvie came over to me and rubbed my back through my towel. "What's wrong?" she asked.

"What's wrong?" I paused, waiting for her to realize how stupid that question was. " 'What's right?' would be an easier question to answer. Everything is wrong!" It felt strange to be this emotional and not about to cry, but I was more mad than upset. Like, angry at the entire summer.

"OK. How about we just focus on getting into your cover-up clothes and heading to the next activity," she urged. "You'll feel better when you're not at the scene of the . . ." Her voice trailed off as she tried to think of the right word to capture the atrocity of the Color War. "Incident."

I nodded, even though I didn't think she was right at all—I would never feel better no matter where I was—and slipped on my shorts.

It took me so long to get dressed that by the time I was fully clothed and ready to head out the gate, the next session of instructional swimmers were already making their way into the pool area.

Sylvie and I stood by the side to let the stream of them in.

My depression onset was so distracting that I didn't even notice when Ryan and Eli walked in until Sylvie called out to them.

The two guys walked over. Eli gave us both huge waves hello.

"What's going on, ladies?" Ryan asked, clearly not noticing my scowl.

"What's going on? I'll tell you what's going on." I was shouting more loudly than I meant to, but I couldn't help it. I was so fired up. "This whole camp can't get over the fact that I can't swim—it's like the most exciting thing in the world here and everyone's talking about it and I'm beyond sick of it."

Ryan gave me a sincerely sad look. "Not everyone, Laney."

"Yes," I contradicted him. "Every single person. Even the little kids."

I relived the instructional swim subzero-level recommendation story for the three of them.

"Well, that's barely anything compared to what the boys our age are saying about you," Eli retorted with way too much honesty. Ryan shot him a dirty look for the overshare and then tried to hit him with his towel.

"What?" I whined. "What are they saying about me?"

"Nothing. It's just stupid jokes about your swim strokes being so bad correlating to your other stroking skills," Ryan said. "It's lame and will pass by the end of the day, don't worry about it." I looked at him, so entranced by the kaleidoscope of light and dark browns that made up his chocolate eyes, I almost forgot how miserable I was, but not quite. My eyes dropped from Ryan's stare.

"Don't worry, Laney. This'll be over soon enough," Eli said.

"Totally," Ryan added. "Someone will take a dump in the pool or something and that'll be the new talk of Timber." Seeing that he wasn't doing much to help my mood, Ryan shrugged and gave up, walking into the pool area with Eli.

By that evening, I'd had way more than enough of the Color War–related snickering and pot shots, especially from Hayden. It was a particularly painful shower hour. She was taking forever to get ready, trying on and modeling six different pairs of butt shorts for her devoted duo before they decided that she should wear the pair that wedged themselves the deepest into her crack. Mandi was standing at the door, hollering at the group about schedules and time management and this being dinner, not fashion week. "Why are you moving so slowly tonight, Hayden? Let's go."

"Yeah, I don't know. It's like I'm moving at Laney-in-the-swimming-pool-at-Color-War speed," Hayden said, flaring her nostrils like the villain she was. She shot her eyes over my way to see my response.

I completely snapped. Ignoring everything Disney Channel young adult sitcoms had taught me about handling bullies, I gave her exactly what she wanted: a big reaction. "That was witty, Hayden. Well worded. Really rolled off the tongue," I deadpanned, shaking with how heated I was. "I personally would have gone with something that actually had some humor in it and wasn't just blatantly cruel. Like maybe 'slower than a swimming Laney, more unskilled than her doggy paddle, able to lose daylong competitions in a single race.' You know, but the direct-to-bitchfest route you took suits you better. Well played."

I was so upset that I couldn't even stand to be in the same bunk with these girls. I rushed past Hayden, slamming my shoulder into her as I headed out the door, and made my way to dinner on my lonesome. I ran down the stairs sniffling and trying to hold back tears, which I knew was probably impossible.

Sylvie sprinted to catch up with me. "You shouldn't let her get to you. She's just a girl with bad fashion sense and horrible hair." She paused for a second, considering what she had just said. "Wait, that describes me too. I meant that she's a bitch with a bad attitude."

I pouted, not feeling any better. "I'm just . . ." Tears started to trickle down my face and I could barely finish my sentence. "I've never had this many people talking about me before." I thought back to the end of my freshman year, when I went to prom with Hect VanRider, the hottest senior, and wore that phenomenal Michael Kors halter dress. "Like saying bad stuff about me."

"I don't know if this is going to make you feel better or not, but Hayden would find something to mock you for even if you had totally won Color War. There's nothing you can do with that turdbucket."

I laughed, ending my all-day perma-frown. *Turdbucket* is probably the single hilarious-est slam in the English language. "Just so you know, this laughing is not about me feeling better."

"OK, maybe this will make you feel better. Today officially starts the one-week countdown until camp's over." She smiled at me, waiting for me to explode with happiness. Which didn't take long. My eyes seriously started welling up with tears of joy. The only other time I'd been so happy I cried was the one fight that Dr. Mark and my mother had where he threatened to move out. "So we can muscle through these next seven days, OK?" Sylvie grabbed my hand and squeezed it. I squeezed back and nodded.

We walked hand in hand the rest of the way to the mess hall. I didn't care that it might have made us look like lesbians. Although that probably wouldn't help with the horrible rumors circ-ing the boys' bunks.

• • •

In an unprecedented move, we were given an entire hour of free time after dinner. When the director shouted the announcement into the microphone, I almost spit my powdery mashed potatoes across the table and for the first time, joined the rest of the camp in post-announcement whooping. Free time? Choice in my own activities? Implementing actual free will? Making my own decisions felt overwhelmingly unfamiliar . . . kind of how Michael Cera might feel if he ever got cast as a heartthrob and not the cute but dweeby underdog. Like, I knew this was a good thing, but I needed a sec to get used to it.

"Want to come with me up to archery for the free time?" Sylvie asked as we cleared our table. "I only need two more bull's-eyes and I'm totally making it in to the archery bull's-eye club."

Eh, so much for making my own decisions. I was still tender from my shower hour mental snap and didn't want to be alone. "Sure, I'll come and watch you point and shoot your way into the Guinness Book of Timber Trail Records."

The post dinner cleanup went super quickly, no one wanting to waste a second of their free time. Clearing the plates took all of three minutes, even though most of them were still piled with food, as Aiden, Aidan, and Hayden had collectively decided to go on a diet at some point before dinner. And then I wiped down the table—a task which normally grossed me out to the point of gagging—and didn't even think about vomiting once. The mess hall quickly emptied and Sylvie and I shuffled out too, starting on our way directly to the archery range.

I saw Ryan jogging up to us from a distance and Eli following at a much slower pace. Ryan was kind of in silhouette with the sun setting behind him, totally looking like the hot and unattainable guy in a romantic comedy. This scene was doing nothing to help my forced just-friends mentality.

"Hey," Ryan said as he approached, getting impossibly cuter in that alternative Dan Humphrey I-wear-two-hoodies-at-once kind of way with each step. "Just the ladies we were looking for." I felt myself blush a little, but then realized that he was only playing his role as Sylvie and Eli's cupid, not kicking game my way. Eli was still a good twenty paces behind, but Ryan continued to speak for his amigo. "We"— he gestured to his less-than-hustling compatriot—"were wondering if you two would care to spend your hour of free time with us canoeing on the lake." Eli finally arrived, panting like a dog in heat. Before he said anything, he took a long drag from his inhaler.

"We can't. We're heading . . ." Sylvie stopped as I interrupted her with my water sandal smushing her toes. And I knew I'd told her I'd stop love-matching, but I just couldn't. It was like when Patricia Arquette tries to stop seeing dead people in *Medium*. She can't, because it's a skill she was born with. Me either. I couldn't ignore my God-given gift.

"That sounds awesome. Thanks for asking," I interjected. Even though I loved Sylvie, I thought perhaps I should start charging for my matchmaking services. Isn't eHarmony like fifty bucks a month? That would cover the DVD set of *Hannah Montana* I was going to have to buy to catch up on what I'd been missing this summer. What? Admit it. It's a good show.

Ryan smiled my way and then headed off to the boats with Eli at his heels. Sylvie and I stood where we were for a few minutes, her trying to send me evil-eye looks for love-bugging her when I said I'd stop, and me attempting to look innocent even though I was so obviously guilty. I finally gave up and made my way to the dock with Sylvie not far behind me.

"OK, how should we divide up the boats?" Ryan fake asked once we arrived, knowing full well that he wanted Eli and Sylvie to wind up in a boat together.

"Well, maybe you three could go out together and I could take the smaller canoe by myself, since I'm the best canoer," Sylvie offered, again forcing me to leave sandal imprints on her left foot. I was pretty sure she was sabatoging herself to spite me now. Like that wine guy my mom told me about who decided to sell his way successful vineyard for two dollars right before his divorce so that when his wife got half of what he was worth, it would only be one dollar. But that was a stupid, spiteful move. And you know what? The only people that benefited from that were bored high schoolers who had good enough fake IDs to buy cases of the cheapo wine from Trader Joe's and play Edward Wino Hands during lunch. Was that what Sylvie wanted? To help senior slumpers instead of helping herself? I sure as crap wasn't going to let that happen.

"Or I could go just with Ryan," I said. "I got a letter from our New York friend with all of the goss that's been going on this summer, and I've been dying to fill him in on it. So I guess that leaves the two of you together. Is that OK?" It was a total lie. I hadn't heard from Kennedy in forever. And I didn't really care if Sylvie thought this was OK. She was getting in that canoe with Eli alone. Period.

Sylvie and I exchanged looks; she eye-told me that she knew what I was up to and I squinted back that I couldn't help it if I had gossip and needed to be in a boat alone with Ryan.

"Is the pollen aggravating your eyes as well, ladies? I was thinking about taking a trip to my bunk to get some drops. I can bring them back for your use," Eli offered obliviously.

"Thank you, Eli. But it's not the pollen that's aggravating me. It's something else," she said, her gaze locked on me.

Something else was aggravating me too.

"Well, maybe the pollen or whatever it is isn't trying to aggravate your eyes. It's trying to help your eyes," I said. I stood with my hands on my hips, not breaking eye contact with her.

"Yeah, well, if I recall"—she pointed to herself—"I distinctly told the pollen that my eyes didn't need any more help." The boys backed away from our nutso talk and walked over to pick up paddles and life vests for us.

It was getting to the point where I felt like a crowd should be chanting "Jerry, Jerry, Jerry," and considering this was over helping a friend with her crush and not sleeping with my baby daddy's sister-in-law's second cousin who was fifty years my senior, that was just ridiculous.

My voice got a lot softer and I tried to explain. "Well, the pollen can't help but to try to help, and she's sorry, but the pollen thinks the one-on-one time will be really fun for you and your eyes."

"Hey, let's cut the crazy, ladies," Ryan interrupted. He was leaning his weight on two paddles, with two life jackets in the other hand. It would totally have been a J.Crew catalog shot if his shirt hadn't been splattered with flecks of his dinner gravy. "How about we get to canoeing before they change their minds about the free time and make us all play dodge ball or something."

This was logic that neither of us could argue with. I gave Sylvie a weak shrug.

"Fine, let's just go, OK?" she conceded, heading over to Eli's boat. And I knew this mini fight wasn't about winning, but I totally wanted to jump up in the air and scream "Victory!" Instead, I just gave myself a mental pat on the back.

Sylvie and Eli took a canoe and paddled off, and Ryan and I followed. Actually, I stopped paddling a few yards into the lake because Ryan said I was stroking backwards and just making us spin in circles. So he paddled and I tried to make myself look attractive in my life vest.

He stopped when we got to the middle of the lake and I turned around to get a better look at what he was staring at: the other two in their canoe.

"So do you think it's going to happen between them or is this entire summer going to be a waste?" I asked.

"Even if it doesn't happen with those two, I'm pretty sure this summer wasn't a waste." I felt a jolt of flutters run through my body. He was talking about getting to know me not being a waste, right? This was totally him making a move. But before I could answer with "Yes, Ryan Bellsinger, I'll marry you. Thank you for making me the happiest woman in the whole wide world," he said, "I mean, you have those awesome FART tie-dye shorts, right? Those are pretty special."

Wait, what? Farts? I was not only in the friend zone, I was so deep in the friend zone I was in the nosebleed he-doesn't-even-realize-I'm-a-girl zone. I cursed my mother for not packing any padded bras.

"Yeah, I guess." I looked away, trying not to let him see how deflated I was.

"And I mean, I'm really glad that we got a chance to

hang this summer. I hope we keep it up back in the city." He backstroked us away from a low tree branch we'd drifted near.

"Really?" I perked up, again feeling the wedding proposal coming on. Well, not really that, but maybe a kiss or a handhold or a thigh rub. I scootched myself forward to the middle bar of the canoe to give easier access for any of the above.

"I mean, yeah. Now at least I'll have someone at Conrad's parties to talk to aside from the dip. But seriously, you should try it sometime. Aunt Marge makes a killer bean dip."

Again I deflated, my anticipation coming down faster than J.Lo's weight after the twins. Being on this canoe was like Mr. Toad's Wild Ride through my insecurities, and I wanted off. I briefly considered jumping into the sea urchin/urine water and swimming to shore, but with my gag reflex and swimming skills, that didn't seem like all that reasonable an idea.

He must have been sensing my awkward vibes, because suddenly, he was itching to get out of the situation too.

"So, how about turning around and heading back?"

I nodded and silently moved to the front of the canoe, careful not to rock the boat too much.

"And since we want to turn now, you should paddle for a few strokes."

I had to laugh at that and then I stuck my oar in, stroking until we were pointed toward the dock.

"Nice work, L."

Why did my body have to react to him calling me by a nickname? I immediately got the warm tingles running up and down the core of my body, but my brain was telling me to just ignore it. I mean, he probably called Eli "E," so this was just a friend thing. I consciously decided to respond in the jokey friend way instead of what I really wanted to do: french him.

"Yeah, well, when you've got guns like these"—I flexed my nonexistent biceps—"a little canoe spin ain't no thang."

OK, could I have sounded any more like a weird substitute teacher just then? With wit like that, no wonder he wasn't into me. I hated that I was doubting myself into a mess of self-loathing and then realized hating that only added to the self-loathing issue.

Ryan interrupted my crisis of confidence. "Hey, check them out."

Wait, maybe he was into this lame joke. I struck another *American Gladiators* pose. "Excuse me, sir, do you have tickets to this gun show?"

"What? No, not your muscles. I meant check them out." I flipped my head around to see him pointing to Sylvie and Eli's boat. After an initial wave of blinding embarrassment at my bicep blunder, I saw what he did. Eli and Sylvie both had their lips pursed and they were only millimeters away from each other.

"It looks like they're going to kiss. They're so close," I narrated. "Closer, closer. Oh my God. Miracles do happen! They just kissed!" I was prouder than a mama bird when her chick learns how to fly.

"Wait," Ryan interrupted, "it kind of looks like they were doing fishy faces and then the boat rocked and they smashed their heads together accidentally." His hand was over his eyes, shielding the sunset glare as he examined the pair.

I squinted and saw Eli rubbing the blood off his mouth where Sylvie's retainer had cut him. Crap, Ryan was right. "Whatever. It was still non-CPR mouth-on-mouth contact. And that means success in my book!" I held a hand up for a congratulatory slap.

Laney,

That place sounds every shade of awful . . .
including chartreuse. You so should have gone on a teen
tour instead.

Sorry I haven't written. The surgery totally wiped
me out. I'm not even sending a pic now because I'm
still so swollen. You'd be shocked, like when we on-
demanded Clueless and couldn't believe how fat
Brittany Murphy's face was. That's how puffy I am.

Anyway, hope you're surviving and managing to
avoid that freak Ryan all summer. Remember,
eyebrows are a crucial part of your face and he'd
probably pluck yours out or something.

Can't wait to see you again. I promise, all we'll do
is sit inside and watch brain-liquefying reality TV, OK?

Kisses,

K

Chapter 18

Back in the bunk, I couldn't believe there really was a letter from Kennedy waiting for me. It made me feel a little better about my white lie to Sylvie. But as I got to the part about Ryan, my heart dropped at a rapid 9.8 meters per second to the bottom of my stomach and splattered. Obviously, that would be Kennedy's reaction to Ryan's presence, and I knew that on some level. Still, I guess my feelings kind of made my memory of my posse's cliquiness a little fuzzy. Calling Ryan a freak totally brought it all back into focus. I let out a huge sigh.

"What? Did Manhattan sink into the Atlantic or something?" Sylvie asked, her voice muffled by the ball of tissues she was holding to her still-bloody lip.

"Um, no. Not that."

"Then did Fifth Avenue turn into low-income housing?"

I shook my head, still unable to shake my sour puss.

"Then what? What's making my wittle Waney-Paney sad?" Her voice was high and squeaky and she pursed her lips out like a super-concerned babysitter.

"Oh nothing." I didn't want to talk about this with anyone, not even Sylvie, so I changed subjects. "OK, now that you're close to clotted, can we talk about your ride in the love boat? How was the kiss? And how not annoyed are you at me anymore?"

She crinkled her face. "Hello, a kiss? Most people would look at my face and think I was abused." She continued, but I could barely hear her over my inner monologue. It was like since I hadn't heard from back home in so long, it almost didn't exist anymore. And me liking Ryan—or even just being friends with him—was kind of doable. I mean, why not? He was fun and nice and alt-cute and probably a really good kisser. And all of those reasons were of course, well, *reasonable* here at camp. But back in New York, those reasons were anything but. Like who would we hang out with? My friends? I mean, what would I do? Bring a Ziploc of bean dip and baby carrots wherever we went to keep him entertained? And his friends? No thank you. I feel like I need to be deloused whenever I go below Fourteenth Street, and his friends are like at Fourteenth and under at all times. Plus, they probably hate me. It just wouldn't work. It was all very Romeo and Juliet, but I guess minus the him being in love with me part. And even though he so clearly wasn't into me, just thinking about the rush I got when he said my name and the way my body seemed to turn into a jelly of mini-explosions when he touched me and the overwhelming anticipation I felt for the next time I was going to see him . . . Saying goodbye to all that the second I stepped back on NY pavement was going to hurt. But I knew that there was totally no other way. We just couldn't mix in the real world. Like oil and water or Kelly Osbourne and a bikini . . . just not meant to be.

"Where do you think his orthodontist is sourcing his materials? A barbed-wire fencing company?" Sylvie finished her rant and looked at me for a response. I just nodded, not knowing what she'd been saying for the past five minutes.

"All righty, ladies of mine. We all ready for drama?" Mandi pranced around the bunk, trying to psych us up. I kind of felt like I was already deep into a drama, so I might actually be all right at this activity. Plus, drama didn't seem to require bracelet weaving, sweating, or getting wet. Something told me this was too good to be true. What was next, an hour of online shopping?

A few minutes and a dirt path later, I found myself in the rec hall, the crime scene of the dance and first time I saw Ryan. Well, saw him as a person and not a blemish on my metaphorically Proactiv-perfect social scene. I caught myself smiling at the memory and then quickly upbraided myself. So never going to happen with him on a jillion levels—one being that he didn't like me, two being that social stigma prevented it. (A jillion converts to two in the metric system, by the way.)

We were standing in the dusty room, waiting for drama

to start. I was spending the downtime focusing on my split ends. Through the drapes of hair I'd pulled in front of my face, I saw a guy gallop through the rec hall's double doors. He clapped his hands to get our attention. "Ladies, ladies, sorry I'm late, but perfection takes time, you know." He spun, letting us take in his perfection. And perfection was exactly what he was. Like the statue of David, but actually cut out of flesh. And he clearly knew it, having dressed himself in tight workout gear that he'd obviously altered himself to make even shorter and more abs-bearing.

He jazz-handed us all a wave. "Hello, hello." For being so huge, his voice was shockingly high. "I'm Tommy and I'm Timber's resident drama mama."

"He's really talented," Hayden said snidely and directed completely at me. Though I wasn't really sure why she felt the need to bark that my way.

Talented Tommy clapped his hands. "Let's get started right away with a warm-up. Let's all join hands and pass the power." He pursed his lips and waited for us to assume warm-up position. Hayden, Aiden, and Aidan practically clawed each other bloody racing to get spots next to him. If I didn't know that lions couldn't have acne, I would have sworn I was watching one of the attack scenes from *Untamed and Uncut* on Animal Planet.

"Yes!" Hayden said to herself as she clutched one of his huge paws, and winked at Aiden, who was also holding a hand. Aidan moped over next to Hayden and grabbed her hand, and Mandi, Sylvie, and I joined the circle.

"All right, I'm going to start the power and I want you guys to close your eyes."

Basically, pass the power was a game where we passed a

squeeze around the circle. Per Tommy, this would bring us together as a unit and help our collective consciousness on-stage. I didn't want to tell him that even a massive superglue spill couldn't bring this bunk together as a unit, so I closed my eyes and got ready to pass the power.

"I'm going to give you ladies an emotion," he explained, "and I really encourage you to imbue your power with passion before passing it on."

This seemed more like cult initiation than drama, but no one was mentioning Kool-Aid or polygamy or body-dwelling aliens, so I felt relatively safe.

"All right, ladies, let's imbue our power pass with effervescing joy. You know, that explosion of emotion you get when you find out that the guy you like likes you back." Why did he have to pick *that* emotion? I barely remembered what that even felt like. Still, I squeezed Mandi's hand when the power came to me and passed it on. "And now let's go with guilt. Like when you're watching TV and one of those feed the children for a dime a day commercials comes on and you're wearing J Brand jeans and you realize that you could feed the entire child population of Ethiopia with the cloth on your ass." Again, this one didn't apply to me because I never watched TV in jeans. I was elastic-waist-only in front of the tube . . . velours or pj's. But I passed the hand squeeze with as much emotion as I could anyway. "And now all focus on fear. You're in the bathroom about to step into your shower and you see a huge bug. Like so huge that you're convinced that the dinosaurs aren't extinct and you shriek with terror." He waited to feel the squeeze come back to him.

"OK, open your eyes, sisters! Time for another game. We're all going to be a machine working together. So we each pick a repetitive function and a corresponding sound and then one by one we step into the machine. It'll be like a phantasmagoria of sound and movement. Let's start with you"—he pointed to me—"in the clown pants costume."

"They're culottes, not clown pants," I clarified, although for what purpose, I don't know. I took the few steps to the center of the circle. I kind of felt self-conscious and then suddenly decided that this was the only activity I'd participated in all summer that didn't terrify me—no chance of heart palpitations from exhaustion, no drowning possible, no falling backwards into the waiting arms of an archenemy— and I was going to rock it. I kicked my legs up and let out a yelp and punched the air at the same time. As soon as my feet hit the floor, I propelled myself right back up. Sure, I one hundred percent looked ridiculous, and if anyone from home saw me doing this they'd probably put a spoon in my mouth so I wouldn't swallow my tongue, but it felt good to be doing something balls out. It wasn't studying or socialing or fashionista-ing, which I typically do full throttle, but it was something. And after an entire summer of half-assing, this was refreshing. For those few minutes that we were playing this insane game, I was actually enjoying myself to the point where I could temporarily forget about how angry and annoyed and embarrassed I was this summer and unclench emotionally.

As I seizured and yelped myself into an Academy Award, the rest of the girls joined the machine one by one. Sylvie did a sort of sliding-door motion and whooshing sound, and Mandi binged and bobbed up and down. Hayden joined in, rolling up her shirt for three beats until you could almost see her bra and then making an "uh-uh" sound and unrolling it.

Aiden did something similar, but in reverse and even creepier, with her shorts. And Aidan entered the game by body-rolling on the floor and moaning. Suddenly, those three had changed the drama machine game into the closest I was ever going to get to starring in kiddie porn—and I'm not just saying that because I'm aging out of the demo in the near future.

After a few minutes of jiving together as a machine, we disassembled. Tommy congratulated us all on a class well done and then sent us on our merry way to tennis.

And I legitimately was merry. Not completely sucking at an activity was a real treat.

"So that was really fun. I wish we did drama all the time," I said as I tripped my way down the rocky pathway.

"I guess. But what was going on with Hayden and her squad? That was creepy. The whole thing should have been shot in night vision and then leaked to the Internet." Her face was contorted in disgust, like she'd just been tricked into drinking rotten milk or watching an entire marathon of TLC's A Baby Story.

I shuddered, thinking back on their sexytime routine.

"Yeah, that was real weird."

The porn posse caught up with us, prattling to each other at volumes that probably interfered with astronaut communication in space.

"Tommy is so hot."

"And talented."

"And talented at being hot."

The trio giggled. "And we were definitely holding our own when it came to the hot competition," Hayden said.

I'd be embarrassed for myself if I ever had thoughts that

were this stupid. The fact that these girls were totally un-abashed not just saying, but practically yelling these strings of inane ridiculousness was completely shocking to me. And completely compelling. I inched closer to them to be sure I didn't miss a second of it.

"Wait, it was a competition?" Aidan asked, chewing on her hair.

Hayden made a guttural why-do-I-have-to-explain-everything sound. "Yeah, whenever you're with your friends and there are boys involved, it's always a competition. Survival of the tit-est."

Sylvie looked over at me, her eyes wide with disbelief. I just shook my head. And I thought growing up in the city was supposed to give you a tough exterior. But these subur-ban girls were at a whole other brutal, callous level.

"Well, he totally loved us. We were totally turning him on with our moves and skills and stuff," Aiden said, ignoring that there was no *us* in *slut*, unless you were dyslexic.

"I'm pretty sure that when he was saying that thing about a boy liking you back, he was talking about me." Hay-den cocked her head to the side and pursed her lips in a look I'm sure she thought was more fierce and less ducky than it was.

"Like you're a boy?" Aidan asked, zoning in on Hayden's boobs with a question mark look. Was she openly question-ing Hayden's gender identity? I couldn't believe that Hayden wasn't hitting the roof over this.

She explained in a voice brimming with exaspera-tion, "No, like I'm an analogy for a boy." And there was someone who was never going to see the inside of an AP English classroom.

I whispered to Sylvie, "Doth my gaydar deceive me or—"

"No," she interrupted, "he's here and queer and they're there and obtuse."

"Thought so." For a second, I contemplated breaking this news to Hayden and company, just to see their reaction. But I quickly created my own analogy. Listening to this convo was to seeing them deflate over their nonexistent chances with Tommy as Snapple Peach Iced Tea was to Diet Sunkist. Both options were good, but when it came down to one or the other, the choice was pretty obvious. I'd take a trio of loud obliviousness and a Snapple, please.

I shook my head at the situation and then looked ahead to see guys walking up the path toward us. I squinted a little and made out the figures of Ryan and Eli's bunk. I could hear my stomach kerplunk into my, well, whatever guts part was under it. After that letter from Kennedy, I totally didn't want to see Ryan. I mean, how was I going to act around him now? Wait, why was I asking? The answer was pretty obvious: AWKWARD.

"Hey, hey, hey," Ryan called as he approached. He was wearing swim trunks low on his hips and had his shirt twisted up and draped over his shoulder. The only word for the brown, muscle rippled flatness of his chest and stomach was "yum." I tried not to look directly into the six-pack for fear that I wouldn't be able to stick to my guns and act like I wasn't really friends slash in love with him. And even though I had just honed my drama skills, it wasn't easy. "How are my favorite ladies at Timber?"

"We're fine," Hayden answered for her trio.

Ryan smiled politely and waited for our response. "We are too," Sylvie answered for our duo.

"We're on our way to drama," Eli chimed in. "I have Mercutio's monologue from William Shakespeare's *Romeo and Juliet* memorized. I'm hoping he'll let me recite it." Suddenly, my skills in the drama teamwork machine didn't seem so impressive.

"That's a good one," Sylvie replied, genuinely enthralled. "But wasn't that more of a soliloquy?" she added, way less genuinely. I would bet my entire wardrobe—not my camp one, my real one—on Sylvie knowing exactly what differentiated a soliloquy from a straight monologue. This was just her attempt to lure Eli into conversation. My heart swelled. There's nothing more rewarding for a teacher than to see a student apply her education and succeed.

I, however, was proving the adage "Those who can't, teach" with my interaction with Ryan.

"So, how was drama?" he asked, trying to break us away from Shakespeare 101.

"It was good, fine. Like, whatever. It doesn't matter what I say because we're not going to talk." I was spouting awkward at fire-hose force.

"Not talking? Like Tommy made you all do mime stuff? I'm sorry." He pressed his hands against an invisible box and pounded silently to escape. In spite of myself, I laughed. How could I not want to hang out with a guy who's a good mime? I was totally going to miss him when we got back to New York.

"GIRLS, NO TALKING TO THE BOYS," Mandi yelled frantically, running down the path at us. By her hysterical tone, you'd think she was warning us not to push the red button that we'd found in some secret presidential lair.

I rolled my eyes at her yelling but was secretly relieved. As annoying as the no-boy/girl-mixing rule was, at least it meant that I got to end this horrifyingly awkward convo with Ryan.

"WE'RE COMING!" I yelled back, and gave an apologetic smile to the fellows. "We've got to go before Mandi's head explodes all over the place."

"Yeah, counselor brain just doesn't go with this outfit," Sylvie joked.

We were all giggling as we walked away from each other.

Mandi caught up to Sylvie and me a few paces after we left the guys. "Do you girls know why you shouldn't be talking to the boys?"

"That killer strain of cooties that's been going around?" I asked, pushing a bunch of leaves away from my face. Walking three across was far too wide for this little path, and I had to keep avoiding low-hanging branches.

"No. Because it's against the rules." Before I could come up with some sort of response to that, she hustled off and was marching ahead at a super-fast clip, leaving the two of us giggling in her wake until we reached the tennis courts.

We stepped through the gates, still laughing at how psycho Mandi was about camp rules. It was just so weird to be that militant and aggressive with a pink ribbon in your pony.

We stopped at the bin by the entrance to grab rackets and Sylvie stood there for a while, inspecting each one. I just plucked one out without much thought. Considering my athletic prowess, even if the racket had no strings, it probably wouldn't affect my game all that much.

Hayden and Aidan were already volleying on the far court, and Aiden and Mandi were waiting on one side of the near court to play us. They were warming up with knee bends, and Mandi was pointing to herself and then to the net, clearly talking over some kind of game plan.

"So, what's our team strategy?"

"How about I play front? And I'll also play back. And you just try and avoid getting pelted in the face?" she offered.

"So same as our volleyball, soccer, and field hockey strategy." I nodded. "Sounds doable. All right, hut, hut, hike, and break. Let's get started!"

Laney,

Wowsers, camp? I can't believe my daughter is at camp. Just spoke to your mother and she said you're having a blast. Glad to hear it. Everything in California's great. Maybe next summer you can come to camp out here if you like camping so much!

Much love,
Dad

Chapter 19

"*It's the final countdown.*" I was screeching and air-guitaring myself into a sweat right by Sylvie's bed.

She croaked out a sleepy, "What the hell are you doing up? Mandi's only come by three times."

And yeah, it's true that I normally needed Mandi to try and wake me up at least six times and then bounce on my cot until I got nauseous to rouse me, but today was different. Today marked the three-day countdown until the end of camp.

I wish I could say that I had mixed emotions about

leaving Timber. That it had been hard, but valuable. That I learned a lot about myself and about nature. Blah, blah, true meaning of teamwork and tenacity and appreciation for experience out of my comfort zone, blah. But the truth is that all I could think about was getting the eff out of the place.

"*It's the final countdown!*" I repeated, and then pretended to guitar-pick with my teeth. I continued singing, "And I don't know the rest of the words to this song because I've only ever really heard it during VH1 Top Twenty countdowns. *It's the final countdown.*"

Sylvie's feet hit the ground and she sat up in her bed for a second, rubbing her eyes and preparing to get vertical.

"Come on, Sylv. Get in the celebration spirit." I snapped my fingers and jingled, "*The best part of waking up is getting serenaded in your cot.*"

"Do I hear my favorite song?" Mandi asked as she made her fourth wake-up round. I wasn't sure if she was talking about the commercial jingle or my incredibly off-key 1980s hair band cover, but either way I decided to avoid early-morning interaction with Mandi and didn't fess up to my singing.

"What are you celebrating?" Sylvie inquired as she slipped on her flip-flops.

"Um, hello. We only have three more days of internment camp and then we get to join the real world with caffeine and free choice and late wake-ups and clothes that don't make me look like I stepped out of the first season of *Friends*." I felt like the Little Mermaid as she was making the deal with Ursula or like Ashlee when they were unwrapping her face bandages post–nose job. Looking like a normal human was just around the corner.

Sylvie exhaled a huge sigh of morning breath in my direction. I winced. "Yeah, that's going to be so nice. I mean, I am going to miss some things." Another gust of rank breath came my way.

"What are you going to miss? I can't think of freaking anything about this glorified juvie center that I'm going to miss. Especially not your morning breath." I hand-fanned in front of my face.

"Hello? Us. I'm going to miss us." She turned toward the bathroom for a much-needed tooth-brushing. She called back as she walked, "I only meant for that to sound about fifty percent as cheesy as it did."

I sat down on my cot, blown away not just by her stank breath but also by the truth of what she had said. I don't know how I didn't realize it until then, but Sylvie was totally my best friend, and not just at camp. I honestly wouldn't have made it through those five point five weeks without her. And yes, Kennedy was still officially my best, best friend. But I don't think I could have leaned on her the same way I'd leaned on Sylvie all summer—actually, she probably wouldn't have even let me near her with my frizzed-out hair and synthetic shorts. But that kind of stuff was never an issue for Sylvie. She had always been there when I needed her, and not just that, she totally propelled me forward even when I wasn't always aware of it. And that really is what a best friend should do. I was beginning to realize that despite my resistance on the soccer field and in the swimming pool, I actually might have learned something this summer . . . and not just that fluorescent green isn't my color.

• • •

After I'd finished mopping the shower floors—third-to-last time I was ever going to have to touch cleaning products!—Mandi huddled us all around for an announcement.

"Girlies, I am so, so, so excited to tell you that this year, we're doing a Timber lip sync for the last night's show!" And the crowd went wild. Or at least Hayden, Aiden, and Aidan did.

"Counselor say what?" I turned to Sylvie for an explanation.

She cupped her hand around my ear and yelled so I could hear her over the celebratory yipping. "On the last night of camp, the oldest girls' bunk always puts on a show for the rest of the camp. It's a privilege you get for being the oldest campers at Timber, and every year it's kind of different. Like sometimes the older girls do skits or a talent show or an actual full musical. This year we're going to do a lip sync. Like the song is playing and we do a dance routine while mouthing the words."

A *privilege*? This sounded like punishment.

"*We*? We nothing. This is a YouTube mockumentary waiting to happen. I'm going to sit this one out." Sylvie rolled her eyes at me. "What if I run for president one day or something? I can't have that Googling around about me. That's probably more damaging to a campaign than a sex tape. I mean, everyone has sex eventually, but not everyone traipses around on a stage fake-singing."

"Come on, Lane. This is it. The final sprint to the finish. Don't put up your diva guard now. Just muscle through." I knew the end was near, but still, this felt like where I needed to draw the line. I might overdose on embarrassment. "And really, when you look back on this summer, is this little song-and-dance show going to stand out as more humiliating than anything else? I mean, this is nothing compared to last week when you got hit in the head with a basketball three times in one game. There are coma patients with better reflexes than that."

I nodded and shrugged to indicate that she was right. Beaten, I looked over to our bunkmates to join in on the "fun."

The evil trio and Mandi were huddled together whispering and not paying attention to the two of us. I assumed they were planning our act, but I couldn't be sure.

Just as I was about to passive-aggressively cough my way into some attention, the cluster broke up and all four of them looked our way. Hayden took the opportunity to speak for the group. "OK, so we've decided that we're going to do the 'Grease Megamix' for our lip sync." Her brigade was practically twittering with excitement at the selection.

So my diva guard might be down, but the "Grease Megamix"? I mean, come on. It had "mega" in the title. It sounded like those hair gels that dried crunchy.

"You know, I'm not sure if that highlights my vocal range or my not-lameness enough," I countered.

"Yeah, well, it's not really your choice. And even if we did vote—which we're not going to because it's not your choice—you wouldn't win. There are three of us, not including Mandi, and only two of you, and we all want the 'Grease Megamix.' So get used to it."

And that's what we call in the bitch business "throwing down the gauntlet." And I'm not one to let gauntlets fly without a reaction. I was starting to loosen up my muscles for the requisite catfight neck twisting when Sylvie pulled me aside.

"Can you think about this for a second before resorting to street violence? First of all, your street—Park Ave—doesn't give you much cred in the situation. Second of all, this is so not even worth your energy. Even if you win and we get to sync something cooler, how much less humiliating is that going to be? We're still going to be on a stage, shimmying in awful costumes, and mouthing words. Just count this as part of the sprint to the end."

I rolled my eyes and tried to explain just how unacceptable this situation was. "The 'Grease Megamix' is like Holocaust-joke-level offensive to me. I so can't just let this happen."

"OK, so obviously, this is a hill that you're going to be sprinting up. And it's going to be harder than sprinting on flat land, but you're still going to do it. Don't let five minutes of John Travolta's singing derail your final countdown," she pleaded. I think she was genuinely afraid for my well-being if it came to a Billboard Butts throwdown.

I rolled my eyes again, more at the situation than at her. "Fine," I said through clenched teeth, not sounding remotely fine. But Sylvie was right. No matter how much I fought, the lip sync was still going to be a day trip to hell. So, I swallowed my pride, turned back to the rest of the bunk, and managed to croak out, " 'Grease Megamix' it is."

"Great! I'm so glad we came to a unanimous decision," Mandi said without a trace of sarcasm, even though she'd just witnessed my entire exchange with Sylvie. How could she not see that the only unanimous sentiment within these log walls was complete disdain for each other? "All right, girlie girls. I'm going to head to the staff lounge and leave you all to rehearse."

Mandi grabbed a pink hoodie from her bed and sashayed out the door, waving to us. "Good luck with the planning. I know with all the talent we have in this bunk, the show's going to be dynamite!" I was sure she was trying to be encouraging, but I found her blind faith in us more disturbing than anything else.

As soon as she was out the door, Hayden stepped forward as self-appointed dictator. "OK. I feel like I was pretty much born to be Sandy, so I'm going to cast myself as her. You two"—she pointed to her minions—"can be two other girls, the pregnant one and the high school dropout one. And Laney and Sylvie, you guys are, well, the guys. That just seems like a good fit for you two, because the boys have less of a part and need less talent." She quickly turned to look at Aiden and Aidan and they all cracked up immediately.

"Really? 'Cause I remember that one of the boys has a face full of acne craters, so I just thought that you would be more of a natural fit for a boy role, Hayden," I snarled.

"What was that?" Hayden whipped around to confront me.

"I said—" Just then Sylvie gave me a hard punch in the arm, stopping me midsentence and forcing me to look at her sprinting pantomime. Right, the final sprint. I could do it. "Nothing." I rubbed my arm. "Forget it."

We got right down to rehearsing, which was pretty much just hours of hand jiving without breaks. Hayden had the "Grease Megamix" on a CD she'd ripped before coming to camp, but the player that Mandi borrowed for us from the rec hall was so ancient that it didn't even read burned CDs, so we had to rehearse to Hayden's a cappella version of the song.

She wasn't too busy singing to critique us, though.

"Your arms aren't noodles, ladies. Let's keep these moves sharp," Hayden squawked as we moved through her uninspired choreography. "People, people, people. Is this a lip sync rehearsal or is this day care? Because all I'm seeing are a bunch of toddlers with poopy diapers sagging around, not performers. Let's put some pep in our step, ladies."

Mandi popped back into the bunk about an hour into rehearsal. By that point, I was beyond spent. "Hey, Mandi. Isn't it about time for instructional swim yet?" I looked at my bare wrist and tapped it to indicate we were late. "I'm probably going to go through withdrawal if I don't get my daily fix of my urine 'n' chlorine drink."

"Nope, no swim today. I want you guys to have as much practice time as possible," she enthused. "You are going to be perfect."

"Oh." I moped back to my place in the soul train Hayden had just positioned us in.

The rehearsals took precedence over all of our activities for the next two days. Our only respite from Hayden's squawking was at meals, which meant that I actually started looking forward to the rubber chicken and jellied gravy combinations and savored my time in the dank mess hall.

At the end of dinner on day two, Hayden leaned over her plate to shout at us all, "So if everyone's done, let's head back to the bunk to prep—"

"I'm not done," I interrupted, picking my fork back up and attacking the mountain of mushy green beans I still had on my plate. My elbows were aching from all the hand

286

jiving, and I couldn't take another run-through where Hayden yelled at us to smile for seven minutes straight. "You guys can go back and practice one last time. I just can't get enough of these green beans. I wonder if they had to boil them overnight to get them this limp and nutrient-free."

"We so don't have time for a run-through," Hayden corrected me. "Just barely enough time to get into costumes, hair, and makeup. We have to go now." Before anyone had time to clear and stack their plates, she was up and sprinting back to the bunk.

The news that we weren't going to practice the dance anymore was enough to break my binge-eating strike. I hastily wiped down my area and dumped my leftovers. Then I pushed back my chair and trekked to the bunk with Sylvie.

When we got to the cabin, I saw that Mandi had laid out costumes on each of our beds that she'd dug up from the drama costume closet. The girls had pastel poodle skirts and scarves to tie around their necks, and Sylvie and I had jeans and white T-shirts waiting for us. As much as I'd been craving a pair of jeans all summer, the grody peg-legged, acid-washed, dust-mite-ridden pair on my cot was not what I had in mind. I doubled up on underwear before putting them on, hoping that would protect me from whatever diseases the pants were carrying.

"So how do I look?" I struck the Marilyn Monroe coy skirt-pushing-down pose and batted my eyes.

"Probably about as good as I do." Sylvie did a *Napoleon Dynamite* glamour shot fist-to-the-chin move.

"Yeesh." I winced. "Then I think culottes are a better getup for me."

We both burst out laughing at how unattractive we looked. It felt good to laugh at this situation. Much better than crying, which was totally what I would have done six weeks earlier. We finally collected ourselves to the point where we could actually walk in a straight line again and decided to head toward the rec hall. The rest of the girls were taking forever to get their costumes on and their hair and makeup done, and I knew they wouldn't wait for us if we were the ones lagging.

Just as we reached the door, Mandi ran up and stopped us. "*Hello*. You guys almost forgot hair and makeup!"

"Oh, we're the boys. We don't need hair and makeup," I explained.

"That's exactly why you do," she said.

She pointed to Sylvie's bed and made us sit down as she rummaged through her toiletries.

"Close your eyes," she instructed. "I want your final looks to be surprises!" At this point, there was no use fighting. I closed my eyes and waited for a Danny Zucco makeover.

I felt her running product through my hair and then penciling my cheeks for some reason. When we were finally allowed to open our eyes, Mandi was holding up a mirror for both of us to check ourselves out. What was reflected back at me was frightening—like looking at my weirdly birth-defected brother who never was and never should have been. Both of us had our hair greased back into slick buns, and huge sideburns eye-linered onto our cheeks. My first instinct was to run to the bathroom for a shower to get rid of the entire look, but instead, I let Mandi shepherd me out of the bunk and followed the team across the camp to the rec hall.

I seriously hoped we wouldn't somehow see Ryan on our

way there. Never in my whole life had I felt less attractive. Not even when I got my wisdom teeth removed and was drooling blood.

Luckily, we got to the rec hall without being spotted by anyone, which was a small miracle. Mandi rushed us all through the side door that led backstage. The backstage entrance was even more dank and dirty than the main part of the rec hall. It was stuffy and reeked of mildew. No one had probably been back there since last summer's end-of-camp spectacular. I wonder what they performed? Whatever it was, it couldn't have been as atrocious as *Grease*. Mandi turned to us all and shushed us—though her hissing was definitely louder than any noise we were making—as the camp director yelled into his megaphone to start the show and introduce us.

Hayden gave us one last pep talk before we walked out onstage. "Remember, ladies, this is all about presence. So be sure to smile with your eyes. There's a huge difference between this"—she gave us a blank stare—"and this"—she shot another stare off, this time looking vaguely constipated. "Just remember that and we'll be golden."

I wanted to ask her to do the smiles one more time, just to be a jerk and see her make the stupid faces again, but before I could, the megamix started to play and I was being pushed out onto the stage. I listlessly shimmied around in a routine that resembled Hayden's choreography, clapping my hands and nodding my head to the beat. And I did my best to move my mouth at the right times and look enthusiastic. I doubted the audience could tell I was actually mouthing "Please let this place get struck by lightning before we get to the part where I have to spin Hayden."

Unfortunately, there was no lightning bolt and I did spin Hayden at the song's finale. But that also meant that we were at the end of our routine. I kneeled in my designated ending pose, stuck my hands out, and tried to catch my breath. The crowd was actually applauding, which was a huge surprise to me. I looked out to the audience, but with the stage lights, I could only see the front row of seats, which were occupied by the boys from my swimming group. They were clapping, but also giggling . . . probably at my sideburns. Brandt was laughing so hard, I was pretty sure he was about to make the lake warmer right there in the rec hall.

As soon as we hand jived offstage, I heard my name called from one of the wings. And then, out of the corner of my eye, I saw Ryan coming up to me. Effing great. I was actually thinking I might get away without him witnessing this disaster up close. But then again, who really cared? I was New York bound the next day, and this was probably the last time we were ever going to interact. I had nothing to lose.

I turned to face him.

"Yeah?" I answered back.

"Hey, I was looking for you. Great job out there," Ryan said as he walked toward me.

"Yeah, right." I rolled my eyes at him. "I can't wait to get out of here and back to the city, where things are normal and, well, just less campy," I moaned while trying to wipe off my sideburns, turning them into huge black cheek smudges.

"Actually, before we go back, I kind of have one more friend who wants to get set up with someone you know."

Ugh, what was I now, the Virgin Whisperer or something? "Fine. But there's like not even a full day left. Eli and Sylvie took the better part of the summer and I don't even know how successful it was. I mean, a bloody lip and several discussions about allergies to pet dander? That does not a love match make. I don't think I can make it happen."

"Um, actually, well . . ." I could hear his nerves. "The guy is me."

This sour, nauseous feeling instantly started radiating from my stomach. Ryan wanted me to set him up with someone? I mean, I knew my crush on him was all kinds of ridiculous, but still, I couldn't help him date someone else. The nausea dialed up in intensity as I realized that the only people I knew were in my bunk or the little boys in my swim group. Obviously, he wouldn't be talking about my water buddies, and he totally wasn't asking about Sylvie. He was definitely asking me to set him up with Hayden, Aiden, or Aidan. If he had punched me in the face with brass knuckles, I wouldn't have been more hurt and surprised. Trying not to show my angst and queasiness, I turned my attention back to Ryan and casually asked, "And who is the girl?"

He stared down at his feet for a while and then back up at me. "The girl I'm hoping to be set up with is ... ." He leaned in and kissed me before finishing his sentence. The kiss was short and soft and sweet. I was so caught off guard, I felt like I was about to float and fall over all at once. "Well, she's you."

I sighed. Screw how dorky this would make me and how star-crossed we were. He was just so cute, standing there, looking at me with those eyes I could swim in—if I knew how to swim—waiting for my response. There was no way I could not kiss him back. I put a hand up to his shirt, balled a little of the fabric in my fist, and pulled him in. Before I closed my eyes for the actual kiss, I saw a flash of relief on his face. I smiled, wondering how long we'd both been having the same exact feelings and trying to ignore them. And then suddenly our lips were together and I stopped thinking and just existed in the moment. It was one of those magical kisses that make you feel like you should be soaring up and surrounded by glittery smoke like the end of a Disney movie. I finally pulled my lips away and then hugged him, getting my sideburns all over the shoulder of his shirt. Next time, Sylvie and I were going to have to use waterproof mascara for the chops. Wait, next time? Maybe when I got back to the city, things wouldn't be as normal as I thought.

I pulled away from Ryan to the sound of Mandi hollering for us all to line up and bunkward march. All of a sudden, I was back inside my head, nervous and awkward and neurotic. I hoped Mandi was far enough away that she hadn't witnessed the kiss or even me talking to Ryan at all. It took me a second, but I reasoned that she totally hadn't seen anything or else she'd be yelling about a lot more than heading back to the bunk.

"I, um . . ." I was so flustered and nervous and focused on not embarrassing myself by asking if he could tell that I ate three pieces of garlic bread for dinner that I could barely think of something normal to say. Suddenly, I was hyperaware of my drawn-on muttonchops, and I just couldn't believe that he liked me when I looked like this. Actually, how could he have ever fallen in like with me when I was so disgusting-looking all summer? This abrupt onset of self-doubt brought on a serious case of the anxious sweats, which didn't help my smudged-sideburn situation. "Well, I, um, should probably go. I guess I'll just see you tomorrow or whatever." Great. I just had the kiss of a lifetime and I left him with the same words I utter to my mother when I'm going to sleep over at Kennedy's?

"I think you'll be seeing me a lot more than just tomorrow." He winked. Like not creepy old man waiting for the downtown bus wink, just a cute, made-me-want-to-kiss-him-all-over-again kind of wink. And it totally melted me and kind of made me want to get a tattoo of his face somewhere on my body.

I made this weird, hyperventilating chuckling noise and then said, "Yeah, well, see ya!" and started off toward Mandi's beckoning calls.

I wouldn't exactly call it kicking him my A-game, but at least I didn't drool. Which after an entire summer out of practice was as good as I could expect.

As I hustled off, I could feel holes being laser-burned into my back. I turned to see Hayden, Aiden, and Aidan glaring at me with fierce hatred, like extras from the *Blair Bitch Project*. Obviously, they'd seen the entire interaction between Ryan and me, including the totally hot kiss. And while I wish I could say I was mature enough to know that the kiss was really just between Ryan and me and that's what made it so special, I really can't. Their jealousy was like the cherry on top of my Ryan-smooching sundae. It made the entire amazing thing impossibly more awesome. I strutted by the trio. I couldn't have been more obvious about how pleased with the situation I was, even if I had HA-HA! written on the butt of my pants.

"Um, hello?" Sylvie said, speed-walking to get to my side. "Did I just see what I think I saw?"

"That depends on what you think you saw. Did you see me sputtering out a stream of pure awkward at Ryan?" I asked, perhaps going a little too far with the self-deprecation.

"No. I mean, yes, I totally saw that. But I meant the kiss. Did Laney Parker find love at Camp Crappy Trails?" She linked her arm with mine and squeezed as she teased me.

"Love? It was only one kiss. *Love* is a lofty word, but yeah, it totally applies here. You're looking at the future Mrs. Bellsinger," I kidded. "But seriously. The kiss was A-MA-ZING! Like just indescribably unbelievable. It was almost like an out-of-body experience. And right after the kiss, I wasn't even myself. I was this geeky, bashful, super-awkward nerd and he was Captain Cool, Calm, and Collected."

"It sounds like a *Freaky Friday* swap."

"Exactly. Which would make me Lindsay Lohan before anorexia, when she still had boobs." I stuck out my ribs and tried to act chesty.

Sylvie giggled at my barely A's in action, which I'm sure looked especially ridiculous with my man hair and mutton-chop smudges. "But seriously, that's just what happens when you really like someone. It certainly happens to me around Eli." She paused for a second. "To be clear, I'm talking about going into awkward mode, not growing boobs."

I smiled at her, and then my smile got even bigger as I thought about Ryan and the kiss to top all kisses. We followed Mandi's marching orders and filed out of the rec hall and into the warm night.

I floated back to the bunk, barely even noticing my knee pain as I climbed the stairs. Falling asleep was so easy, being totally content with how things were going to work out with Ryan and with it being my last time sleeping in a bunk bed ever, unless I got sent to jail at some point in the future.

Dear Mom,

I know that you're probably going to see me before you get this, but I just had to write and tell you to STOP SPREADING RUMORS ABOUT ME! I got a note from Dad that said you told him I was having a great time at camp. Why would you tell him something that heinously untrue? Have you not gotten any of my letters this summer?

Even still, I'm super pumped to see you so soon! I've missed you and New York and Perez and even your cooking.

> Still your daughter even when you tempt
> me into disowning you,
> Laney

Chapter 20

I woke up the next morning nowhere near as pumped as I thought I'd be for my final day of camp.

Noticing I was awake, Sylvie turned her head on her pillow to look at me. "Shouldn't you be doing some sort of victory dance right now?"

Clearly, we were so on the same wavelength.

"Yeah, I should," I said, shocked at my own lack of last-day enthusiasm. "But I'm just not that pumped for some reason. Like all of a sudden going back to my normal life seems daunting."

"More daunting than a seven-mile hike followed by hand-scrubbing a toilet and then swimming with a school of six-year-olds?" she asked, sitting up on her bed.

I rolled my eyes. "No, of course not. I'm not saying I want to stay for another session. I'm just not as eager to get back to Laney Parker status quo as I was even like three days ago."

"First of all, you totally don't have to be Laney Parker status quo when you get back. Go back and be Laney Parker 2.0, still yourself but better. I mean, you haven't really learned how to swim or run without looking like a panicked chicken—"

"Hey," I interrupted. And then I gave it some thought. "Wait, you're right. Panicked chicken is actually dead on. Continue."

"As I was saying . . ." She faked being annoyed. "But you did learn other stuff this summer. You can't ignore that and go back to New York one hundred percent the same as when you left, you know?" I nodded. This one was wise well beyond her fifteen years. "And you're going to be Laney 2.0 plus Ryan. That's going to be pretty awesome, right?"

A wave of nerves crashed over me as soon as she said his name. I mean, I totally didn't care about what other people thought about us. Well, I guess the pseudo–panic attack brought on just by saying his name meant that I actually did care. But whatever. Even if I was a wee bit nervous about coming out as a Ryan-crusher, I'd decided that didn't mean that I wasn't going to do it. So that was a very Laney 2.0 step forward.

"Yeah." I nodded slowly, still mulling everything over. "It will be pretty awesome."

With this new self-awareness, I was ready to tackle my last day at Timber. And the day seemed to be going in fast forward. Breakfast was a blur, and then we went back and packed. For me, that took almost no time. I piled most of my undesirable clothes into the bag Mandi laid in the center of the room for donations to the drama closet and actually packed very little. I carefully folded my FART shorts and placed them in my duffel along with my aqua socks. I wasn't going to wear either item again, but since I hadn't had my phone to take any pics all summer, I needed at least a little something to remind me of my internment.

The bus for Long Island was scheduled to leave right after lunch. Parent pickup was a little later in the afternoon, and Sylvie's folks were coming to get her. I dragged my duffel down to the mess hall, with her trailing behind, demanding to help me carry something the entire way. But lugging a half-full duffel was the one thing this summer I was sure I could do on my own.

We ate lunch in silence. I knew that Sylvie and I were quiet because we were upset about leaving each other, but neither of us wanted to break down and cry into our fish sticks. As for the other girls, I bet they were terrified of going back into the real world, where they probably didn't have any friends and everyone treated them like the bottom-feeders they really were. Or maybe they were sad about leaving each other too. I don't know.

We walked out of the mess hall and toward the bus that was waiting to cart me back to where the concrete was greener.

"Well"—I looked back at the mess hall—"that's one part of camp I definitely can say that I'm one hundred percent happy about never seeing again. No mixed emotions there."

Sylvie giggled a little and grabbed my hand, and we walked like that the rest of the way, both of us sniffling.

I looked at her through my tear-fuzzed eyes. "Hey, what are we crying about?" I was trying to be light about our split, but leaving her side felt so weird and kind of foreign. Like when I go to another country and they call eggplants "aubergines." And I get really flustered ordering and wonder why everyone can't speak American even though I know that's beyond unreasonable and it's just homesickness talking. Right then, I wanted to throw a hissy until she decided to come home with me to New York and never spend any time apart. But I knew it was just Sylviesickness talking. "Obvs we're going to see each other again. Come to New York next summer or sooner, like tomorrow-ish. Really, you're always welcome, and we'd have such a kick-ass time."

"I know, I know," she said in a sad, soft whimper. "I'm just going to miss you until I see you again."

"Not as much as I'm going to miss you." And then tears started slowly falling from my eyes.

We hugged. "OK, goodbye," I croaked out.

"Just goodbye for now. Right?"

I nodded.

She slowly turned to head back to our bunk and wait for her parents to pick her up. As she walked away, I saw the boys charging from the mess hall to drop their bus contingent off.

"Hey," I called after her. She turned around and walked back toward me. "Why don't you go say goodbye to Eli?" I tilted my head toward the oncoming male brigade. I was pleased that I could squeeze in a final love lesson. "And give him a kiss. Like a real one, without any oral injuries this time."

She rolled her eyes. "I can't do that."

"Just go for it, Sylv," I urged her. "What have you got to lose?"

She heaved a loud, guttural sigh. "I don't know. What if it's totally awkward and he's embarrassed or something?"

"Come on. Don't let my entire summer effort be for nothing, lady. First of all, it's the last day of camp. Who cares if it's awkward? Secondly, what's he going to be embarrassed about? It's just a kiss, not like you borrowed his iPod and found out that his Favorites playlist is only 'It's Peanut Butter Jelly Time' on repeat." I nodded in his direction and then shouted after her, "Make me proud!"

She gave me a pained look, to which I responded by flopping my hands forward in a "go forth and flirt" motion. She turned toward him, hesitated for a hot second, and then after one false start finally made the approach and tapped him on the shoulder. My girl didn't waste any time with pleasantries. She just leaned forward and planted one on him. I wanted to cheer or something, but refrained. Turning making out into a cheering sport might have made Sylvie a bit uncomfortable.

I felt my mouth curling into a smile, and I couldn't stop myself from thinking about just six weeks earlier, when I'd stepped off the bus in this very same spot. I knew that I was such a different person, and I knew that once I got back to the city, my changes would be a million times more apparent. Pre-Timber me wouldn't have given Ryan extended eye contact, let alone a kiss. I never would have thought I'd have so much in common with a girl who didn't own a stitch of designer denim. And I never would have found a weird comfort in knowing that I could survive out of my element.

Would I do it all over again? To be honest, probably not. But now that I've done it, I definitely wouldn't undo it if I had the chance.

Decently content with my summer, I scooped up my duffel and swung it over my shoulder, ready to step onto the bus. Just as I was about to take a step, I felt a warm hand on my shoulder. Without turning around, I knew who it was, and a wave of electric energy flushed my body.

"You weren't going to leave without saying goodbye, now, were you?" his deep voice asked. I knew Ryan's parents would be picking him up later in the day, just like Sylvie's, and I wouldn't see him on the bus.

I started sputtering an explanation. "Well, no. I mean, you live near me, so I didn't think . . ." But when I turned to face him, I stopped talking. I inhaled deeply and decided to take a lesson from Sylvie. I grabbed both of his shoulders and tugged him in for a long, completely perfect kiss. How could I have even thought about leaving without a kiss like this to hold me over until New York?

I pulled away slowly and stood silent in front of him for half a second. "Well, goodbye," I said.

His entire face turned up with a huge grin and he brushed a lock of my hair behind my ear. "Bye. How about I call you tonight when I get home?"

"I'd like that a lot." Inside, I felt like fireworks were exploding. And I just couldn't stop smiling as I headed toward my freedom wagon.

I threw my bag in the bottom compartment and walked up the stairs and onto the bus, turning to wave to Ryan for a second.

This time, the bus was wide open with seats. It looked

like everyone was still saying their goodbyes. Brandt was already on board, and I took the seat next to his.

"So, Brandt, did you have a good summer?"

He removed his finger from his nose. "It was all right." He went back to his booger dig for a second and then asked me, "Did you have a good summer?"

I looked out the window to see Sylvie, Eli, and Ryan standing in a row, waving at me. The second they saw they had my eye, they all turned around and bent over, revealing that they had each Sharpied one word of WE'LL MISS YOU on their butts. When they turned back around, Sylvie was holding up a permanent marker in triumph. Wow, a kiss and a butt fondle in one day? This girl was on a roll. I was so happy for her. I let out a quiet laugh.

I looked back down at Brandt. "Yeah, I actually did have a good summer."

Dear Sylv,

I'm somewhere in the middle of Pennsylvania right now. . . . There's a billboard for a Cracker Barrel and a TCBY—sound familiar? Anyway, I'm holding my phone. That's right, as soon as we pulled out of Timber, I got it back. A lot like a prisoner who makes bail and gets his confiscated belt and watch back, no? Wanted to let you know that even with communication to the real world right on my touch screen, I really only wanted to write you. I was a little too close to all-out bawling to say it when I left, but you seriously made my summer, woman. Without you . . . I kind of don't even want to think about it. You've become so much more than a friend. You're my best friend. And if our friendship can make it through a Timber summer, a couple hundred miles between us isn't going to mean anything. We probably can hike it and meet in the middle. (Obvs kidding. My legs actually got sore just thinking about that.)

Love you like a sister,
L

PS—Oh, and send me your number. How the eff could Mandi make a contact sheet with just mailing addresses? Who's Amish now, right?

ACKNOWLEDGMENTS

If I were a hugger, I'd hug these folks: My superstar of an editor, Krista Marino. The extraordinary Ms. Elisabeth Weed. My friends who always go above and beyond the call of friendship duty: Ashley Messick, Julie Hochheiser, Kissy Hardeman, Kelcye Ball, Gabi Arnay, Emily Roumm, Jessie Zerendow, Vanessa Bayer, Shallon Lester, Cristin Stickles, and Lauren Jaffe. Phil Frankel, Angela Carlino, Beverly Horowitz, Random House Children's Sales, Rosy and Tom Khosravi, Grandma and Grandpa, Mom, Dad, and Andy.

Jane Steinberg

Julie Kraut lives in Maryland. Growing up, she loved summer camp and willingly wore skorts, embarassingly enough. Today she's enthusiastic about cheese, Googling herself, and writing. *Slept Away* is her second book for young readers. To learn more about Julie, visit www.JulieKraut.com.